THE DEATH
of an IRISH TINKER

THE DEATH
of an IRISH TINKER

A Peter McGarr Mystery

BARTHOLOMEW GILL

William Morrow and Company, Inc.
New York

Library of Congress Cataloging-in-Publication Data

Gill, Bartholomew, 1943–
    The death of an Irish tinker : a Peter McGarr mystery / by Bartholomew Gill.—1st ed.
      p. cm.
    ISBN 0-688-14184-6
    1. McGarr, Peter (Fictitious character)—Fiction. I. Title.
PS3563.A296D436 1997
813'.54—dc21   97-12889
                                                  CIP

Printed in the United States of America

First Edition

1 2 3 4 5 6 7 8 9 10

BOOK DESIGN BY SUSAN DESTAEBLER

Strike one Tinker, you strike the whole clan.

—AN IRISH COUNTRY SAYING

PROLOGUE

Des Bacon had been a bully up until his fifteenth birthday, when he returned to Gibraltar after his summer holidays and found that the wankers and wallies he'd been thumping—steadily, daily, just for the laugh of it—had grown.

Suddenly many were bigger, if not stronger, than he, and they rounded on him in a group, shoving him around a circle, punching his face, his ribs and stomach, spitting and even pissing on him when he fell and couldn't get up.

Finally, the biggest snatched him up by the neck and held him off the ground, like a stuffed doll, while the others took turns kicking him in the nuts. The yard master only looked away, later saying, "You had it coming, Paddy."

"Buck up, son!" his father had roared in his heavy Ulster burr when Desmond was released from the med bay with his neck in a cast. "I've a remedy for a runt like you. Them bastards are to know, because you've got to show 'em, that you're treble fierce.

"They truck with you again, you're to pay 'em back in blood. Not all of 'em, mind. Not even some. Just the one as an example, but make it good."

It was the only real advice his father ever gave him, but it was more than sufficient. It was an education in itself.

When in the buttery at school the one who had held him by the neck nicked his elevenses from his tray, Des Bacon did not hesitate. Taking three forks from the utensil bin, he went straight to the machine shop, where he sharpened the tines on a speed grinder. Back at the mess table, he tapped the oaf on a shoulder. "Good scoff?"

"The best. Know what makes it special, Paddy?"

Desmond waited.

" 'Twas yours."

The others laughed.

"In fact, it weren't enough. I'm hungry still. Get me another, double chips."

Suddenly everybody was quiet, eyes darting at each other, gleeful. They were together; Des was alone.

"But me money—I'll have none for meself." The Irishisms were on purpose to separate himself further, to make himself into the wild, unpredictable, and dangerous loner. "What'll I do for me prog?"

The boy shook his head and tsked. "You know what they say in Ireland, Paddy: Do for yourself or do wi'out."

It was then that young Desmond Bacon realized what a rush revenge was. The forks he was grasping in a fist behind his back were power, what would put him in control again. And control was everything.

"I want to get this straight, so I know. So we all know." His free hand swept the table confidently, and he rejoiced in seeing their smiles crumble. Something was wrong; the fragging wasn't going to form. "I'm to do for meself?"

"S'right, Paddy. Off wi' you now. Chop, chop. Chips, chips."

"Then I'll do you."

When the bugger placed his hands on the table to get up, Des plunged one fork as hard as he could through the git's right hand, sticking it to the table. And before the bastard could even cry out, Des did the other. He waved the third at the crowd. "Anybody else?"

Kicked off the Rock, Des was given two years in a reformatory in England where his father's advice proved even more valuable. First day he picked up a bench and nearly killed the wog bugger he found going through his kit. And would have too, had a guard not come running with a truncheon.

They tacked on another year with no chance of early release, but it was worth it. He'd proved he'd try to kill, if you messed with the Toddler. It was his name from the first day he walked down the reformatory hall.

Des Bacon didn't care—the Toddler, the Tod, the T. A handle was useful. You could take charge all the easier if people thought you were a thing and not a person.

When the Toddler got out, he discovered that his parents did not want him back, which was good. Instead he was sent off to California to some of his mother's relatives, where he enlisted in the U.S. Marines instead of being drafted.

Sent to Vietnam, Lance Corporal Desmond Bacon became a paid killer. All the more spectacularly when selected to become a scout/sniper—part of Captain E. J. "Jim" Land's 1st Marine Division squad that assassinated Charlies, sometimes firing at ranges up to 1,125 yards. He became one of Land's most competent killers.

Mustered out in 1971 with a chestful of decorations, the Toddler was given the choice of flying back to any destination in the world. He chose Dublin, where his other granny now lived and where customs inspections for "Yanks" during the tourist season were lax.

With two duffel bags stuffed with China White heroin but his dress blue uniform spangled with medals, the U.S. Marine war hero sailed through Dublin Airport. And was in business. The Tod had chosen well. The whole "drug thing" had not yet hit Ireland, and the police had no clue how to enforce the few laws on the books.

Also, other laws protecting personal rights, searches, and seizures were tailor-made for a careful operator who could afford the best legal representation that piles of drug money could buy.

But the Toddler knew what was key: control. Of himself, his product, and of what his Marine training had taught him were "the conditions of the kill." With that edge, you were everything; without it, just buggered.

And should be.

PART ONE

1984

1
CHAINS

 Peter McGarr had not always been afraid of heights. In fact, he had not known that he was. But this was different.

He was perched 175 feet up—Miss Eithne Carruthers had said—in a giant sequoia that without a doubt had been taller before lightning had struck, shearing off its top and creating what amounted to a nest in the remaining bowers.

It was she who had noticed the crows circling the top, she whose dog had found a human hand by the trunk, she who had rung up the Murder Squad a few hours earlier.

McGarr looked down into the nest.

At first glance it looked as if some immense prehistoric carrion bird had dined upon a sizable repast. Many of the bones were bleached, the skin dried out, the flesh well past the first foul reek of decomposition.

But yet there lay what had been a human being.

Naked on its back with arms and legs stretched out, it had an iron—could it be?—cangue around its neck, like something from the ancient Orient. And stout shackles on its wrists and ankles. They too looked rather antique and were also made of iron, which was now rusting, like the chains that pulled the shackles tight to lower branches.

It was then that a blast of wind, bucking through the scree of the two tall mountains to the west, struck them. The top of the sequoia heaved and surged, and McGarr held tight, not daring to look down.

In dramatic descent to the east lay a wooded mountain valley, then Powerscourt—the vast demesne and garden of exotic plantings, like the sequoia itself, that had been laid out by Eithne Carruthers's great-great-great-grandfather, she had told him—and the lush Glen of the Dargle River.

Farther still, McGarr could see the seaside town of Bray with its several tall church spires and massive headland. Toward the horizon was the deep blue water of the Irish Sea.

He could barely breathe, the wind was so strong.

"Chief, you okay?" Detective Inspector Hugh Ward had to shout, even though they were only feet apart. A dark, wiry, and athletic young man, Ward was riding one of the surging bows calmly, easily, with one hand no less. In the other was a camera.

"What I can't figure out"—Ward had to shout, and still McGarr could barely hear him—"is why he struggled so violently if it was a suicide. And how could he have closed the final shackle if he bound his feet first, then one wrist, the neck, and finally the other hand? How could he have done that—locked the other hand?"

And who was he? There was nobody missing locally or in the village of Enniskerry, a few miles distant. McGarr had checked.

Now he forced himself to look more closely.

The corpse was nearly a skeleton at this point, picked clean easily because of its nakedness by carrion crows, seagulls, the passing hawk, he imagined. The neck hung loosely in the canguelike device, and the mouth had dropped open in a kind of tongueless, toothy leer.

Even the eyes had been pecked from the head. Yet the hair, which was long and flailing in the breeze, was glossy brown and had been sun-bleached streaky. A small man? A large woman?

Surely the pathologist would be able to tell with one glance at the pelvic bone, which was obscured by a dried flap of some internal organ that the birds had declined to consume and what looked like another collection of smaller bones. But all other appendages that might reveal its sex were gone. Only some viscera remained, and the skeleton, which was well made.

Climbing up on the other side of the body and farther out on narrow branches than McGarr would ever dare, Ward pointed down at the wristbone that was closest to McGarr.

The hand was missing. Ward had to shout as loud as he could, as they pitched and heaved in the wind.

"My guess is . . . whoever did it either tricked him up here on a dare or something, then managed to get those clamps on him. Or they hoisted him up here unconscious. When he came to, he struggled so mightily he fairly well wore away that wrist."

So it looked. Even the bone had been abraded.

"Later, after the birds and decomposition and all," Ward went on, "the weight of the manacle on the damaged wrist made the hand come away, and it fell to the ground. In fact, I'd bet with all his struggle he opened up the wrist and bled to death."

Ward, who was new to the Murder Squad, was only testing his investigative wings. In matters of mortality, McGarr had ceased to bet. Here he doubted they'd ever determine the exact cause of the victim's death. If he was that. Or she.

One thing was certain, however. At some point before the person died, he had understood or rethought his situation and tried everything he could to free himself from his bonds. His chains. Naked on the side of a mountain in Ireland in winter, perhaps with a wrist opened up and bleeding, he could not have lasted long.

McGarr's second thought was how altogether romantic the whole scene appeared for a murder, if a murder.

There Ward was above him with the wind flattening his features, fanning back his dark hair, and his one hand gripping the lightning-charred stump of the tree trunk. In all, he looked like some big dark eagle ready to pounce. Or, worse, a vampire. When he spoke, his teeth looked like fangs.

It all smacked of some myth or other that McGarr could not recollect at the moment. The whole scene was bizarre. No, grotesquely bizarre. And if it was murder, the murderer or murderers had to work to get the victim—all twelve or thirteen stone of him, McGarr guessed—up into the perch. Using what?

"Block and tackle," Ward said, as though having read McGarr's thoughts. But then, McGarr had trained him.

A blast of wind now struck, and the top of the tree hurtled toward the valley and the ocean beyond. Ward had to avert his head and wait until it subsided.

McGarr felt vaguely nauseated. His brow was beaded with sweat in spite of the breeze.

"See the marks on the bark of the trunk. Just below you."

A horizontal band of fresh scarring wrapped the tree just below the "nest."

"With a come-along or a pulley they hauled him up here, no problem."

Which was overstating the possibility, although the "they" was accurate. It would have taken at least two people, one to pull the rope, the other to guide the unconscious or semiconscious body up through the branches that made the tree so easy to climb.

And once they got him as high as they could by that means—to the line of scarring—there had remained the additional four or five feet into the nest, which would have taken no little strength and daring. Finally, the cangue and shackles had to be fixed and the chains fastened to the branches below.

In all, the murder—if murder—had required time, planning, more than one person, hard labor, and a detailed knowledge of the tree, the house, the estate, and the habits of Miss Eithne Carruthers. As well as some extraordinary animus to have taken such pains to kill in so dramatic a way.

Another possibility was that the murderers had gone to such lengths to make a point or send a message.

Unless, as Ward had mentioned, it had been part of some . . . rite or other, and the man had climbed the tree willingly, allowed himself to be yoked, only to have second thoughts when it was too late.

The band of scarring on the tree suggested otherwise.

"Well done, Chief," the climb team leader of the Tech Squad said when McGarr reached the ground. "But don't expect any combat pay in your packet this week. It's all in a day's work." For them, he meant. Now the Techies would have to remove the shackles, then bag and lower the gruesome cargo to the ground.

"The places we've been," said McGarr, "the things we've seen. Sure, it's a wonderful life."

The others laughed, and McGarr found it an actual pleasure to walk again—out of the copse and across the wide lawn toward the handsome Tudor-style house built of limestone block.

The short, square man with a long face and an aquiline nose slipped his hands into the pockets of a tan windcheater. A waterproof cloth cap to match was on his head.

Bald now in his early fifties, McGarr kept what hair remained rather long. It was a deep red color and curled on the nape of his neck. His eyes were gray. Glancing back at the tree, he felt rather proud and amazed that he had climbed it, now that he was back on the ground.

"Who would have known about the tree—the condition at the top, how easy it is to climb?" he asked the Carruthers woman in her large modern kitchen, where he found her speaking to her cook.

"Oh, everybody, I suspect. Don't you watch television?"

When? McGarr thought. His wife sometimes put on the evening news, and he had watched the All-Ireland Final last year. Or was it the year before?

"That tree was in a drinks advert for Veuve Cliquot." A tall woman well into her sixties, Eithne Carruthers was still lean and athletic. She was wearing a riding costume—tight black jacket and jodhpurs—and her boots had tracked mud over the kitchen tiles.

"First you see a young man and woman on the top of that mountain, drinks in hand." She pointed out the window. "Then they're in the top of that tree. Voice-over says, 'You don't have to scale the highest mountain or climb the tallest tree to enjoy Veuve Cliquot. But when you do'—at that point you see them sailing a lovely yacht and then finally seated at dinner in the Westbury Hotel—'celebrate the moment with Champagne Veuve Cliquot.' They gave me nice check and a case of their bubbly. It's quite good. Would you care for a glass?"

McGarr smiled and checked his watch. "It's rather early. Let me rephrase: Who would have known that they could climb your tree with impunity and be in it for hours without being seen?"

The woman hunched her shoulders. Her eyebrows were plucked, and the taut skin on her cheeks suggested a face-lift. "Again, probably anybody. I spend January and most of February with my"—she smiled—"*father* in the Midi. Apart from the groundskeeper, the rest of the staff is on holiday."

"Who would have known that?"

She shook her head. "The staff, of course, and their families, my near neighbors, and our local guards. I call into the barracks on my way to the airport. But otherwise I don't make a practice of telling people—shopkeepers and the like down in the village, if that's what you mean. We had a break-in two years ago."

"Much stolen?"

She closed her eyes in mock horror. "Only *everything* of any value. Your colleague said they were professionals. They even closed and locked the gate on the way out."

Which was not unusual these days, thought McGarr. Several gangs of well-equipped, highly skilled thieves were operating in the Dublin area. But what they needed were touts—people who knew the habits of the rich, like Eithne Carruthers, and who were willing to say.

"What about the chains and shackles?"

She averted her head. "Enda, my groundskeeper, told me about them." He had been the first to climb up and peer into the "nest." "Like something out of the Inquisition. You expect to see that stuff in Spain and Portugal, but certainly not in this country."

Why not? thought McGarr, thanking the woman and moving toward the door. Ireland had suffered its own Inquisition for close to a millennium with no end in sight.

"Will you keep me informed?"

"If you like."

"It's not often one finds a dead person chained to the top of her tree."

And one who had not wished to die like that. But apart

from the approximate age of the corpse, McGarr knew nothing else.

When he got home to his house in Rathmines a few hours later, he placed the folded evening newspaper on the kitchen table and stepped into the pantry.

"Who was the ancient hero who was chained up in the tree for birds to eat?" he asked his wife, Noreen, who was preparing dinner at the stove.

"Prometheus."

McGarr reached for a glass and the bottle of malt on the sideboard.

"But it wasn't a tree, and the bird was an eagle that feasted upon his liver. Eternally, since Prometheus was himself immortal."

McGarr was glad they weren't having liver tonight. From the aroma in the kitchen he could tell Noreen was cooking her own home-cured pork sausages simmered in seasoned bouillon. She served them with boiled potatoes, pea beans, sauerkraut, and a variety of mustards.

Suddenly famished, McGarr raised the glass to his lips and wished he did not have to go back into the office. But the volume of unsolved cases had increased dramatically along with the burgeoning drug problem, and only plain, dogged police work would close them.

"What was his crime?" McGarr stepped around the door to watch Noreen at work over the Aga that was making the kitchen toasty. It was the hour of the day he enjoyed most.

"It was one of commission: He went too far. Jupiter gave him the order to make mankind out of dirt and water."

And when he did, he must have had you in mind, thought

McGarr. A redhead like McGarr himself, Noreen was a diminutive but well-knit woman with alabaster skin and green eyes.

A full fourteen years younger than McGarr, she managed her parents' picture gallery in Dawson Street and was a devotee of the arts in every form.

This evening she was wearing a black kimono that pictured a bird of paradise on the back in vibrant detail and black Japanese slippers with brilliant red piping. In all, she looked like a member of some smaller, finer, and more colorful race.

"But Prometheus took pity on our sorry state," she went on, while moving between stove and fridge, "huddled shivering and fearful in the darkness when night came on. So he stole fire from the heavens and carried it down to us. Of course, it was more than just fire. It was light, heat, and eventually culture and civilization."

"And for that he got the max?"

"Well, max enough. Nothing was ever the max in the classical world, myths being subject to amendment." Noreen turned from her labors to regard McGarr: the rumpled khakis that he'd climbed the "Cliquot tree" in, what amounted to a two days' growth of beard since he'd been up most of the night before, and the rather full glass in his hand.

"Prometheus himself might have ended his agony at any time," she went on. "By submitting to Jupiter's authority and telling old Jupe what he wanted to know. He was a clever lad, you see, who knew a thing or two. *Chief* among which was not to drink more than one of those things in your hand before having tea. And, two, he might spill the beans about how

Jupiter would beget a son who would displace him and end the hegemony of the Olympians. Are you with me, tatty one?"

McGarr wouldn't be without her, but now he really *did* want another.

"Needless to say, Jupiter required more detail, which Prometheus refused to supply."

"Being the stand-up guy maker that he was."

"Well, he liked the odd skirt, as did Jupiter. In fact, with Prometheus all chained up on the mountain, Jupiter couldn't keep his hands, et cetera, off female humans, which was the other little thing that Prometheus knew."

"This is getting racy."

Noreen raised an eyebrow. "Human beings, as it turns out, are not the only racy lot, and Prometheus knew that if Jupiter kept messing with mere mortals, there'd come a day that a human would give birth to a Jovian by-blow who would grow up to be a peerless thug and who would set Prometheus free. Therefore, he could wait."

Turning back to her cooking, Noreen continued. "And that new superlout was none other than Hercules, who at the time was himself a human and had yet to gain his immortality via the twelve labors."

"So, Prometheus was freed by his own creation. The one that Jupiter ordered him to make." McGarr shook his head. "The irony of it all."

"Well, let's say the 'Byron-y' of it all. It's probably the taliped bard's best poem. Are you ready?"

McGarr smiled. Noreen was without a doubt putting on a show, but it always amazed him that she forgot almost nothing of what she read. Or at least not what she called "the good parts." He swirled his glass. "Work away."

Setting down her stirring spoon, she placed one foot before her and raised her chin dramatically. She then regarded him, her eyes suddenly glazed. "It's my look of cosmic disdain."

> *The rock, the vulture, and the chain,*
> *All that the proud can feel of pain,*
> *The agony they do not show,*
> *The suffocating sense of woe,*
> *Which speaks but in its lowliness,*
> *And then is jealous, lest the sky*
> *Should have a listener, nor will sigh*
> *Until its voice is echoless.*

Thinking of the corpse he had viewed earlier in the day, McGarr could not imagine the agony that the man had endured, his wrists and ankles being the evidence.

When McGarr now only nodded his appreciation of her performance and did not utter a quip, Noreen twigged on the possibility that he might have had some "professional" reason for asking about the myth. No detail of his investigations was uninteresting to her.

"Here, let me top up that glass." She moved toward the pantry and the bottle. "Don't think you're going back to the Castle; don't even imagine it. Day's over, end of quest. It's nasty out there, and you look . . . destroyed is not an adequate word."

McGarr watched mutely as she topped up the glass. Demolished would be more accurate, were he to drink it all. "I don't think you want to know."

"Try me."

When he had finished, Noreen shook her head. "I can't believe it was murder. I think your first thought is more likely. That it was something he or she went along with willingly but then thought better of.

"How else could they have got him up there, naked and—I assume—in the middle of the night? Even if nobody was home, that tree can be seen for miles." She waited for an answer, but McGarr only stared down into the brimming cup.

"I mean, how many murders have you ever investigated that were actually carried out in a manner so elaborate? And why would anybody go to such lengths when a knife or a bullet would suffice with a minimum of attendant risk?"

McGarr reached over to the kitchen table and opened the paper. Banner headlines declared:

CROW BAIT
NAKED MAN CHAINED TO TOP OF CLIQUOT TREE

"Something like Jupiter did with your man—"

"Prometheus," Noreen supplied.

McGarr nodded. "To send a message. To show who rules and what could happen to anybody who thwarts his will. Thirteen generations of pain is a long time. I bet it felt like that to the man in the tree."

2

BANG!

Dublin
February

 It had begun six months earlier in the dead of winter. With the men who put the other man down.

They could not have seen Biddy Nevins. She was on her knees across the street with a large concrete planter between her and them.

Kneeling on the footpath, she was counting the change people had tossed her for her colored chalk drawing of a page from the Book of Kells. In fact, it was the page that was presently on display in the Trinity College Library at the other end of Grafton Street.

Around noon Biddy had called into the college and glanced at the book, a new page of which was turned every day. She had then drawn the page perfectly on the pavement, the ornate Celtic design and complex Latin phrasing letter perfect. Biddy herself, however, was illiterate and unschooled, even in art.

It was a talent that she had discovered while in hospital, recovering from the gear—as heroin was called—that had marred six years of her young life. Biddy needed only to glance at a printed page, a painting, a person, or a thing once, and she could draw it like a photocopy.

It was also the talent that had led her to be called the Queen of the Buskers, her own Mickalou with his music being the King of the many sidewalk artists and minstrels who plied Dublin's most fashionable commercial district. Closed to traffic, Grafton Street was usually thronged with shoppers; now, as a cold winter evening set in, however, nearly all had gone home.

It was a shout or a scream that caused Biddy to look up from her take and over at the men. Streetwise since her Traveler father had dropped her off in Dublin during the winter she turned nine—to "harden" her, he said—there was little that could occur around Biddy that she did not ken. Which made what was happening on the corner across from her stranger still.

Standing in deep shadows by the gates to St. Stephen's Green were two big *shadogs*, called shades by Biddy and her other Traveler friends. Dressed in their winter blues, their broad chests were spangled with the silver buttons of the Garda Siochana, Ireland's national police. But it was the man between them who was crying out, "Jesus, no! Please! I beg yeh, I'll do anyt'in'! Name it, Tod. Just fookin' name it, and it's fookin' yours. Isn't it enough you've already fookin' crippled me?"

It was then that Biddy noticed that the two shades were holding the man up, as though there were something wrong with his legs. And a fourth man—the man he was appealing to—now stepped out of the shadows to look up the street in the direction that the traffic flowed around the large park in the center of Dublin. There was little traffic at this hour of a winter evening, when most people were having their tea, but the lights of an oncoming bus caught the short, dapper man whom Biddy recognized immediately and loathed.

Called the Toddler because of how he was built—round and wide—and how he walked, which was flat-footed, he was without a doubt the biggest drug dealer in the country. "And one wily fooker altogether," said Mickalou, who had got straight with Biddy and had once run for the Toddler when he had no other choice in life.

Biddy stopped counting, scooped up the remaining change, and tossed it into her chalk box. She did not want to be anywhere near the Toddler, even across a street, and she had Mickalou and their four-year-old daughter to get home to in the flat they rented off Patrick Street, about a half mile away. She'd pick up a few bangers, a cabbage, and a loaf on the way, and they'd eat in for a change on such a bitter night.

But Biddy had only just closed the lid when the man cried out again, "No! Please! I have a wife, a fam—" And the two cops rushed him out of the shadows toward the double-decker bus, the front of which now lurched around the corner. They hurled him headfirst under the large back wheels.

There was another pitiable cry that was cut short by a sharp, cracking sound, like a balloon bursting or a backfire, and the bus roared off toward Dawson Street, where it would turn.

It had been the man's head. It was flattened on the tar, his popped eyes lying side by side like a cutout with a halo of blood and brain. And yet one arm now jerked up, as though to feel the damage, before falling back onto the tar.

Biddy did not realize that she was now on her feet and had taken a step or two toward the street until the Toddler turned his head to her. It took only a moment for both of them to react.

Like a salute, the Toddler's hand darted at her as Biddy turned to flee. "Get her! Get that Tinker bitch!" And the two shades—who couldn't be shades—sprinted across the street, one angling off to keep her from running into King Street toward the shopping arcade there. The other one came right for her.

Down the dark brick promenade of Grafton Street Biddy Nevins plunged, her chalk box under one arm, the heavy woolen greatcoat that she wore against the cold flapping behind her. Now nineteen, she was a tall, thin woman with yellow gold hair that formed tight natural curls she wore long. Like some other Travelers whose clan had "married close," she had one blue eye, the other brown. But her high cheekbones and fine, even features were those of her mother's prominent Traveling family, the Maughams, and she looked all of what she was: an exotic creature in every regard.

Who could shift, because she had been forced to and fast for most of her life. She pegged by Cathedral Street and Moore Lane, which were too narrow and too dark to enter and hope for help if she was caught. And the one, the smaller shade, was right on her heels.

With her heart in her mouth and her chest bursting, Biddy rushed by Bewley's Tea Room and the lighted display windows of Dunnes and Switzers and the Brown Thomas department stores, before cutting into Wicklow Street. If only she could find a shade, a *real* shade, but that wouldn't help her either if there was only one.

Madly she racked her brain for a refuge down the streets and laneways where, as a child, she had begged and stolen and run in a wilding pack with other abandoned children. They had terrorized tourists, stolen cars and anything that wasn't nailed down, and booted drugs, which was the beginning of the end for so many of them. And now maybe for her, here where it all had started.

But would she want the police? she asked herself, glancing back to find that she now had a half block lead on the only one of them she could see. God, no. Not if she could avoid it. Cops would mean giving her name and later detectives, who would come around when they put together why she was running with who she was, with her work, and with the dead man. Biddy only ever drew Book of Kells pages there on the wide squares at the top of Grafton Street.

No shades could protect her from the Toddler when no shades had been able to put him away for lo these many years. He was, like, immune or in with them—the shades—who, some said, now worked for him. Could this be proof? No— in spite of all that had happened to her, Biddy refused to believe it; otherwise . . . there'd be no point in carrying on.

There had to be somebody out there in "Buffer Land," as Mick-alou called the settled society, who was good. Who believed in right and wrong. They couldn't be all like the politicians—on the take.

Bang. Biddy ran right into him—the second shade who was not a shade. He must have circled around through William Street and run fast. Bouncing off his broad chest before he could grab her, Biddy shot the box of chalk and change up into his big rough pan, shouting, "He's not the police! He's *not* the police!" at a car in William Street that had slowed to watch the altercation. "He's a fookin' *murderer!*"

And her hands—they came up hacking, scratching, punching at his face, churning—fast, faster—so he couldn't grab her. Her boot—she got that in too, right between the bastard's legs. Once, twice. He roared and lunged for her. Christ, where was the other one? He couldn't be far behind.

But the big one had caught hold of her lapel and now began lifting her off her feet with one hand while cocking the fist of the other. Spinning, Biddy slipped one sleeve and then the other, as the hand, the arm, the fist punched past her ear. She pivoted and left him crouched there, holding the garment.

To hell with it, she thought, as she sprinted down the slight hill and toward the many headlamps she could see lashing by at the other the end of the street. Like any other "Tinker bitch," she had a closetful of cast-off clothes back at the flat. The heavy thing had only been slowing her down.

It was then she heard the shots, not one but a bunch of them booming like a cannon in the tight pack of buildings along the narrow street. A shopwindow near her head cracked, a second bullet knocked out a piece, and Biddy only just jumped into the road when the whole works—a wall of glass—crashed into the street.

Bolting right out into the busy Dame Street as she had years ago after nicking some buffer's billfold, Biddy ran right at the oncoming cars where no sane person would follow. All she could think of was Mickalou and her baby, the only two people who mattered in her life. It was plain now they would kill her; hadn't the shots proved it?

The Toddler would have stopped at her chalk drawing and would now know who she was: Mickalou the Gypsy minstrel's girl. The "Tinker bitch" that he'd already called her. Another junkie and therefore expendable, somebody the Toddler had been killing slowly for years and now would finish. No—now had the *right* to finish, like the man he put under the bus.

Didn't the Toddler and his gear *rule?* There was graffiti like that—THE TODDLER RULES or TOD'S TOT, THE *TOTAL* GEAR— all over the city. Or the drawing that was printed on glassine tabs, of a smiling Toddler with top hat and spats, holding something (Biddy knew what it was!) behind his back.

Written on the bottom was the sentence they all said to each other so often nobody gave a thought to what it meant: IT'S *DEADLY!* It was scrawled in shooting galleries, in pub loos, on walls where people were poor and stupid, the way Biddy herself had been for all those years.

And the expression on his face? That said, Come and get it, you stupid dead fucks. Come into my world and let me kill you slowly. I'll take everything from you, and after it's mine, I'll take what's left of your worthless lives. If I choose.

With one phone call the bastard would learn where she

and Mickalou lived, and he'd take away Mickalou and hold him until he got her. Then he'd kill Mickalou too, and maybe even the baby. It was her fear speaking to her. But why not? Why not a baby? It would add to the way people spoke of him, to the terror. The awe. It was said that the Toddler never killed the same way twice, and it was always never certain that he had. Only that the people he wanted dead got dead. Sometimes horribly, like just now at the top of Grafton Street. God, why hadn't she packed up sooner and gone home?

Back on the footpath now, rushing by the gates to Dublin Castle, Biddy could see a guard in the kiosk, and she thought of turning in. He too could make a phone call. There was even some class of guard office right there on the grounds, as she remembered. But would he or any shade believe her, a Tinker and former junkie, a pavement artist with a long record and now a tall tale? How long would it take her to convince them that what she said was true and send a car to the flat? Too long, she decided. And had she not learned never to trust the shades again? Not after what they'd done to her those first few months in the city when she was nine.

Raped repeatedly, night after night, by the boys in the gang of Traveler children who were living by the dump in Ringsend, Biddy had hemorrhaged and fainted in the street. The shades took care of her all right; out of the fat into the fire. From the Richmond Hospital they took her to a "shelter" where she was molested every night by the superior of the place. To give the nun credit, she was gentler than the boys. Sometimes.

Christ, a limo now poked out its bonnet at the top of the street. It was a Merc, long and black with tinted windows and an amber spotlight that the driver was playing along the footpath, as the car drifted toward her.

Biddy nipped into the Castle Inn, the bar, not the lounge, and noted how conversations stopped the moment she appeared in the doorway. Sure, she must have color in her cheeks after all her running, but to appear hatless and coatless on such a bitter night and dressed only in a fisherman's knit jumper and a long plaid kilt with her tangled blond tresses and two-color eyes, Biddy could be only one thing. "Knacker," she heard somebody mutter.

Her eyes darted first to the other doors: to the lounge, another in back of the bar that seemed to lead to a kitchen, and a third that was the men's room. Next she scanned the crowd to see whose eyes were still on her good chest. Without her coat or chalk box she had no money, and she should ring up and warn Mickalou while she still had the chance.

She turned to a middle-aged man who was sitting against the wall. A whiskey drinker who had on a good suit, he was probably some bureaucrat from the nearby City Hall or the Castle. "Please, sir, for the love of God, could you give me a bit of help? It's a matter of life and death," she whispered in a chesty rush, words that she had heard her mother and so many other Traveling women utter over the price of a bottle of milk, but here what she said was the truth. "May I fall down paralyzed dead, if I'm tellin' you a word of a lie. I've to make a phone call. Two lives depend on it, and I came away without me coat and purse."

"You there, woman," the barman called to her. "Out, out with yeh now! No beggin' in here."

But she had fixed the man with her eyes that she knew would tell him truer than words. There was a long moment on which her entire life seem to hinge, as the barman came around to put her out in front of the Toddler's Mercedes and the man paused to decide. But his hand reached out and shoved a fifty pence coin toward her.

"God love ye, sir. You're a savior." She turned toward the phone.

"It's not God's love that I need tonight," he said to a companion.

"Being a sinning savior."

They had a laugh.

In an undertone the barman said to her, "After that—out. Or I'll toss you out myself."

There was no answer at the flat, which was good. Maybe Mickalou had not got home. On the other hand, maybe they had already lifted him. Their child, Oney, was being minded by the woman in the flat below, whose name was Morrisey.

But when Biddy opened the telephone directory and turned to the M's, she despaired when she realized that she did not know how to spell the name or the street—John Dillon—that the building was on. She had never attended school, not for a day, and nobody in her family could read.

Her father was proud of it. "Buffer voodoo," he called the written word. "I need only know where I am, when I am, and what's bubblin'," he once bragged when drunk. "The rest is pox."

Biddy was wasting time. Slamming shut the directory, she turned to see one of the Toddler's murdering shades coming in the bar door, and she stepped back quickly into the shadows, then opened the door to the lounge.

"Did any of yous see . . ." she heard him ask the bar in a harsh Joxer accent, as the door closed. For muscle the Toddler hired only North Side Dublin gougers, Mickalou had said. "The rougher the better. While he sounds like somebody off the BBC."

Turning around, Biddy expected to find the other one coming into the lounge from the street. Instead she found only an old woman finishing a pint. "If anybody comes in searching for me, for the love of God, don't tell them I'm here. I swear on my child they're not guards, and they're only after murdering a man on Stephen's Green. Now it's me."

Biddy rushed to the back of the long dim room and toward the ladies' she could see over a door. But the sign wouldn't stop them; they'd look there.

"The other door," the old lady said. "Go down the stairs and out the back. Guards is scum."

Biddy had only closed the door when she heard, "She go t'rough here?" Then louder: "You—old one!—she go t'rough here? The girl. Blond, a Tinker. Which way?"

"I'm deaf. I can't hear you."

"Did a Tinker bitch go t'rough here?" he roared. "Fook wi'd me, and I'll pop yuh!"

"Is that a gun? Will you shoot me?"

In the utter darkness Biddy had to feel her way down the stairway into the cellar that stank of rotting porter lees and rats' nests. She heard the door to the loo bang open and then the metal doors of the toilet stalls. Finally the door above her went wide, and the stairway was flooded with light. But by then Biddy had found the back door.

She waited to see if the man would start down, but when he didn't, she stepped into the night and lit out, running as fast as she could through the dark side streets and lane-ways.

3

CRUSH!

 At Patrick Street, a main and well-lighted thoroughfare four blocks distant, Biddy paused until traffic eased before sprinting through the cadmium haze to John Dillon Street, which was hard by.

There she concealed herself behind a parked lorry and waited for less time than she should but more than she could afford. When she was satisfied that there appeared to be nobody about or nothing unusual in the street, Biddy made her way around to the alley, scaled the wall, and dropped down into the back garden.

At the kitchen door she listened to the sounds coming from the frosted glass panel of June Morrisey's kitchen door. Among the voices of June's five children, she could hear Oney, which meant that Mickalou had not stopped around to collect her and was not home. She rapped on the door.

"Jaysus, Biddy, you gave me a fright. Did you forget your keys? Where's your coat and hat?"

Oney came running out to Biddy, who picked her up and hugged her within an inch of her life. There for a while she thought she would never see Oney again. But she'd have time enough for hugs and thanks when the three of them got clear.

"I'm in big trouble, June." Biddy stepped into the kitchen and began walking toward the hall door. "Someday I might be able to tell you about it. Right now I have to go upstairs, put some clothes together, and leave. We won't be back. If Mick's not back before I go, could you tell him—" Biddy racked her brain for what she could say that would not make June a party to what had happened but would make Mickelou understand that he too had to shift. There was no other way. "Tell him the *g'ami shadogs* is *toreen, crush!*"

"What?"

"It's Gammon," which was the Traveler secret language that was as old as there had been Travelers, Biddy's grandmother had told her, and that was over a thousand years. Mickalou, who knew such things, said it had been spoken first like Irish and now like English, but with Gammon words that could be understood only by their own.

Travelers used Gammon while buying or selling to buffers or in court or when shades were in camp. It was also a way of telling a real Traveler from some traveling buffer. The sentence Biddy had said meant, "The bad police are onto us, clear out!"

Biddy repeated the statement. "Can you say it?"

June tried but only got a part of it right.

"Maybe if you wrote it down for me."

June hunched her shoulders. "I don't have a clue how to spell them words, but I'll try."

Biddy carried the note upstairs with her and propped it on the kitchen table. She then threw together three kits, one for each of them, and poured all the money from the fish bowl into a plastic bag that she stuffed in her coat. It was all the money—less expenses—that she and Mickalou had made in the last few days and hardly enough to take Oney and her far from Dublin.

Mickalou would have whatever he made that afternoon, which was always more than Biddy, and she rued the day that she let him talk her into a bank account. "Banks is for buffers," she had complained. "What happens if we have to shift in the middle of the night?"

Said Mick, "That was our other life"—when we were shooting dope, he meant. "This is now." And them the King and Queen of the Buskers. "We'll leave only when we want to. And when we do, our savings will give us the legs for shifting properly. We might even emigrate."

Even then Biddy had thought Mickalou had forgotten who they really were to the settled people who mattered. Just two poor Tinkers, who did not. To the lot of them, Tinkers were scarcely human. "Itinerants" was the word that they used on the telly. At first Biddy, like most of her people, had not known what the word meant, although it sounded bad. And was.

Placing Mickalou's kit on the table near the note, where he'd see it first thing when he came in, Biddy stopped for a moment to look around. There was the cooker they had scavenged together, the lino on the floor his father had put in, and all the Traveler detailing Biddy had painted over the doors and in the tiny sitting room in brilliant red and yellow, the Travelers' colors. She'd painted horses' heads, scrollwork, fruit clusters, and lucky horseshoes. They had even bought a wee budgie that was sleeping in its cage and they'd never see again.

Biddy had been happier here than she had ever been in her life. In Mickalou she had found a man who was different from the common run of Travelers and muckers she had known—not selfish and brutal and demanding but kind and considerate and fun to be with. When she was not, it was as if there were a part of her missing.

And then she also loved him because he loved—as she did herself—something that was not himself, that was "exalted," he explained to her. For him it was Irish music and the bagpipe, which he worshiped beyond distraction; for her it was drawing where she could and did lose herself for hours on end. It wasn't work.

Jesus Christ Almighty and all the saints in heaven and sinners in hell, she prayed silently. Please help us through this. If you do, I'll—Biddy did not know what she'd do, but she'd do something religious and deserving.

She switched off the lights and had nearly closed the door, when she remembered IDs that she had been given along with the "effects," the police had called them, of a friend she had gone into rehab with and who had hanged herself the day they got out. Beth Waters had no family that they could locate back in England, but she'd had a driver's license and national health card. With those in her pocket, Biddy locked the door and rushed down the stairs.

"Can't you tell me about it?" June asked.

"Believe me, it's nothing you'd be wanting to know."

"Is it drugs?" "Again," went unsaid, since Biddy had told June about the recovery meetings they went to nearly every day.

Biddy shook her head and pulled two jumpers over Oney's head, then added a thin jacket, a medium-weight jacket, and finally a stout winter coat. Traveling people had known, years before ski clothes came in, that layers kept you snug. The child was falling asleep, and Biddy picked her up in her arms.

Biddy regarded her smaller, older friend, who had been so helpful to her. "If anybody calls round, guards even, say nothing. You don't know me; you never did. Mick and me were just two Knackers who lived upstairs, and you're glad to be rid of us."

June's face was drawn in disbelief; settled people just did not leave like this. "But where are you going? Can I call you a cab?"

Biddy shook her head. Cabs kept records, and cabbies took tips, the larger the better. The Toddler would only need to circulate the message that he had a hundred pounds for whoever knew where the "Tinker bitch" had gone, "the one from the top of Grafton Street. The blonde with the chalks and the pictures." Biddy would make her way back to her people by herself and leave off her daughter. Then she'd quit the country altogether. It was her only chance.

She handed June her key. "There's the budgie. Don't let her die. In two weeks, before the rent comes due, go in and take whatever you fancy. Or take it all and make a few bob. We won't be needing a thing."

Tears popped from June's eyes. "Then you're serious."

Biddy shrugged and picked up Oney. It was what it meant to be a Traveler—even a straight, honest, law-abiding, working, bill-paying Traveler who was Queen of the Buskers. Nothing was permanent.

It was then they heard the front door to the building open and men's voices in the hall. One was Mickalou's, and he was speaking loud and Tinker-theatrical, as if to warn her. "Amn't I after tellin' yeh now she don't be home? There's not a light showing in the flat. I can bring you, now, to where she might be. I know the pubs, the spots. She'll take the wee drop, yeh know, and it's there she must be."

Hearing Mickalou's voice, Oney woke up and cried out, "Mickey, Mickey!" which is what she called him, before Biddy could clamp a hand over the child's mouth.

"We'll have a look for ourselves, if you don't mind. Lead the way, like a good chap." Biddy didn't have to peek out to know; it was a soft, intelligent-sounding voice. Neutral in accent but maybe a bit Yank. The Toddler.

Biddy did not know what to do: stay where she was or go out the back, the way she had come in, and chance the alley. But could the Toddler have covered that too, thinking she might bolt?

Now they heard footsteps climbing the stairs and the jingle of keys as Mickalou opened the door. "See, look for yourselves."

There was a pause and more moving about, as the two "cops"—Biddy supposed—searched the flat. Because they heard the Toddler plain, when he said, "What do we have here?"

"My kit."

"You're off, then? Where to?"

"See me folks."

"And where would they be?"

"In the North."

"Where in the North?"

"Campin' in the North. I'll have to ask round to catch them up." Ask other Travelers, Mickalou meant, although he was only being dodgy. His parents were camped near Glenties in Donegal, far to the west of Dublin.

"And this. Could you tell me what this says?"

It was the note, Biddy was certain.

There was another pause, in which they could hear things being tossed about deeper within the apartment.

"I dunno. She leaves me notes, but she can't write. She's illiterate, not a day of school in her life. But isn't it the thought that matters?" It was just like Mickalou: There he was in danger of his life, yet he was having the Toddler off.

"Now here's an interesting word, *toreen*. What does *toreen* mean?"

"Beats me. Like I said, it's gibberish. And *crush*. Now, there's a good word for my situation." Mickalou went on loud down the stairs, as though telling Biddy what she should do because he'd heard the baby and suspected she was in with June. *Crush* meant "clear out." "It's how I feel, Tod. You pull me off the street, you sit on me, and all I hear is Biddy. What she do? How'd she offend you? Tell me, so I can make it right?"

"Ah, my young friend. You'll do that and more, if we don't find her soon. But not to worry. I have faith in you. Weren't we once partners? Now, come along. We'll visit these 'spots' you spoke of."

Biddy despaired at leaving Mickalou with the Toddler, but there was no other choice short of giving up all three of them. Also Mickalou had an easy way of getting on with people, even the likes of the Toddler, whom, after all, he had once worked for. And finally Mickalou was a party to none of what had happened there on the corner and knew nothing about it. Why would the Toddler want to harm him?

Thanking June with her eyes, Biddy made straight for the kitchen door, which she opened quietly. She stepped out, waved once, and fled through the back garden.

The alley was empty and led to a quiet street and another alley and so forth—all places that Biddy had begged, door to door, in years past. It was her one advantage: knowing how to move through the city in a way that no car could follow.

Yet she had the feeling that she was being followed. All the more so when, at Harold's Cross a long mile distant from John Dillon Street, she chanced to step out of the shadows and wait for a bus that would take her to Tallaght, where she did not know what she would find.

The Toddler or her parents or, worse, both.

4
CAW

 Winter came early that year with cold winds and lashing rain that began in September and scarcely let up for whole weeks on end.

By November Dublin was blear and chill, as though a permanent pall had fallen over the city. Conversation was muted, voices were hushed, and even lifelong Dubs seemed beset and without hope that the short days would ever brighten.

On one such morning a telephone call came through to the Murder Squad that was fielded by various staffers and finally routed to Detective Sergeant Bernie McKeon, the squad's chief of staff, who dealt with most difficult callers.

A rotund but powerfully built man of middle age, McKeon listened for a while, asked a few questions, then turned his head to glance into the cubicle where Chief Superintendent

McGarr was presently staring down at a cup of coffee, as though attempting to divine some secret from its rising vapors.

McGarr had slipped his hands into the pockets of his dark suit, and his hat—a bowler now in winter—was still on his head, even though he had arrived a full half hour earlier.

Seated to his immediate left with an arm on the desk and a newspaper opened in his lap was a much larger and older man who was nattily attired in a pearl gray vested suit and black brogues. Superintendent Liam O'Shaughnessy—McGarr's second-in-command—was also wearing a hat, a magnificent homburg that matched the suit.

True, it was chilly in the old building that had once served as a barracks for the British Army, but the early-morning scene—the coffee, the staring, the newspaper, the hats—was a ritual that McKeon knew better than to disturb without good cause. Or at least until McGarr produced the bottle of malt from the lower right-hand drawer and topped up his coffee. "The Chief," as he was known to the staff, had been up all night investigating another suspected murder in Lahinch in distant Clare, and he could be . . . irascible was not quite a strong enough term, when tired.

Omertà, they called it jokingly: the "code of silence." Once it was broken, their day of work would begin with a formal meeting in the cubicle and questions from the two that would keep everybody hopping often long into the night.

"I'm sorry, the chief is tied up. Where are you now? Oh. I realize it's a long way, but could I ask you to call into our office here in Dublin Castle?" McKeon listened some more, then said, "Yes, he will see you. Personally. It's just that he's presently in a, er, planning conference. It's quite important, but I can assure you he's most interested in what you have to say. In person would be best, if it's not too much to ask. Another possibility is for us to send out a detective to interview you. In private, of course."

It was the technique McKeon employed to separate crank and scurrilous tipsters from those who truly believed they knew something. Those willing to show themselves at least had the courage of their convictions, which was the operative word in the office.

An hour went by, then two, then six and eight. Utterly exhausted now, McGarr was about to reach for his hat and drag himself home for a hot meal and a long sleep when McKeon appeared in the doorway.

"There's a Tinker woman in the dayroom, Chief, who says she wants to speak to the 'head *shadog* and nobody else' about what she thinks is a murder. She rang up this morning, and she's come all the way from Ballinasloe. I tried to get the story, but she won't tell me any more than it's about two people"— McKeon glanced down at a slip of paper—"Biddy Nevins and Mickalou Maugham."

"The bagpiper?" Who was also a Tinker, which was the term McGarr thought more traditional and apt but was now used mainly by people of his own generation and older. "Traveler" was a more recent term that the Traveling people now used to describe themselves. "Itinerant" was used by the media, and "Knacker" by bigots.

McKeon shook his head.

Could there be two people with such an unlikely name? Mickalou Maugham was, arguably, the finest musician in the country on the uillean pipes, the Irish bagpipe, which was inflated by means of a bellows under the arm rather than by blowing into a bladder. McGarr's own grandfather had been a noted piper in his native Monaghan, and McGarr occasionally took out the instrument, which had been left him. But he played only poorly.

Maugham's touch, on the other hand, was sweet and deft, and McGarr had a number of his CDs. More to the man's credit, he had set about at an early age to record the music of his own people, the Travelers, and later to set down in musical notation all the unrecorded bagpipe music in the rural parts of Ireland and Scotland. A series of articles in the *Irish Times* had detailed the technique he had employed to extract the tunes from bagpipers in isolated areas where people were suspicious of strangers. The effort was nothing short of brilliant.

Setting himself up in the principal pub in a village or wherever people congregated on market day, he would make a show of pulling his bagpipe from his kit. Then he would take great pains to tune and adjust the instrument—all to make sure that he had an audience. Finally he would begin to play, running through simple songs to more difficult numbers and ending with the most complicated and difficult music that he knew. Only when he could not continue would he stamp his foot on the floor and say in English, Irish, or Scottish—depending on the venue—"Beat that!"

Some local piper was sure to pick up the gauntlet, and the competition would be on, sometimes lasting for days as word spread of Maugham's presence and additional pipers appeared. Later on, when the others had gone to bed, Maugham would stay up late into the night, writing down what he had heard. Every now and then for over a decade a small press in Dublin would issue a book in his name titled *The Pipe Music of Ulster* or of Iona and Mull or the Eastern Highlands, where Maugham would play the Scottish pipes. McGarr had them all.

But because so much of his time was spent in pubs, where—McGarr supposed—he was bought jars by appreciative listeners, Mickalou Maugham developed a drink problem that later led to drugs, "which are more efficient," he told *The Times*. It was a thought that had never occurred to McGarr, and he remembered. Fair dues to the man, however: He put himself into hospital, kicked his habit, and had remained drug-free for a number of years at the time the article was written, which was a good few ago. Four or five.

He had married another Traveler, a tall, pretty young woman whom he had met in rehab, and she had gone on to become the premier pavement artist in Dublin, always drawing a page from the Book of Kells there at the top of Grafton Street across from the gate into Stephen's Green. Because the other street musicians called Maugham the King of the Buskers, she became the Queen. Although McGarr had often tossed her a few pence for her drawings, which were remarkable, he had never known her name. But it occurred to him now that he had not seen her or him for quite some time, even though he walked up Grafton Street at least once a week after visiting his tobacconist on College Green.

"How old a woman?" he now asked McKeon, meaning the woman out in the dayroom.

"Forty-five, fifty, though she looks like seventy."

No, that couldn't be the wife, who was still only a girl.

"Show her in then." McGarr sorely hoped that nothing had happened to Maugham.

"Well, I'd say it's more a matter for Hogan's," which was a pub not far from the Castle that some of the squad frequented. "She looks scared to death, and she's asked me twice if we 'do be holding' her if she was to help us 'shades.' Maybe she'd be more forthcoming in another setting. And then . . ." McKeon glanced at the clock. It was time for him to leave, and his first stop was always Hogan's.

McGarr saw no harm in the change, and the woman seemed relieved when McKeon told her she could have her chat with the chief superintendent in a pub. "It's that time of day, and he thinks you might be more comfortable there. This isn't much of a room."

McGarr asked Ban Gharda Ruth Bresnahan, who was the squad's newest recruit, to accompany them and take notes.

"But when will I get this done if I'm off to a pub?" As the least senior and still-uniformed officer she had been assigned clerical duties, which she had railed at, wondering aloud more than once about the implications "of one woman pickin' up the dorty details for a pack of men. Can't someone else do a piece of work around this place now and then?"

By whom she meant Hugh Ward, who had only climbed out from under the mountain of paperwork with her coming and was not about to dive back in.

"Think of it this way, Rut'ie," McKeon now observed in the pancake accent that marked him as a Dubliner; he was a stocky man with a full head of corn blond hair and dark, mischievous eyes. "It's an *investigation*, what you've been telling me all along you joined us to do. And afterwards, why, you'll have the office virtually to yourself—to type up your notes and get on with all that bother. Without *us!*"

Which was cruel, really, but every new man (or, here, *person*) had gone through the unofficial hazing process. And if she could not take it, then she wasn't fit for the job, and there would always be somebody else willing to fill her . . . well, shoes.

McKeon now watched Bresnahan rise reluctantly from her chair and reach for a steno pad and pencil. A big red country girl from Kerry, she filled out her light blue blouse and dark blue uniform dress rather amply. Otherwise she was pretty, and McKeon imagined that with some care taken, the fiery young woman might have some potential in the way of form.

But far be it from him to suggest it. Father of an even dozen himself, he had met WOMAN enough for one lifetime, and the decision was still in daily doubt as to who would supervene.

Down in Hogan's, McGarr ordered three whiskeys and a lemon soda for Bresnahan, who was in uniform and could not drink. The Traveler woman had no qualms. She tossed hers off in a swallow and turned to McGarr.

"My name is Maggie Nevins, and I was born in Tuam, County Galway, forty-eight year ago come December first. Me da was given a waste house when I was young, and they've stayed there ever since."

McGarr thought he knew what she meant. During the fifties, emigration from places in the West had resulted in a number of abandoned houses, some of which were awarded to Travelers in an effort—largely successful there in Tuam— to settle them. He tasted his drink.

"But I married a Travelin' man who fancied the road, and we've been on it ever since."

Which was apparent. From sun and wind, the skin of her face was creased and lined and the color of dark tea. Yet it was once a handsome face with clear brown eyes, prominent cheekbones, and a strong chin. Her nose, which was long, was bent to one side, as though from an injury. Battering was an all-too-common feature of many Traveler marriages.

She was wearing a bright scarf over her head, reminiscent of the full shawls that older Tinker women used to employ. McGarr could just see the glint of thick gold "Gypsy" earrings. Her winter coat was new; her boots were rather stylish and made of some supple leather. In all, she looked like a woman who had spent her life on the road, but those roads, at least in recent days, had been in and around Dublin or some other large city.

"How long have you lived in Dublin?" McGarr asked Maggie Nevins.

"Permanent like? Nine year up until ten month ago. Before that we tried to stick the country. But there's nothing for Travelers in the country no more. It got so we couldn't even keep all our own childer."

"And how many would that be?"

"Sixteen in all. Four is dead, six still with me, seven counting me oldest daughter's daughter."

Bresnahan's head had come up from her notepad, and she regarded the woman down her long, straight nose with unveiled contempt. The daughter of a "strong" farmer from Kerry, she was very much a settled personality in every way.

"There in your caravan in—Ballinasloe, is it?" It was a city in Galway that was about a hundred miles from Dublin.

"Aye. But"—Maggie Nevins's eyes darted timidly at Bresnahan—"it's not been as bad as the telling would have it. Not by half. I'm alive, amn't I?" That seemed to cheer the woman for a moment, before her brow glowered. "It's about her—Oney, the little one—that I come. She do be Mickalou and Biddy's child, and I'm freckened she'll be needing a da."

"She's also your daughter's daughter?" McGarr asked, remembering that the pavement artist had been noticeably pregnant—when?—four or five years back. "The girl, the one who does the Book of Kells at the top of Grafton Street?"

She nodded, her eyes shying toward the bar. "Biddy. I'm a born Maugham myself, you know."

"Here, can I get you another wet?" asked McKeon, now that she had begun her story.

"That's grand." She handed him her glass, and McGarr eased back into the cushions of the banquette, recalling what he knew of Tinkers. A few years before, he had chaired a Garda commission to establish police guidelines for dealing with the over three thousand families that constituted the "Traveling community," was the current phrase in Ireland, and he was acquainted with their history.

The word "Tinker"—by which those people had been known until recently—had been taken from the sound a hammer makes when striking metal. But there was only so much work in any given area, and they of needs had taken to the road.

As early as A.D. 400 smiths were traveling throughout the

country, and in later times, when famine, poverty, and evictions swelled their ranks, Tinkers offered other services to the resident population. They became seasonal farm workers, horse traders, minstrels, storytellers, thatchers, and chimney sweeps—whatever it took to get by.

Contrary to current opinion, they were not shiftless vagabonds. Tinker women brought isolated farm wives news, gossip, and swag—small manufactured items, such as needles, combs, hand mirrors, etc.—that could not be had otherwise in rural Ireland, while their men provided needed skills and services and were, by and large, honest brokers. They had to be. Vigilante justice was swift and harsh, and in most quarrels officials took the side of the settled party, no matter the wrong.

The pattern of Tinker life, however, changed drastically after the Second World War with the appearance of cheap metal and plastic goods and mechanized farming that replaced seasonal labor. Forced to shift to the cities, Travelers were cramped onto small plots heaped with rusting auto parts, trash, and such. The men went on the dole; the women begged in the streets.

But the greatest tragedy—to McGarr's way of thinking— was the effect city life had on Tinker children. Schools for them were segregated and poor, and few attended. With little to do and no place to play, many took to roaming the camps and the city. Vandalism led to more serious crime, drink, and drugs.

Government efforts to improve the Travelers' lot had largely failed. Only half of Dublin's seven hundred Traveling

families were housed, usually in squalid, ghettolike neighborhoods, and the percentage and conditions of life for them
countrywide were little better.

But McKeon had returned with the drinks, which he carefully lowered to the table in front of them.

"You were saying about your daughter and Mickalou
Maugham?" McGarr prompted. "Ten months ago."

Maggie Nevins nodded and picked up her new drink. "It's
what I come to tell you about. A Thursday last February. The
very hardest part of the winter, though we were in great
heart—me and the kids—since Ned had come back to our
caravan from the Labor with pockets of money and a nice feed
for us from the chipper.

"But I should have known better, for what did I hear when
I opened the door"—she paused dramatically—"chatterin'
magpies." Her eyes swung to McGarr, who shook his head.
He did not know what she meant.

"Trouble comin', and I should have known. For the truth
is, I only got the washup done and the kids in bed when the
door opened. Who should it be but Biddy in a huff and Oney
in her arms, saying she had trouble and had to shift? Could I
take the baby for a while? She'd send for her when she could;
she was going to get out of the country as quick as she could.

"With that Ned, who had nodded off, wakes up and asks
her what it's all about, but she says she can't say. 'If they
thought you knew, you'd have to run too,' was her words. And
she scarcely said good-bye. 'Speed it! Put it going!' she gave
out to Ned. And they left in a rush for Rosslare and the ferry
to Folkstone.

"And"—Maggie sighed and looked down at her now-empty glass—"they be no sooner gone than an awful thumpin' comes to the caravan door, and some man starts roarin', 'Get out o' that! Get out o' that, you Knackers!' And another thump that fairly knocked the door off its pins.

"I look out and there's two big *shadogs*, uniforms, buttons and all, the one with a big gun pointin' right at me head. My God, the fret it give me. I was in bits, only half alive. 'Open up, you Knacker bitch!' he calls me. 'Or I'll blow yeh away!'

"I see lights goin' on in other caravans, and I says to meself, says I, 'If mindin' me granddaughter be a crime, they can take me off.' So I opened the door, and didn't the one peg me from the top step right down into the mud at the feet of the other with the gun.

"He shoved it against my temple, roarin' pure savage, 'She in there? She in there?' at the top of his Joxer lungs. 'Who? Who?' I got out. 'Biddy, you fookin' Knacker cunt!' " Maggie Nevins turned to Bresnahan. "Sorry, miss, but them was his words.

"The other one was already inside the caravan with a big white torch, shinin' it around and tossing things about. Some of the kids was cryin'; the others was screamin' for me. But nobody came out from the other caravans to help, and I don't blame them with the uniforms and the guns and all.

"When I tried to get up, the one with the gun roared, 'Down on the ground! Down on the fookin' ground!,' then cut me legs out from under me and stood or somethin' on the small o' me back. When I howled out in pain, what did he do?"

The three of her listeners waited—Bresnahan's pencil poised—while Maggie Nevins, obviously shaken even to recount the incident, tried to gather herself. She shook her head; tears had filled her eyes.

Suddenly the bar noise was almost palpable.

"Didn't he spin me around and punch the bloody gun into me gob, pushing it down until I was chokin'?" With a finger she pulled down her lower lip to reveal two lower front teeth that had been snapped off at the gum.

"It was then a shadow came between me and the lights in the caravans. Legs it was. Trousers. That was all I could see. Then a voice said, 'We'll start with the youngest. Bring the youngest one out.'

"I was clawin' at the gun that was like a stake pricked through me throat. I couldn't breathe. I was gaggin'. When the shade in the caravan came to the door with Oney, the third one said something, and the gun was ripped out o' me mouth. I'd swallowed me teeth, and didn't they come up in a cough. I was rollin' in the dirt, gabblin'. I could hardly see for the pain in me throat.

" 'That your child?' the third one asked. What I saw of him was smaller than the others. Older. Different-soundin'. 'Isn't she young for an old woman like you?' I still couldn't talk. I'd never been hurt so sorely in me life, not even in childbirth. It was like he quenched a poker in me lungs.

"And all I could think of was poor little Oney. She was so tired from running with her ma that through it all, she was still asleep in his hand and him holding her up—you know, over his head like a stone or somethin'." Maggie Nevins raised a hand to demonstrate. "Like he'd rear back and chuck her into the night."

Again she had to pause, and McGarr could not keep himself from thinking what a powerful witness she might be, could she be persuaded to testify, which he doubted. Travelers simply did not help the police, and those that did were never again trusted by their own. Added to that was the fright she had taken; obviously it was still with her.

"Then he—the little, older one—squatted down to look in me face, smilin', mind. 'I'll ask but once,' he says in a voice soft as butter. 'I make no idle threats. If you don't tell me, he'll kill the baby. It's hers, isn't it? Biddy's?'"

"I was at sixes and sevens what to say, grass on me daughter and save her child, or play dumb and chance he wouldn't. But I figured Biddy at least had been gone for a while, and she had her father with her. And when I looked into the man's eyes, I could tell he meant what he said—that little smile and them devil eyes. That's what they were. Happy like.

"Says I as good as I could through the blood, 'She come in, gave me Oney, and begged her father to take her down the country. That's all I know.' And he knew I was lyin'.

" 'When?' " he asked.

" 'An hour? Maybe two, maybe three. I fell asleep.' "

" 'Really?' says he, sounding like a laird. "Two or three hours ago she was still drawing at the top of Grafton Street. You must not care for your granddaughter very much. Did Biddy tell you where she was going?'

"Me mind was racin', tryin' to suss out what I could say that he'd believe and keep him off Biddy and Ned. The car they'd come in was big and rich-lookin', and if I said Rosslare, they'd catch Ned's old van sure. At last I decided to tell him the truth, or part of it. 'She said she wouldn't tell me that either. "If you knew, you'd have to run too." Them was her words.'

"That seemed to satisfy him. He stood. 'What about in there?' he asked the one in the doorway holding Oney. 'Nuttin'.' 'Put her back.' And the bollocks just tossed her back into the caravan, where she cut open her head and started wailing.

"Says the little mahn, 'Will you remember me?' Says I to him, 'I can't even see yiz.' With that, he turns, like he was going to walk away, but instead he spins and kicks me in the ribs. And what a kick! I thought he dropped a stone on me heart. 'Now I think you'll remember not to remember. And buy a newspaper from now on. I'll be sending Biddy a message just for her, down in the country.' "

Maggie Nevins turned her eyes to McGarr. "Now, this is why I'm here. When he opened the back door of the car, who did I see in there but Mickalou? He was lyin' on his side with his face on the seat, and all he could raise to me was his eyes that was"—she shook her head—"all muddied up. I never saw the like.

"And it was then—come closer while I tell yeh—didn't I pipe the man? The little one."

"The one who kicked you?"

She closed her eyes and nodded. "The Toddler, he's called. I'd know him anywhere, because of the way he walks. And a viper. Years ago he'd come round with weeks of free gear for all our childer, and him with a gang of rough Joxers, so's nobody could do nothin' about it. And wouldn't. Didn't he murder Paddy McDonagh?"

McGarr cocked his head. "Who?"

Maggie Nevins repeated the name, and McGarr glanced at McKeon. He didn't recognize it either.

Said Bresnahan, "Paddy McDonagh was the name of a Traveler who either fell or was defenestrated from a high floor of Switzers in Grafton Street just about this time last year."

It was true that all reports of questionable death passed across Bresnahan's desk before being processed. But McGarr wondered how much her command of seemingly every detail of every case was a matter of interest and acumen as it was simply overcompensating for being the squad's only woman.

"Shall I go on?" she asked.

McGarr opened a hand and closed it—his gesture for "Why not? But at your peril." He did not suffer tyros gladly.

"There was a question about how McDonagh managed to get the window open and himself out of it without being seen. It was a heavy thing without a counterweight and would have had to have been propped open. But it was found closed."

"And all for thirty-three pounds fifty," Maggie Nevins put in. "Which was what he owed the shagger."

"You were a witness?" McKeon asked.

Maggie Nevins shook her head.

"You know of a witness?"

Again. "And I fancy there wasn't one. It's not the way that yoke works. But it was known about Paddy and him—the money owed."

"For what?"

"Ah, the bleedin' gear. Didn't most of the young ones that were let run loose end up with the Toddler, one way or other?" Her eyes swung to the bar.

Bresnahan cleared her throat. "May I ask a question?"

McGarr nodded, competence having its rewards.

"Do you remember the date that your daughter came to your caravan and you were attacked?"

Maggie Nevins set her empty glass on the table. "Darlin' girl, I don't go by no calendars. I couldn't read one if I tried."

"Could it have been the eleventh of February?"

"It could. But all I remember is it was rare bitter and the ground where I fell was froze."

"I mention the eleventh of February, Chief, because that was the evening Gavin O'Reilly was knocked down and killed by a bus at the top of Grafton Street, just there at the corner and the gates into Stephen's Green.

"Isn't that where your daughter—"

"Biddy."

"—did her chalk drawings?"

The older woman nodded.

To McGarr and McKeon, Bresnahan added, "O'Reilly was a known drug dealer. Small time, compared to Desmond Bacon, but he was competition nonetheless. Word on the street was he'd been peddling to the Toddler's clients. That's evidently a no-no, punishable by death."

"Who's Desmond Bacon when he's at home?" Maggie Nevins asked, now seeming a bit tight. She pulled a packet of cigarettes from her purse and offered them around. McGarr took one, it being bad form for all of them to refuse.

"Desmond Bacon is the Toddler," Bresnahan continued. "O'Reilly's Achilles tendons had been cut, and he would not have been able to walk. The file says it's difficult to imagine that the man had crawled out into the street. Also, the driver of the bus swore he saw nobody in front of the vehicle, but he did see a group of men on the footpath when he turned the corner, including two uniformed guards. The conductor said he saw them too.

"Minutes later it was reported that guards were seen chasing a young blond woman in Wicklow Street, where one of them pulled out a gun and fired at her, knocking out a plate glass window. She ran out into Dame Street and presumably escaped. But there was no report of any guard firing a weapon on the evening of the eleventh anywhere in the country."

This time the look that McGarr and McKeon exchanged was more lengthy, as though to agree that Bresnahan might be more valuable than simply note-taking and office help.

Maggie Nevins shook her head. "And to think them bastards would have killed Biddy."

And you and the baby, McGarr was now certain. "Who filed those reports?"

Bresnahan shrugged one shoulder and looked away. "Inspector Ward." There was something between those two, and McGarr wondered if it was professional jealousy alone.

"In the morning I want them on my desk. And everything you can find on this Toddler yoke. As Toddler. As Desmond Bacon. The works.

"But discreetly. Don't request any files from Drugs, until we decide how to proceed." He meant the section of the Serious Crimes Unit that was known as the Drug Squad.

McKeon smiled. Folding his arms across his chest, he began humming a little tune. This Toddler was too cute by half. And in making his thugs don Garda uniforms to commit murder and felonious assault, the man had crossed a line, and he would pay, one way or another. McKeon hoped it would be the other.

"And tear up those notes, Rut'ie. It was after hours, and we came here to Hogan's for a jar or two. There was a woman sitting here—you forget her name—and we spoke."

"Just chat," McKeon put in.

"Chat," Bresnahan repeated, suspecting that some decision had been made but having no clue to what. And then she was a bit flustered, having been called Rut'ie by the chief for the first time ever.

"Where's Biddy now?"

"England."

"Where in England?"

Maggie Nevins only closed her eyes and shook her head.

5
CONTROL

 "No drugs for him. Doesn't drink, smoke. No-body's even seen him take tea," said Tom Lyons, who was their contact from the Drug Squad. "The ten months I been scoutin' the yoke, I've never seen him in a chipper, cafe, restaurant. Just the pub there, where he sits in a corner and watches things. Eats with the granny at the house, or at least he must."

Since Desmond Bacon did not look in need of a meal, thought McGarr, who was standing with a clutch of other men on the roof of the Cadbury chocolate factory about a half mile away from the Toddler's pub in Coolock. It had just been raided. A baker's dozen of mainly young people were lined up on the footpath by the door to the bar. Along with the Toddler.

Six uniformed guards were looking after them, while a team of detectives combed the pub for anything illegal. Anything at all. McGarr needed an excuse to "interview" the man, his way.

He adjusted the eyepiece of his binoculars and focused in on Desmond Bacon, alias the Toddler.

Bacon was a short but heavily muscled man with a round build. But he was not fat. Rumor had it he was a health and fitness buff and a martial arts expert, though that had yet to be corroborated.

Balding now at twenty-nine, he kept his remaining hair, which was dark, clipped short. He was wearing a gray double-breasted suit with the jacket open. Beneath it was a black turtleneck jersey. His black shoes were gleaming, and earlier McGarr had noticed a glint of gold on a wrist.

A dark beard shaved close made Bacon's fleshy face look older. But apart from the grandmother—reportedly an ancient woman who lived two streets distant—Bacon had no family in Ireland. Or any involvements that they could discover, female or male. His *trade* was his life, though he never practiced it himself directly. Those who did it for him were either loyal or dead.

"The most we've ever learned," Lyons went on, "is he was born on Gibraltar, son of a Belfast Royal Marine and an American woman. Got into trouble there, big time. Irish-English thing, the police file says. When the Brits ganged up on him, he gored the leader with sharpened forks, plunged them right through the other kid's hands.

"He was sent to a reformatory in England for two years. First day there he nearly killed another inmate with a bench when Bacon found him going through his kit. They gave him another year.

"From there he emigrated to the States and his mother's people in California. The Vietnam War was on then, and he joined the Marines, where he was assigned to reconnaisance."

"What's that mean?" McKeon asked. "Office work, or was he out on point? You know, alone." He himself had spent ten years in the Irish Army with stints in The Lebanon, and he knew from personal experience that reconnaisance duty as remote observer or sniper or both was perhaps the most hazardous mission in any army during war.

Lyons shook his head. "Dunno. That was all the file said. But he liked whatever it was well enough to reup. And he got medals, awards, citations—the lot. Promotions to sergeant major when his time was up and the promise of officer training were he to stay.

"He decided to get out, and they gave him the choice of destinations, anywhere in the world. They'd send him there gratis. He chose Dublin. And the legend is he arrived here in full dress uniform with a chestful of medals and two duffel bags of China White that were never checked."

Drug surveillance then being nearly nonexistent, McGarr knew, especially for a returning war hero. Or someone who looked the part. He had probably been waved right through customs.

"And he was in business," Ward said.

"What's he doing with his head?" McKeon asked. Both were also holding binoculars to their eyes.

"Dunno," Lyons replied. "It's what he does whenever he's got business. Or trouble."

It was something like a tic, McGarr decided. Bacon kept tilting his head twice to one side, then once to the other, as though trying to pop a kink in his neck. Which made him all the more the Toddler, when he wasn't moving forward, flat-footed but stiff, as though too heavily muscled and "tight" to walk normally. As he did now, stepping to the curb to scan the street.

"He's on the lookout for the solicitor. Probably paged him the moment we walked in."

The small black plastic box clipped to the Toddler's belt was a pager, McGarr knew, though he wasn't sure how they worked. It was a device that had only just arrived in Dublin and that some in the Garda thought the police should have.

"There's not a person who works for him who's not using. Or not on the piss. Pays them in gear and Guinness, it's said."

"Like effin' slaves," said Bernie McKeon, who had a daughter who'd had a problem with drugs; McGarr had a niece and Ward a cousin the same. It was a big problem and growing.

"Owns the pub, the bookie shop across the road. All the shops to either side. Houses as far as the motorway." Which was a throw of two hundred yards with most of the dwellings attached. How many? Twenty-some at least. It was quite a holding.

"There's not a person in them that doesn't think he's God. You know, the god of the syringe or pipe or tablet."

And the god who would make them dead without a qualm, thought McGarr, though Bacon didn't look very godlike—a short, pudgy fella with a tic.

The others?

"They look normal enough," Ward concluded. "For here."

By that he meant for a working-class area on the North Side.

The men were wearing leather bomber jackets or short, tight windcheaters that were left purposely open to display gold chains. Otherwise brush cuts, black crew-neck jumpers, black shoes or runners completed the uniform. And tight stone-washed jeans.

The women wore those too, along with stark white half boots with pointy toes and jackets to match. Those were padded in the shoulder but gripped the waist tight, so as to suggest more bosom than any probably possessed. Left open, the plackets revealed strands of gold chains, plunging V-neck jumpers that were pink in color and made of something like angora, and mounds of skin.

All were blondes, save for one whose hair was some unlikely shade of magenta. Layers of cosmetics made their faces seem lurid even under a pale winter sun, to say nothing of their long, lacquered talons and what McGarr thought of as the "cornered" look: felonious eyes that darted this way and that, as though for a way out. But mainly at the Toddler. Perhaps for direction. Or chemical salvation.

"What about the girls?" McKeon asked. It was a generous description but probably accurate; few were over twenty, but all could pass for thirty.

"Sure, they're renters. By the hour, by the night, long as you've any readies left. Big trade with foreign businessmen looking for a bit of different. It's said he ships them out as well. Middle East, Madagascar, Djibouti—wherever blondes is in. Two birds with one stone. See the odd girl out?"

"With the purple hair."

Lyons nodded. "They call her the Grape. Disappeared for seven weeks, she did. We thought for sure her body would surface in a canal. But when we checked immigration, didn't we find she'd skipped to Syria in September on a Syrian government jet. Came back the same way with four 'diplomats,' each carrying a stuffed diplomatic pouch."

"Business as well as pleasure," McKeon put in.

"She wasn't back a day before the word in the street was 'brick.' And still is." It was another name for hashish. "But far be it from him to sell bricks. Grams is all, and the markup is fantastic."

When the Toddler now tried to step out farther into the street, a uniformed guard put up a hand and gently pushed him back. That made the largest two of the Joxers, who seemed to be guarding the Toddler, move forward truculently.

"Who're they?"

"The Bookends, they're called. Hyde and Hyde. Twin brothers who grew up here, two doors down from the Toddler's granny. Hard cases even before he got back from Vietnam. But shortly after he did, they left school. When the father gave out to them, they thumped him, put him in hospital. Critical. On the mend he wouldn't say word one. Rumor is, they promised to kill the mother if he did. And would."

Again McGarr could feel his gall rising to think that this little gang of—how many?—two dozen or so that he could see had been able to act with such impunity for so long, killing people at will, shooting at people in city center, attacking an old woman and her children while masquerading as gardai.

And here in Coolock the Toddler had virtually taken over the main street.

"Drugs?" McKeon asked.

"Who? The Bookends? For personal use, I'd say so. Anything they want. It's how he keeps 'em loyal. But no trade. Nobody around the Toddler is allowed that. If they do—and some have—they end up in the Liffey."

Or under a bus or up in a tree, thought McGarr. He made mental note to ask Bresnahan to compare the names of murder victims in open cases against known associates of this Toddler. The Drug Squad would have a list. Or maybe it wouldn't.

"He ever been lifted?"

"The Toddler? Not that I know of. Not in this country."

"Why not?" McKeon asked.

Lyons shook his head. "Maybe he's been careful." But his eyes said he didn't think it was his place to say.

McGarr made a mental note to find out why.

"Who's the monkey?" Ward asked.

He meant the small young man who was dressed in a tight black—was it?—chauffeur's uniform. With a dark galways and gaunt body, he looked like a stick figure wearing a paste-on beard. Or an organ grinder's monkey, cap and all.

Lyons lowered his glasses. "Know him?"

Ward shook his head.

"The Monkey is what he's called. And not just for the costume and the beard. He's a heavy hitter, a great one for the gear." With two fingers and thumb, Lyons pantomimed pushing the plunger of a syringe into his other arm. "He's your man's driver. Some say he even provided the car that the Tod-

dler took title to in payment of his heroin debt. Archie Carruthers is his name. He's been driving for the Toddler for—
lemme think—maybe two years."

"*Carruthers?*" McKeon asked.

Lyons nodded. "Comes from an old family down the country."

"Wicklow?"

"Could be."

"Glencree?"

"Dunno. But he's nothing special. Just your common, gar-
den-variety gearman, thinner than most. Do anything to
score."

And probably had in the "Cliquot" tree on his—mother's?
aunt's?—property with the help of the Bookends or some of
the others McGarr could see through the binos.

"Let's lift him," McKeon muttered to McGarr. "Take him
back to the Castle," where McKeon and McGarr would grill
him. They were good at it.

But what if Carruthers didn't come across and they had to
let him go? How long would he last back here in Coolock?
Where he would come. Inevitably. Being a monkey man in
the worst sense and not being able to help himself. Then
again, Archie Carruthers—Monkey Man—had chosen who he
was and how he would live at least two years earlier, when
the robbery had occurred at the Glencree estate.

"I'll break him without even asking a question."

McGarr glanced at McKeon, suspecting he could, but he
had to be certain since the mere act of taking him into custody
would be like signing his death sentence. "Give me a moment."

Down in the car McGarr radioed his office, and Bresnahan patched through a phone call to Miss Eithne Carruthers, who came on the line after a short wait. "Tell me about Archie."

"My nephew?" There was a pause, then a sigh. "It occurred to me I should have said something about him last spring. But only after you were gone. Archie's my sister's only child, you understand."

And you his enabler, McGarr imagined. "How long have you known about his drug problem?"

"Years, of course. We've done everything we can: doctors, hospitals, clinics, even a rehabilitation center over in the States. Two years at enormous expense! Now it's up to him. He's got to want to stop himself."

And be able to. McGarr knew of addicts who'd been helped simply by being put in a place where using was impossible. Like jail. It made *wanting* to quit easier. "And after your break-in, did you tell the police about your nephew?"

There was another pause. "No, I couldn't bring myself to do that either."

"What about the car, the Mercedes? When did Archie steal that?"

"During his last slip. Two years ago. No, three."

"And you reported it?"

Her sigh was audible. "No."

"Why not?"

"Because—because I didn't want it to *be* Archie. Because it *was* Archie—I told myself—why, sure, wouldn't it be his car someday anyhow?"

"Since you have no children."

"That's right."

"And there's only you and your sister." Left in the family, he meant.

"Yes. And she a widow."

Little wonder the Toddler had kept Archie Carruthers close. The Monkey Man had brought him a marque automobile and whatever was boosted from the estate during the theft, and finally he had even helped him commit murder.

No. The Toddler had been nowhere near the murder. He'd been back in his pub or some other public place where people could see him.

"Do you think Archie is involved in . . . was it murder, Superintendent?"

Procedure dictated that McGarr remain noncommittal since her sister and she might hire a solicitor who would only make the investigation more difficult. But maybe not in this case. Maybe what the Monkey would now need was somebody who could talk some sense to him. "It was murder."

"Where's Archie now?"

"About to be taken in."

"And charged?"

"Perhaps. It all depends on how cooperative he is. Maybe it wasn't his idea at all. Maybe it was the drugs."

"Of course. Without a doubt. It was the drugs. Archie may be many unfortunate things, but I know in my heart he's no murderer."

McGarr wished he had a pound for every time he'd heard that.

"Where will you be taking him?"

"My office." He thanked her and rang off.

A few minutes later he pulled the unmarked blue Ford Granada into the curb by the pub where the Toddler and his minions were still lined up. Climbing out, he removed his Garda ID from a pocket and flashed it at the other guards, saying, "Peter McGarr, Murder Squad." Loud, so the Toddler and his solicitor would hear.

With the laminated ID still out, he made directly for the Monkey Man. "You must be Archie Carruthers."

The young man's eyes shied toward the Toddler, as though seeking permission to acknowledge his own name. Carruthers had narrow shoulders and a thin chest. On him the galways ring of dark and curly facial hair looked almost comic, truly like some monkey or leprechaun or pooka. But not like a real human being, which was fitting since he was not a person. He was an addict, a true Monkey Man.

"I asked you. Are you Archie Carruthers?" Out of the corner of an eye McGarr saw the Toddler nudge the solicitor, who stepped forward.

"What's this about? I represent this man."

"Since when?"

"Since this moment."

"And do you represent the rest of these people?"

"I do. Aye." The solicitor was a tall gray-haired man in a splendid tailored overcoat.

"Without even knowing their names. Tell me—what's the name of that undoubted felon over there, the one with murder in his eyes?" McGarr pointed to one of the Bookends, who was glaring at him. "Or the young woman beside him. A renter, I hear. Fancy her yourself?"

McGarr waited, studying the man, trying to remember who he was. But there was no reply.

"Ah, then, you're a rare, generous man for someone in your line of larceny. Fee free to unlimited, anonymous clients. Be honest, you take it out in trade."

Still nothing, which was strange. McGarr had seen the solicitor before, but he could not give the fleshy but handsome face a name. The man's color was high, his nose streaked with veins.

McGarr turned to the Monkey. "Archie Carruthers, you're to come with me." He took hold of the young man's gaunt arm. Under the chauffeur's jacket it felt like a thin branch.

"On what charge?" Finally the solicitor had found his voice.

"Oh, the very worst. Monkey business one, as premeditated as it comes." McGarr turned back to the man, aware that the Toddler was hanging on every word said. "Square with me now, solicitor. Be uncharacteristically honest, and I won't run you in. D'you fancy the odd glass of bubbly?"

The solicitor's head went back, aware of the ruin of his nose. "Bubbly?"

"Champagne. From the look of you, I'd hazard you do. Veuve Cliquot—know the brand? They say it's wonderful, the very best. Gets you up there. High. Makes you feel like a body in a tall tree, all chained and shackled. Had that effect on Mickalou Maugham. Sent him straight to heaven on the eleventh of November last." Hand still on Carruthers's arm, McGarr spun him around. "Or was it the tenth, Mr. Monkey Man?"

Again Carruthers's eyes appealed to the Toddler.

Whom McGarr now took one long step toward, dragging Carruthers with him. "No, that's wrong." They were nearly nose to nose, the Toddler and he. "The murder of Gavin O'Reilly was the tenth. He was the man you put under the bus. Maugham was the eleventh. He couldn't have lasted more than a day chained naked in that tree.

"Tell me something: Did you find the chains and shackles up there? Or had you thought of it earlier? You know, being just the sort of *gear* you'd need to send a message when the next offender presented himself."

McGarr's eyes remained locked into the Toddler's—small, dark, clear, and unworried—for the longest time. Nobody else spoke; not even the solicitor intervened.

Finally McGarr said. "You a betting man, Mr. Bacon? I know you're a chancer. Care to wager how long he'll last?" McGarr pulled Carruthers toward him, then shot the Monkey at McKeon and Ward, who had just arrived.

"That your car?" McGarr meant the long black Mercedes that the Monkey had stolen from his aunt, Eithne Carruthers. It was the model that was used by heads of state, bank directors, and here North Side drug kingpins.

Still, the Toddler said nothing.

"Then you don't mind if I impound it."

"On what grounds?" It was the solicitor again.

"That it's twice stolen. Once by him"—McGarr pointed at Carruthers, whom Ward was placing in the back seat of one of the patrol cars—"and then by him." He swung the finger at the Toddler's face, but the man did not flinch.

The solicitor's brow furrowed, and he looked down at the footpath, as though sorry he'd got involved. McGarr now remembered who he was: Cornelius Duggan by name, who represented only the class of accomplished criminals who could afford him. Well-known politicians, corporate and bank directors, and here a drug mogul. But auto theft was clearly beneath him.

"I hope Mr. Bacon is paying you cash, or could it be something more immediately rewarding?"

Duggan only looked away.

As they drove away, McGarr kept his eyes on the Toddler to see if he would motion Duggan to tag along. But he kept his vigil there on the footpath outside his pub, in his village, in his domain.

Hands in trouser pockets, eyes watchful. The head moving twice to one side, once to the other. The Buddha Toddler. Who'd been in fray before, that much was plain.

6
HOT SHOTS

 "So, tell me," McGarr asked Archie Carruthers the moment they got him into the dayroom and the monkey hat off his head, "how long you been on the gear?" McGarr leaned back in the chair, put his feet up on the table, twined his fingers behind his head, casual like. They had time to kill.

But Carruthers did not answer. Instead he stared at McGarr with a look of haughty, modish disdain for a bald, old, bent-nose cop who had to work for a living and probably believed in all the verities of society that kept people in chains. All the stupid and timid toilers out there who were afraid to live on the edge.

But it was also a look that McGarr had been studying and breaking now for many a year, all the easier in this case since Carruthers's look was of the most fragile variety. It was the look of modish *narcotic* disdain, and the monkey in him would crack first. His junkie pride would crumble in hours and put him on the floor, groveling.

"I won't judge you," McGarr went on. "I won't even tell your aunt. Did I mention I have a niece who was on the gear? Clean now five year this May, please God."

Carruthers flinched at the mention of the deity and turned his eyes with their pinprick pupils to the dusty glass wall on the other side of the table. Like a mirror in a fun house, it distorted things, and he obviously appreciated what he saw. The thin, bearded person sitting at the table looked different. Shorter, wider, hip, strong.

"She's into the twelve steps and all," McGarr went on. "Serious like. Carries this little book around with her, something like a missal. Reads it religiously. She gets a craving— you know, for the gear?—she pulls it out, reads it. Doesn't matter where she is. Grafton Street, the DART. Soothes her, she says. Lets her know God's with her wherever she might be. Gets her back on the proper path.

"No pubs for her. Ever. She stays out of them on principle. Hangs, she calls it, only with people like her, recovering people." McGarr waited for a moment, watching Carruthers's eyes swirl in mock discomfort. "Strongest thing they drink is coffee, and plenty of it, I'm here to say. Wouldn't she like to get her hands on you? She'd set you straight.

"Look"—McGarr lowered his feet to the floor—"as long as we're here, why don't I go get some of the literature, she calls it? We'll go through it together. Maybe I can do you a favor. You ever been to a rehab? Something tells me there's one in your future. Or something *like* a rehab." By which McGarr meant jail.

"Maybe I could call you a priest."

Carruthers couldn't help himself; he sighed and swirled his head.

"Or a minister."

When he glanced at McGarr, it was with a look of pity. Sure he'd been to rehabs, the best. Talked to priests, cops, counselors, ministers, shrinks, and other assorted sky pilots and witch doctors. But the Monkey Man knew what was best for Archie Carruthers, and he'd won out every time. Got them right back on the needle the moment they hit the street. Victorious and wired.

But Carruthers's sigh was enough for McGarr, who knew he was on the right track. He would not ask Carruthers a single question about Glencree and the death of Mickalou Maugham. Rather, he'd let the Monkey—the little fearful, crazed animal inside Carruthers who did not like God or any talk of Him—do the work for him. Or higher powers. The Monkey knew what his higher power was called: HEROIN.

And if the Monkey couldn't or wouldn't or didn't cooperate, McGarr would just toss the both of them—Archie and the Monkey—out on the street, where the Toddler would do the work needed. And maybe put *himself* away, McGarr could only hope.

"Right enough," he said at the door. "You just relax. I'll go see if I can dig up the brochures, the *Big Book* and all. Can I tell you I like this work? Ever since my niece recovered through the charity and grace of God, I think it's my"—he gripped his chest with his fingers—"duty to bring some measure of relief to . . . poor, little, murdering, stupid, dead fucks like you."

He waited until Carruthers's odd-looking head with its curly hair and chin whiskers swung to him.

"You mean, you don't *know* you're dead? You should. Ask yourself this: Where's your mouthpiece, your solicitor? Or, rather, the Tod's solicitor? Ah, the Tod, he's such a stand-up guy. Takes care of his own, he does. You can bank on that.

"Make you a bet?" Now McGarr had Carruthers's attention. "We won't see Corny Duggan's great coat and shiny tasseled shoes within a good mile of this place. Like you, the Tod is just waiting. In forty-eight hours, hey, you're out of here for a reunion. D'yeh have any idea what *Tod* means in German? Course you don't. Chemistry is more your thing."

McGarr opened the door and stepped out. "If there's anything you want—the definition even—give us a shout. We'll consider anything but what you'll soon need." And "be begging for" went unsaid.

It's only two days. I can do it, Archie Carruthers told himself confidently. Hadn't he only just popped three cc's of coke to get him up, then leveled off with a bag of the T's best smack, one of twenty he did in a day. Or would have.

And it was still with him. Enough that as he sat here in the shit being questioned for murder, only one thing was bothering him: that he might make it through the two days, only to find himself back before the Toddler jonesing.

Because the one thing Archie Carruthers knew was his habit. In fact, after his present world-class, nearly four-year run—no breaks—it was about all he knew. Or wanted to know. He ran through how it would go, to be prepared. To steel himself and be strong, the way he looked there in the glass.

Six hours, maybe less, it would come on him: the notion that things weren't quite right and he wasn't where he should be. He'd feel a bit jumpy, anxious, out of sorts, then suddenly, horribly, he'd realize that there was something far wrong with him altogether.

He'd begin to sweat. His nose would run; his eyes would start watering. He'd yawn, again and again, suddenly tired but wide-awake, trembling, his body aching as if he'd been caned or something. All over. Or sneezing uncontrollably. Once in Scotland, where he'd told his mother he'd gone hiking and spent every penny she gave him on dope, he had sneezed so long and hard he'd shattered capillaries in his eyeballs.

Then cramps. His muscles would knot up brutally, and he'd have to try to keep on his feet, rubbing himself, stumbling, falling. He'd upchuck until reverse peristalsis came on and/or he shit himself until he could shit no more. Then maybe a convulsion and hospital. Once at the Beaumont he'd been pronounced dead and given the last rites, and him a bleeding Methodist. Or *from* bleeding Methodists. Coming to, he gave the priest a right Protestant start.

Carruthers smiled, thinking of it. Still and all, the Monkey was a bit worried. With the run he'd been on—over fourteen hundred hooked-up days—anything was possible, thanks to the Toddler, whose gear for "friends" was free and primo. Carruthers had been good with numbers in his time. He could figure.

From behind the glass wall, which was a one-way mirror used by the staff of the squad to observe interrogations, McGarr, Ward, Bresnahan, Swords, and Sinclaire—each in turn—stood watch over Archie Carruthers for the next two days.

They made sure he was provided with food, hot drinks, a comfortable cot with warm blankets, even soft lighting when he complained about his eyes. When he vomited, a steward quickly cleaned up. When he became incontinent, a clean prison uniform was provided, and his street clothes were sent to a laundry.

The squad also made sure that the two television cameras at opposite corners of the ceiling continued to film the Monkey as his condition deteriorated. For the record, if ever needed.

Sitting behind the glass with them at all times was a nurse trained in the treatment of opiate withdrawal syndrome. They also had a physician on call. Before Carruthers's nausea or now—as the Monkey Man approached his thirty-sixth hour and roared for "Char! Bring me some hot bloody *char!*" in an accent that revealed the years he had lived in England—they began placing notes on his tray.

"Chin up," one said. "I'm trying to get you out." It was signed, "T." Another; "Duggan's on the case." Yet another; "When they let you out, see me straightaway."

"The Tod didn't write that!" Carruthers screamed at

McGarr, clipping the tray with a hand and pitching his dinner onto the floor.

McGarr raised his hands in mock horror. "He didn't? Well, maybe not, now that you mention it. It's just a doodle I do. (Something wrong there.) You know, like friction. But I'll wager you this—"

Carruthers was shaking uncontrollably, his eyes sunken, his face gray.

"—he's thinking it this very moment. Came to me like telepathy, it did. He's beside himself, doesn't know what the Christ to do, till his Monkey Man is back behind the wheel of *his* Merc, driving him down the country. Someplace wild, romantic, and isolated, like a lake where the water's deep. You know, beyond the Scalp." It was a barren, rocky defile in Wicklow.

"Know what I'm going to do." McGarr went on. "I, me, personally—I'm going to drive you right up to Coolock my very self, the moment you get out, and deposit you in front of his lordship the Toddler. Drug baron and forgiving, benignant deity that he is. But not to worry. I won't tarry and stay for a pint. Won't embarrass you in any way, shape, or form. I'll take myself off, instanter. Who am I to stand between friendship?

"And won't he be glad to see you sick and shaking or even fine, calm, and hale after having been given—correct me now, if I'm wrong, I'm certain you know more about this than me— naloxone, clonidine, or even methadone?"

Magic words. Carruthers raised his head, and his eyes cleared, even though he was shaking so totally he had to hug his body to keep himself from spilling out of the chair.

"Can I ask you a question? Under these circumstances it doesn't much matter how you answer it. The entire statement, signature and all, would be tossed out of any decent court of law. Were you along for the ride the night Mickalou Maugham was put up in your aunt's tree?"

Carruthers blinked.

"Who was with you? The Bookends?"

Again he blinked.

"What about Desmond Bacon?"

Carruthers shook his head.

"But Desmond Bacon, the Toddler, ordered the killing?"

He nodded.

"Say it."

"Say what?"

"Say, Desmond Bacon ordered the killing of Mickalou Maugham. Raise your head and speak directly to the camera." McGarr pointed to one of the two video cameras that were hung in opposite corners of the room.

"Desmond Bacon ordered the killing of Mickalou Maugham and the Hyde brothers did it. Now—methadone."

"Will you swear to that?"

"Do I have a choice?"

"None that I know of. We put you back out up in Coolock, you'll be dead within hours. And you know it. Or you should."

"Maybe I want to be dead."

McGarr moved toward the door. "Your choice. But I think what you'll choose is methadone, which will be served after your statement. Instanter—my promise."

•   •   •

Two days later, while in restricted confinement, Archie Carruthers was served something else altogether. It was in a plastic bag under a warming tin on his dinner tray.

With the tin still raised in his hand, the Monkey was frozen by the sight, unable to do anything but stare down at the 3 cc syringe filled with what he knew was cocaine hydrochloride and a little glassine bag of Mexican brown that he'd do after, to mellow out. And it came with works: second syringe, butane lighter, spoon, and strap.

Carruthers tried to put it together—how the Toddler managed to smuggle it in, what that said about the *juice* he had even within the police. And finally the big, the *essential* question: Would the T send him more, regular like? Enough to last through whatever was coming?

It even occurred to the Monkey that it might be a hot shot, like the cop, McGarr, had kept saying about what the Toddler wanted for Archie: to be dead. But it was only a passing thought. Why? Because unlike the Toddler, who didn't use, the Monkey was expert in dope. Nobody shot gear like the Monkey, who would know if it was right or not.

To the Monkey's way of thinking, the methadone that he was receiving by tablet was not a true drug. True drugs, real drugs, the only drugs that mattered were not swallowed; they were shot.

In one motion he swiveled himself and the tray away from the observation slot in the old iron door. And in less time than you could say, "TOD'S TOT, THE TOTAL GEAR," the Monkey had whacked the load into the one vein in his left arm that still worked.

But not all at once. Instead he plunged the coke in and out of him, over and over, like the in and out of intercourse, manipulating the spike to repeat the intensity of the rush. Every time he pulled back the plunger, some of his blood was sucked out and mixed with the coke and was zapped back in him like a thunderbolt to the heart.

And his head! Man, it was as if it kept exploding. Lights, bells, gongs, whistles—the lot. Even the hair on every part of his body felt it, standing out from the skin like the quills of a porcupine! Or the pelt of a *blasted* monkey!

But he'd hardly begun, it seemed, when it was gone. It was always the way with a good thing. Not a drop left. Suddenly, precipitously the Monkey began to feel jumpy and anxious. Then nervous and jittery. Which was where the gear came in.

He had to act fast. Soon he'd be shaking and unable to cook the bag. Also, the only vein he had left without taking off his clothes was in his neck, so he'd have to aim. He could use the warming tin as a mirror, feel with the fingers of his other hand, and then plunge. The vein was big; he wouldn't have to pop it dead on. Though he'd try.

But even in his condition, which was now jangly, the Monkey knew he should check the gear. Mexican brown was mean shit. Also, if the cop was right about the Toddler, it could have anything in it—not just impurities but strychnine or powdered battery acid. A mix of the two was the hottest shot of all.

But it was hard to tell by taste. Strychnine, like heroin, was bitter. Powdered acid was hot—or so the Monkey had heard—but Mex. brown was too. Archie had snorted enough of that to know for himself. He ran a little across his tongue: bitter and hot. He waited as long as he could, and there he was still on his feet. All he could feel was his jones.

So the Monkey asked Archie Carruthers, who was shaking so violently he could barely keep the spoon and lighter steady, to say nothing of filling the needle and raising it to his neck: Do we have a choice?

And the warming tin—when he got it propped on the tray—it was so dim he could barely see himself. No problem, said the Monkey. We've done this before by feel. Which was when they got a break. Under his fingers the vein felt blessedly knobby. The Monkey pinched it, plucked it up, then rolled it between his fingers to make it swell, to hit the thick part, to make a good connection.

Out in the corridor beyond the door, he heard the squeal of hinges and the clank of keys. The bloody guard was coming back to pick up the bloody tray!

Christ! He couldn't be found with a needle sticking out of his neck. Or, as bad, nodding with the rush of the fix. He should clean up the spoon and strap and shit and wait until the guard was gone.

But the Monkey in Archie Carruthers would not be put off. He was now in control and decided to have just a bit, enough to get him through the tray and get the guard back down the hall. Then they'd shoot the whole bag. And feel like himself.

Jabbing down, he spiked the vein, tapped the plunger, and sent a jolt of strychnine and powdered battery acid slamming up into his brain. Roaring, spinning for the door with the needle sticking from his neck like a silver barb, Carruthers clapped his palms against his temples, staggered, and fell. Dead before his body even hit the floor.

Or so speculated the pathologist who conducted the post-mortem exam. "Strychnine was once used as a rat poison. It kills by incapacitating the medulla oblongata, which controls breathing and the other involuntary functions of the body, like heart and lungs. An intravenous jolt like that would create instant paralysis. Of course, the battery acid just eats up every vein and organ it touches. Scorches, burns."

The pathologist shook her head. "If the point was to kill him, then the bolus of strychnine he shot would certainly have proved sufficient. The battery acid was . . . over the top."

Which was the Toddler's MO, McGarr knew. To send the message, which was fear.

Also, there was the matter of the man's "connections." Wondering why Desmond Bacon had never been lifted, much less hauled up on charges, McGarr had made his own discreet inquiry both on the street and within the Garda, only to learn that the man was "connected."

"Connected to who?" he asked Tom Lyons, the guard on the Drug Squad who had accompanied them to Coolock.

Lyons shrugged. "Proof's the problem. If I had it, I'd say more at the proper place and time." By which he meant to the commissioner, McGarr gathered.

Connected. Enough to have been selling dope and murdering anybody who threatened him for over a decade now. Connected enough to have obtained Garda uniforms for the Hydes, who then fired a handgun in Wicklow Street and beat Maggie Nevins the night that Gavin O'Reilly was chucked under the wheels of a bus and Mickalou Maugham disappeared.

And now connected enough to have murdered Archie Carruthers in a secure holding cell in a prison that was known for its security. The guard was out, McGarr decided: Not only did he have a spotless record, but he had nearly returned to the cell before Carruthers could inject the dose that killed him. He had struggled valiantly to revive him and was plainly distraught by the entire episode.

The kitchen was another matter. "We're understaffed," the prison cook said, waving a hand at the baker's dozen workers under her supervision. "I don't hire them yokes, and I can't be watching all of them all of the time."

Over a two-day period, McGarr questioned each of them at length, ran background checks, even asked for and obtained urine samples. None was a drug addict. One, however, had a son who had been treated for drug addiction. Another lived in Coolock not far from the Toddler's holdings. But there was nothing to indicate that either woman had anything to do with Toddler or the needle that had killed Archie Carruthers.

"Why don't we just lift him?" said Bresnahan, who had been elevated to the status of contributing to morning meetings.

McGarr canted his head dismissively, since it would be counterproductive without cast-iron evidence. The Toddler was careful and on his *guard* in every sense.

In the meantime he had another idea how to smoke him out.

"Rut'ie, how's your art?"

"My *what?*"

"Art. You know, drawing and so forth."

The big redhead blushed in an ingenuous manner that re-minded McGarr that she was still very much a country girl of—what?—only twenty-three years of age. "Nonexistent. I can't draw a straight line."

"Not to worry." McGarr thought of his wife, Noreen, who would know somebody they could commission for a few days. "What about your hair? Would you consent to becoming a blonde for a few days?"

"Who have more fun," Ward put in.

Bresnahan's handsome head swung to him, "Are you brag-gin' again, Inspector? Or is it just another of your prurient clichés?"

Eyes were raised; glances exchanged. In recent weeks the rivalry between the two young staffers had become less one-sided.

"If I can help as a blonde, Chief, blonde it is."

"Good lass."

7
BANG 2

 Ruth Bresnahan did not know how anybody could possibly remember the thousands of details in a page from the Book of Kells, much less draw it exact.

Especially not an illiterate Itinerant girl and heroin addict, as she knew Biddy Nevins was. Or had been. Biddy's mother had not heard from her for months and was afraid she had met with foul play. Like her "husband," Mickalou Maugham. Could they ever have been formally married before a priest in a church?

Ban Gharda Bresnahan rather doubted it. She was on her knees at the top of Grafton Street, staring down at the foot-path at one of the large flags on which an artist—hired by the squad—had drawn a page from the Book of Kells so early in the morning that nobody could have seen, not with the streets blocked off.

Now Ruth was supposed to color it in, but even that was beyond her, the difference in shades being so slight. She had to keep glancing at the photocopy that she had concealed in the "Tinker's muff," where she had also concealed the 9 mm Glock—a light but powerful weapon—that Chief Superintendent McGarr had given her the loan of.

Tomorrow, she vowed, she'd make sure the artist completed all the hard bits of coloring and left her only the big patches to fill in, if there was to be a tomorrow. She only hope the Toddler lived up to his reputation for vigilance and murderous vindictiveness. She was no nun, and there was only so much kneeling on the pavement she could tolerate, albeit on a padded rag that Chief Superintendent McGarr had thoughtfully supplied.

Pushing the brass-bright ringlets of dyed and permed hair out of her eyes, Ruth reached for a piece of amber-colored chalk and compared it with the crib sheet that was a photograph of the photocopy.

"The next shade darker," said a voice in her ear. Hugh Ward placed a lidded paper cup on the footpath beside her.

"What's that?" She pointed to the cup.

"Coffee. Blond. I thought you might prefer it that way this morning. Having fun? I bet there's not a handful of artists in Dublin who make a living doing their stuff. And here you are, fresh out of a hair salon, making a go of it." He tossed a coin into the tin she had brought with her for alms.

Bresnahan shook her head, her brow wrinkled in disbelief.

"Something wrong?"

"It's a mystery to me how it's said you're so successful with women."

"Not by me."

Bresnahan piped a small note of pique. "Don't give me that, Inspector. It's said—and you take pride that it's said—that you're the quintessential swordsman."

"By whom?"

"Ach, the squad over their tea, the lads down in Hogan's. Sure, you must know it's all over town. Which some women actually find tempting. Can you believe it? But of course, you do."

"What? Me? Christ! I don't, I never say boo. Something like that, getting around, would—" He left off, having said too much.

"Only be counterproductive?" Bresnahan laughed a bit. "Can I tell you now, so you know? I really admire you. The way you've stuck—you stick to your, er, guns. You know what you're like? You're like some throwback to a bigger, grander, more heroic age."

Ward waited. He'd never heard her so glib. Was she setting him up, or could she actually mean it? Or was she coming on to him?

No. That wasn't possible. She had no chance with him, even though, he now realized, she looked better than she ever had *as a Tinker wench busking on a footpath*, which revealed just how far she had to go to attract his attention.

Ward romanced only women who looked like women, who dressed like women, and who comported themselves like

women in regard to *him*. And busting his . . . chops, albeit play-
fully, humorously, maybe even flirtatiously, was something he
only permitted from women who *were* women.

Still, he couldn't keep himself from asking, "And what age
would that be?" Knowing he'd made a mistake even before it
was out.

"Why, the age of the troglodyte, since you asked. You'd
fit right in doin' the Darwin number all over cavedom."

Ward sighed. "Certainly not with you."

"Of that you can be sure." Bresnahan turned back to her
drawing. Or rather her coloring, having scored one for mo-
dernity. Pity there'd been nobody close enough to hear.

She could imagine the sort of vain, stylish, self-absorbed,
up-market tarts who would find his sort of modishly sullen,
saturnine masculinity irresistible. Hugh Ward was simply too
full of himself and his physical presence, from the way he
trained and pampered his body to the care he took with his
clothing and suits that fitted him like a manikin in a window.

That was it: He was like a walking, talking, shopfront
dummy, albeit a frightfully handsome one. Reaching for a
piece of chalk in the proper shade, she bent to her task.

Thus it went for most of the day. Ruth would color a little,
and every so often a coin would clank into the tin. With food
and drink provided by Ward.

Around two she was relieved for an hour by McGarr's
missus, Noreen, who, dressed like Ruth, was herself in Traveler
mufti, filled in the dicey bits and made the whole presentation
look more like the page from the book. Even the money in
the tin increased. Tomorrow Noreen would come earlier, it
was agreed.

"May God save you," Ruth muttered every time a coin descended, "and the devil take the Toddler."

Who entered the southeast corner of St. Stephen's Green, diagonally opposite the Grafton Street gate, at half six, feeling more like himself than he had in a long time, in spite of the way he looked.

Dressed like an older American tourist in a bright, striped blazer, bow tie, straw hat, and sunglasses, he was also carrying what anybody would think were two dozen long-stem roses in a large white box wrapped with a blood-red bow. He even stopped often at the many gardens in the park, as he made his way slowly toward the Grafton Street gate. But he hardly glanced at the flowers.

Instead he concentrated on the gate itself, studying it from different perspectives in order to establish the best possible firing angle. It had been ten years since Vietnam, but it was as if he'd never skipped a beat. Quickly he discovered a small, dense copse of—could it be? It was—bamboo by the side of a duck pond that would conceal him once night fell and from which he could pin down the entire Grafton Street corner, should he need.

Think of the coincidence! Bamboo had been his friend in Southeast Asia, providing him cover and even food on one occasion when the NVA had overrun his fire base, no chopper could get in, and his only way back was on his feet. And belly. It had taken him nearly two weeks to crawl eighteen miles.

Now sitting on a bench a good seventy yards from the

gate, the Toddler concentrated on the strollers and the others who were sitting on the benches. He was looking for "plants."

Who moved? And who did not? Who was actually reading a paper? Did they turn the page? And in this day and age who of the women actually had a baby in the pram? Did she feed it a bottle or chuck it under the chin? There were women guards now; witness the tall blond "Tinker" bitch on the corner across from the gate, the one who was "playing" Biddy Nevins.

The Toddler checked his watch. It would be dark in an hour. "All out! All out!" the attendants would call, making sure everybody had left, even ringing bells that they carried in their hands. After all, Ireland was a quaint even backward and un-suspecting country, which had made everything so much eas-ier for Desmond Bacon, alias the Toddler, lo these eleven years. But he hoped he'd be well away before they locked the gates.

And if not, former Sergeant Major Bacon—winner of a Silver Star, a Bronze Star, two Vietnamese Crosses of Gal-lantry, to say nothing of numerous Marine Corps commen-dations—had a set of keys himself. They were in the box with the roses, along with a change of clothes, and the rifle. It was a Remington 700 with a Zeiss scope that had been used in World War I by the famous (or infamous) German sniper Cor-poral Unertl. Both items, which the Toddler had bought at a gun show in Houston some years before, were among the best ever made.

For ammo he had five 173-grain boat-tailed bullets that would achieve a 2,550-foot-per-second muzzle velocity and would strike any target in the same spot with every shot, shot after shot after shot. As backup, he carried five more in the stock, in case he ran into trouble. But that he doubted.

Sitting there in the full spring sun, watching the gate and the activity around the "Tinker" woman on the footpath across the street, the Toddler decided that he would never again allow anybody, like the Bookends, to do his killing for him.

Look at the potential problem they represented, exactly double the trouble that Archie Carruthers might have brought him.

As shadows lengthened and night came on, Ruth Bresnahan had to struggle to remain in a posture that allowed the blond ringlets of hair to obscure her face. Other buskers, packing up their kits and instruments to go home, stopped to make conversation, mentioning how sorry they were to hear about Mickalou and how good it was to have her back.

Ruth only nodded, muttered thanks, and with one insistent woman even pretended to wipe away tears.

Now, as night fell, she glanced up at a window in one of the nearby office buildings that was the Murder Squad command post. McGarr, who was standing there in the darkness, held his hands to the windows and flashed his ten fingers twice: twenty minutes more. It was getting too dark for the drawing to be seen, but they also did not think the Toddler would make a move until it was night and there were fewer shoppers about.

Ruth had only reached for her chalks to begin packing up when a pair of shoes appeared in her line of sight. Black, shiny, large, official. The kind of sturdy walking shoes that she her-self had worn a few years back when in uniform and on patrol.

Another pair now stepped to the other side of her. Still, Ruth did not glance up; they shouldn't see her face.

"Did yi' t'ink we'd forget?"

"Nah, don't fault her. We're guards. We're supposed to be sht-yew-pid."

It was the North Side, Joxer accent, like the one Maggie Nevins had described the "guards" who had beat her as having.

"Come along now." The one on the right reached down for her arm. "You give out, and we'll kill your babby."

"We know where she is," the other put in gleefully.

"With the granny. Why did she not move?"

"And there they call themselves *Travelers*."

"Fookin' shite. Yiz is layabouts, is all."

"Welfare spongers."

The Bookends, Bresnahan assumed; they pulled her to her feet.

"Wait—me muney."

"Fook yehr muney."

"Ye'll not be needin' it where ye're headed."

"Unless Mickalou needs a fix." The one began chuckling, which was picked up by the other.

"Christ, no, he's *been* fixed."

"Permanent like."

"But the tin, me chalks. People will see them and know something's amiss. Promise me you'll leave me babby be, and I'll go along quiet like." Bresnahan felt one arm release her and then the other.

Bending for the chalks, she pulled the Glock from the

Tinker's muff and, spinning, pointed it at the one brother's head. "Move and I'll blow your head off. Now the both of you sit down right where you are and place your hands on your head."

The one Hyde brother glanced at the other, deciding against her, she could tell when the larger nodded slightly. "You wouldn't shoot us."

Bresnahan was hoping—Jesus, she was praying—that McGarr and the others would get there soon. She had never so much as struck, much less shot, another person.

He took a step toward her, his left hand coming up. "Remember the babby."

"And the Toddler," said the other. "He's out there. Anything happen to us—"

And did. The bullet—was it?—thwacking into the big one's chest sounded like a carpet struck with a bat. And the flesh, blood, and bone, issuing from his back in a plug, nearly knocked his brother down. His face was covered. Blinded momentarily, he batted at the gore.

Bresnahan stared down at the one who was sprawled on the drawing on the footpath limp, lifeless, like some big, dead, beached thing. Then she looked at her Glock. Had she fired it?

Lowering his head, the remaining brother rushed her but took only two steps before he was driven back, right off his feet.

He came down in a sitting position, his hands wrapped around his stomach. When he opened them and raised his head to Bresnahan, she could see the problem. His entire midsection was a red, wet hole.

Suddenly he lost the top of his head. Cleanly. As though a cleaver had been taken to his scalp. Evenly at the hairline.

Then, from out of nowhere, a figure appeared and tackled Bresnahan. He knocked her to the footpath and rolled them up against the large concrete planter there at the corner.

It was Ward virtually on top of her. "Somebody's out there with a high-power rifle," he whispered in her ear. "The chief's called for help, but we'll stay here until the area's cleared."

Bresnahan was confused. She could scarcely put it together, and all the blood—"But who?"

"The bloody Toddler, who else? Cleaning the slate. First it was Archie Carruthers. Now the Bookends. He must have been put wise to what we were about here. And to get rid of them right in our face? That's the Toddler style right enough."

Sending yet another message, Bresnahan thought. People on the street would hear about it. And know. "Will he try to kill us?"

Ward shook his head. "Not now, not with us here. But if he'd fancied, you'd be dead already."

And you not—was it?—on top of me. Yes, Ward was actually lying on top of her, whispering in her ear, and it felt . . . well, it was not unpleasant. Apart from his knees, which were digging into hers. Bresnahan spread her legs a bit, and he slipped between them.

"Don't move," he said.

How? she wondered. Being *covered* as she was. And why? It was a thought that she tried to clear from her mind.

And could not.

•   •   •

When McGarr arrived at the Toddler's residence in Coolock thirty-five minutes later, he found Desmond Bacon wearing a cardigan sweater and house slippers. "We're having tea in the kitchen, Superintendent. Would you care for a wet?"

McGarr followed the round but heavily muscled young man as he swayed, flat-footed, side to side down the hallway. The house was a typical, attached, older county council cottage with scuffed lino on the floor. The sitting room, which they passed by, was furnished with overstuffed chairs with doilies on the arms. A budgie was singing merrily in a cage.

Apart from what looked like picture gallery–quality drawings, photographs, and paintings that could be seen on most walls and lining the stairway to the second floor, the house was not what one might expect of a major—no, *the* major—drug dealer in the country. And accomplished murderer.

The kitchen-cum-scullery was barely large enough for a table and—now—four people. A large framed photograph of Pope John haranguing a crowd hung over a big antique television. The screen was covered by a sheet of yellowing plastic.

"And who have we here, Desmond?" asked the granny, who was an elderly woman barely able to raise her neck because of the hump on her back. Her hair was snow white, her eyeglasses were some designer frame with sequined wings on the temples, and the ring on her finger was large and looked like a diamond.

There were playing cards on the table, the third hand having been dealt to Cornelius Duggan, the Toddler's solicitor, who looked uncomfortable. He was staring down at the table and had not so much as glanced McGarr's way.

"This is Chief Superintendent Peter McGarr, luv."

"From the guards? Is it a social call ye're payin', Superintendent. Or something . . . official?"

"A cup?" Bacon pointed to a teapot on the stove.

McGarr shook his head. "Ah, no. I'd like nothing better,
but I can't stay. Nor can you. If you'll get your jacket, we'll
be off. It's a bit chilly tonight."

"Off where?" asked the granny.

"Just down to the lab."

"What lab? Why?"

"A Garda lab. I'd like to perform a little test on your grandson." McGarr raised a palm. "Mind you, nothing invasive."

"What class of test?"

McGarr glanced down at Duggan, wondering what had
happened to his tongue.

"Ballistics. I'd like to know if Desmond here has fired a
weapon in the last few hours."

Depositing a primer residue of antimony, barium, and lead
on the hands of a shooter. Even washing could not remove all
of it. But the test had to be performed within six hours of the
event to have any value in a court of law.

"A weapon? If you mean a *gun*, why, he has surely, sir.
Corny and Des spent the afternoon plinking clay pigeons at
the Donabate Field Club. Did you not, Corny?"

Duggan flapped a hand to mean yes.

"And since then?"

"Why, we've been playing bridge, as you can see. Can I
let you in on a little secret, Superintendent? I've won a few
bob, so I have." She tapped the pile of pound notes in front
of her. "Most of it from Corny here, who don't have a head
for cards at all. At all."

Duggan nodded, his hands gripped tightly before him. McGarr studied him: a handsome middle-aged man with a full head of steel gray hair corrugated in precise finger waves. Duggan's face was flushed, his eyes were bloodshot, as though he'd been drinking.

Three columns of numbers had been noted on the pad. A biro was stuck in the spiral binder.

"You know, I'll take that cup after all. Where's the rush? Have you been here all day?" he asked the old woman.

"Where else would I go, cripple that I am?"

"Down the shops, say. Who perms your hair?" McGarr glanced at the careful arrangement of blue-white hair that looked like a confection.

"My grandson here is a one-off. He has whatever I need sent in. Does the cookin', pays the bills." She gazed fondly at the Toddler, who was standing at the stove pouring McGarr some tea. "The very best lad in all Coolock bar none. Broke the form when they made him."

One would hope, thought McGarr.

"I'm ninety-one now, don't yeh know? And me pins isn't what they should be."

"But your mind—how's that?"

Her old gray eyes rose to McGarr's. "How's your own, son? And I mean no offense."

"None taken. So, you and Solicitor Duggan and your grandson here have been playing cards—how long?"

"Hours. Since the tea."

"Which was when?"

"Early. Half five. I get tired so." She squinted at the clock over the sink. "It's past my bedtime already."

"He go out at all?"

"Who?"

"Your grandson."

"Not since coming back from the shooting."

"Did Solicitor Duggan take tea with you?"

"Et everything on his plate."

McGarr glanced at Duggan, whose nose was now running, and then over to the sink. It was empty. The rack on the drainboard was filled with dry dishes.

"Dessie, of course. And a slap-up job. Won't he make some lucky girl a right husband one of these days?"

The Toddler set a cup in front of McGarr and then sat on the remaining chair. He smiled, or he tried to. It was more like the baring of teeth. In his round, fleshy face the Toddler's eyes were small, dark, hard, and watchful. Shaved close, the skin of his face was blue. The patch of baldness on his head had the shape of a bishop's miter.

"And what did you eat, Solicitor Duggan?"

The bloodshot eyes rolled past McGarr in what seemed like panic. "Ah . . . chips. That's it—bread and chips. And tea." He raised his cup, which fluttered in his hand. Now his face was an alarming purplish shade, and he bore little semblance to the man that McGarr had spoken with only two weeks earlier.

"Would there be any left?"

"Chips? Of course," said the old woman, still acting as interlocutor. "Are yeh hungry?"

The kitchen was so small that the Toddler, sitting in his chair, could reach over and open the oven door to reveal a heap of chips on a cookie sheeet. "The gas is on." He patted them. "Still hot."

"Did you not have any yourself, Mr. Bacon?" It looked as if nobody had.

"Diet." Without taking his eyes from McGarr's, the Toddler patted his stomach. "I look at a chip, I put on weight. Do you have that problem yourself, Superintendent?" His accent was strange—not identifiably Irish or American or British—and he sounded rather like a man on the evening news.

McGarr stood. "Solicitor Duggan, you'll give a deposition stating that you spent the afternoon and evening with your client here?"

Duggan did not look up at him.

"I say, Solicitor Duggan—"

Slowly Duggan's ruined eyes rose to him.

"I'll need a statement from you."

"As to what?"

"That you went skeet shooting"—which would be easy to check—"and came back here and played—just what is it you're playing here with all those numbers?" McGarr picked up the sheet.

"Bridge," the granny put in too quickly.

"For money?"

"Would that I could spend it. But Dessie never lets me spend a farthing. But sure, it'll all be his soon enough."

McGarr pushed the score sheet into Duggan's line of sight. "Can you recap the winning for me? How does it go? Do you have to bid to win?"

"Or lose, and then you pay everybody." She cackled a bit.

"There's also the honey pot for the best cumulative score. Yeh tot up everybody's winnings, divide by three, and that's what the losers have to pay the woman with the best score."

"I'm new at it," Duggan managed. "I never played but this once."

"Bridge? Or *gambling* on bridge."

Both, it was plain by the ciphers under his name.

McGarr dropped the sheet on the table. "Gamble much, Mr. Bacon?"

Again their eyes met. "Only on games of skill, not chance."

"Like the shooting?"

The Toddler canted his head to the side; it appeared all the more oval in shape because of the miter pattern of his baldness. "I've been known to put a few bob on the barrel of a gun. You must be a fair shot yourself, Superintendent."

"Certainly not up to your caliber. Have you heard about the Hyde brothers?"

Bacon's smile did not fade.

"Dermot and Donal," the old woman said, nodding. "Sturdy lads—they're always so polite."

"To a fault, now that they're dead."

She gasped, and Duggan turned to the Toddler, obviously not understanding until that moment what he had got into.

"When did they die?" Still, it was the granny.

Now the Toddler's eyes seemed almost merry.

"This evening. Early. While you were playing bridge, I suppose. Or could it be while your grandson was shooting?"

She shook her head and tsked. "It's tragic, really. A disaster."

"Any reaction, Mr. Bacon?"

"Oh, I'm devastated. Destroyed. I'll have to do something nice for their mother."

"Because they worked for you."

"Ach, it's more than that, isn't it, Granny? Our families have been close for generations. But since you asked, Dermot and Donal did work for me. And I can tell you without qualification, they were model employees. Loyal, dedicated. And you know, I had the feeling they enjoyed what they did."

"And you've no interest in how they died?"

The smile was back. "Your being here, I can imagine it wasn't pretty. I'm sure I'll read about it in the papers."

"Dessie, you should go over to their mammy now." The old woman flicked her hand at her grandson. "See if she needs anything. See what you can do."

It would make the searches of the house and all the other premises owned by the Toddler that much easier. The operation would begin the moment that McGarr walked out the door with several teams working through the many buildings that the man owned here in Coolock.

"Is there anything else, Superintendent?" The Toddler pushed back his chair and stood. "The number of the sports club? The name of the manager? I'm there so often I even remember the numbers."

From the pockets of the cardigan the Toddler removed a small pad; he reached for the biro on the table. "Ask for Vinnie. Better—interview him. Polygraph. The works." He ripped off the page and slapped it on the table, startling Duggan. "Now then, I really should go over to her."

McGarr was tempted to go with him, just to witness what he'd say, how he'd act.

Instead he waited in his car across the street and watched McKeon and three others from the squad present a search order to the Toddler, just as he was leaving the house.

Nonchalantly, as though he had opened the door to a crew of workmen, the Toddler scarcely glanced down at the papers before stepping aside to let them in. Pulling on a leather jacket, he sauntered out into the night, his short but powerful body swaying from side to side.

At a house several doors up the street, he paused by the gate and scanned the street for a good two minutes before waving to McGarr and making for the door. Without knocking, he entered the house of the two men he had just murdered. Of that McGarr was now certain.

A moment or two later Solicitor Duggan was flushed from the granny's house with what looked like a shoe box in his hand. McKeon would have examined it before allowing Duggan to leave, but McGarr only let Duggan drive his pricey BMW as far as the Malahide Road before pulling him over.

"You've no right to do this. I've broken no law," Duggan complained through an inch or two of open window. "If you persist, I'll have you up on charges."

"Really? Name them, solicitor. Now, step out of the car, please."

"Why?"

"I'd like to see if you're sober."

"That's nonsense. I haven't had a drink all day."

"Then you need one, to steady your nerves. You're shaking. Perhaps you're not well. I'd say a blood test is in order."

There was a pause while Duggan considered his options; cars whipped by them on the busy artery that led into Dublin proper. Finally Duggan said, "What is it you want?"

"The truth. How long was Bacon gone this evening? What time did he leave? What time did he return? I want it in writing. You can say that at the time he asked you to perjure yourself, you had no idea what he was about. He was your client, to whom you wished to be loyal. You might even make some statement about yourself that will elicit the sympathy of the court. I'll give you all the help I can."

Again Duggan waited, as though wrestling with the pros and cons of telling the truth and the penalties either way. Now, staring straight ahead out the windscreen, he drew in a breath and let it out slowly. He shook his head. "I'm a solicitor. Desmond Bacon is my client. Our relationship is privileged."

"Even when he's out murdering? Come now, solicitor, could you be over your head with this man? Think of the others who joined him in murder: Archie Carruthers, who supplied the car and venue for Mickalou Maugham's murder. The Hydes, who helped him murder Gavin O'Reilly and Maugham, that we might have proved, and more than a few others that we could not. Now they're gone. All murdered themselves.

"And here you sit in—what?—a narcotic stupor?"

"Hold on now. I don't care for your tone."

"*Tone?*" McGarr nearly roared. "Good Christ, man, we're not talking tone here. We're talking murder, dozens of them, and cocaine, heroin, crack, crank, hashish. Is that what's in that box?"

Duggan's head snapped to the box on the passenger seat, as though he'd forgotten it. "Hashish?"

"No, of course not. Not you. Not hashish. Cocaine's more your speed, I'd say. Pity he hasn't seen fit to give you something for those shakes. Yet. But there'll come a day. I'm sure he'll know when.

"You don't seem to realize, Cornelius." McGarr went on in a gentler tone, since it seemed to be in question. "You're not back in university or in some club consorting with somebody of your own class. Not even with some of the major thieves and very grand larcenists you've represented in the past.

"And it's not just your career that's in question. That man—the one we just left, who already owns you body and soul? He wouldn't turn a hair snuffing you out. Me to you? He's probably already planned it—you and Vinnie out there at the shooting range of the sports club. Wrap everything up in a neat little packet.

"So you're going to have to choose, and soon, just how much of your life you can salvage. I could be wrong, it could be too late. But like I said, I'll help you every step of the way if you'll let me.

"Now, for tonight, I'll see what's in the box, then let you go. Regardless."

"Your man already has, back at the house. Sergeant . . ."

"McKeon," McGarr supplied. "But he was assuming you were just the Toddler's attorney and not his accomplice in two murders. I know better. Now, open the other door, and I'll get in."

After yet another pause Duggan tapped the electric door latch, and McGarr walked around.

There were shotgun shells in the shoe box—twenty-gauge, No. 6 shot Remingtons. Six boxes of twenty-five. McGarr removed one and snapped on the reading light for the passenger seat. Taking out his penknife, he placed it on the box top and had to punch the blade down to cut through the thick plastic wrap of the cartridge.

Shot, then a grayish powder spilled out. McGarr wet a finger, touched the powder, and held it to his nose. There was no sulfur smell, which was the most easily detectable constituent of gunpowder. He then touched it to his tongue. The taste was bitter, acrid, biting.

His eyes swung to Duggan. "Packs a punch, I'd say. And so well done! The man's a bloody genius, he is. How does he manage the color?"

It had begun to rain, and the wipers came on automatically.

"Hold out your hand."

"What?"

"I said, hold out your hand."

It was trembling, but McGarr managed to slide the powder onto it anyway. "You probably need that to get home." He opened the door. "Remember, I don't want you, I want him. If you help me, I'll help you right down the line, any way I can. And you know you need it.

"Now then, I'll be expecting a call and soon. Keep in mind you don't have much time. Your man is quick to cover his arse."

"And yours," went unsaid.

Two days later Cornelius Duggan disappeared, leaving an apologetic note to his wife telling of a love affair, a mistress, and an "inability to cope with the duplicity of my life." But nothing of the Toddler and murder.

Duggan was never heard from again.

PART TWO

1996

8

RECOVER/UNCOVER

Biddy Nevins had become Beth Waters from the moment she got off the ferry in Folkstone twelve years earlier. But the Toddler had remained the Toddler, even down to the way he looked. The only difference seemed to be his hair, which he'd lost more of.

And there he was, standing in the doorway of the picture gallery on Dawson Street in Dublin, where a show of Beth Waters's work had just opened. They were photographs of women as beauty and porno queens, as rockers and gang molls, the color adjusted, the grain of the print exaggerated to obscure the image and make them look more seductive even than advertising models, no matter what they were acting out in the picture.

Having signed the gallery guest register, Desmond Bacon glanced up at the chrome-framed image of a beautiful young-woman with a strap cinched tight around her arm and a spike poked deep in a vein. She had just depressed the plunger, and now two seconds later her eyes were half closing in ecstasy, her mouth was open, and her full lips were slightly puckered. One of her young nipples could just be seen in the shadow beneath the vent in her blouse. The caption, which was part of the composition, said, "Diabetes, the trip. Can you handle it?"

It was supposed to be blackly humorous, and was, according to a woman critic from *The Times*. She was standing beside "Beth" and "simply" loved "the macabre mise-en-scène and counterpoint of your comment lines. What tension, what . . . dichotomy!"

Watching the Toddler now turn her way, Biddy placed the glass of wine that she'd been holding, not drinking, on a table and looked behind her for a door. She tried to remember what the critic had been saying, so she could respond. It would be not on to alert her to any other type of story.

Or for Biddy to act any different from the bored veteran artist, which she now was, suffering through yet another interview that she'd gone through so many times before in London. It was all part of the "opening act" that an artist had to assume to make a success of herself anywhere—London, Dublin, New York, Paris.

Biddy had been to those places in the last few years. You had to appear above it all, as if there were something beyond their enthusiasm, something they could not see. "Once they think they've got you sussed," another artist had once told her, "you become simple to them, and you're sunk. Keep it all smoke and mirrors. Then they can write what they want, which they like better anyway."

Biddy now smiled and nodded to the critic, not knowing what had been said or what she should answer. Hoping it was enough. All the while madly thinking what she should do. Would the Toddler recognize her? So much time had passed, and she had changed so much, even the color of her eye. The right one, the blue one.

At Cheri's insistence she had gone to an optician and bought a contact that could change the color of the eye to brown. Biddy hated the feel of the thing, riding over her eyeball like a filter. But it was essential whenever she was out of the house.

As for the "Beth Waters" identity, it was the name of the English girl Biddy had gone to rehab with who had killed herself the day they got out. "This is quicker," said the one line of the note she left Biddy. Little could she have known she had given Biddy far more: a way to carry on after the Toddler. The new identity had remained good up until now.

Biddy's first full day in England, she had gone straight to London, where she knew from a dope run years earlier there were shelters for women. Immediately she used Beth's cards to get herself on public assistance. Then one lucky turn after another—based on the schooling of Beth Waters and Biddy's own talent for art—landed her in a small advertising firm where she took over the drawing and helped lay out pages, anything she could do to make herself useful. They loved her drawing, and she'd work around the clock when they had business.

What she liked most was the photographers, getting them props and watching them arrange their compositions when they were shooting, later seeing what came out. It all could be made to seem so real, but unreal. When asked, she would make a suggestion or two, maybe put one thing here and another there. She had only wished to be helpful.

One older woman said, "You seem to have a knack for this. Let's see what you can do on your own." And Biddy did, apart from her utter ignorance of cameras, film, everything about the technical side of photography. The photographer—Cheri Cooke, who was rather well known in advertising circles—remedied that, taking Biddy under her wing in the house that she owned near Reigate outside of London. It also contained a large, well-equipped darkroom.

Next, Oney arrived, at Cheri's insistence. Biddy's child was delivered over to England in 1986 by her father and mother, who took the precaution of driving up to Swords near Dublin Airport on the pretext of buying a new van. They even got out and talked price with the owner to see if they were being followed by the Toddler or any of his thugs. Only then did they dash over to the airport and buy tickets at the last minute for Birmingham, where a Traveler cousin was waiting. Immediately he drove them down to London, taking back roads to make sure they weren't followed. Biddy could not be too careful.

Granted Cheri's house, Cheri's tutoring, even Cheri's money that she gave Biddy as "pay" she called it while Biddy was learning did not come without strings. But as a lover Cheri Cooke was not demanding and seemed to need sharing and companionship most. And after Mickalou and what happened to him, Biddy had given up on men who were always deceiving in one way or another.

Yes, she knew it was wrong to blame Mickalou. After all, he had died, not she, because of a scrape that she had got into herself. But why had he been so foolishly brave with the likes of the Toddler? It was something only a man would do. Women, on the other hand, were dependable.

Once Biddy had mastered her craft, success came quickly for the "Beth Waters" that she had become in the late eighties in London. "Beth" became one of the first "rephotographers," as the technique of photographing photographs came to be known. Clipping shots from magazines, Biddy would arrange the pictures in ways that were visually interesting or erotic or shocking. Some of her larger works—blown up to wall size— fetched prices up to fifteen thousand pounds, and Biddy was suddenly selling nearly all the photographs she made.

But Ireland beckoned. She missed the tranquil pace, and she yearned to provide a better life for her parents, who had lived rough for so long and were now getting on in years. They wanted most to "retire to the road, travelin' here and there, like back when we was young," said her mother, Maggie. But in style and not some old banger of a van. Now they could, since money was no longer a problem, thanks to Biddy.

To be close to them and the rest of her large Traveling family, Biddy—who was now so thoroughly transformed that she sometimes actually thought she *was* Beth Waters—purchased a large house in Ballsbridge, an upmarket part of Dublin.

In the fall of 1991 she quietly moved back with Oney and Cheri Cooke, who now functioned as Biddy's "manager" and little else. Because at the same time Biddy fell in love again—with a man who was a Traveler, like herself, and reminded her not a little bit of her father when he was young.

Fully ten years younger than she, Tag Barry was handsome, sometimes capable, always unpredictable, and not a little bit roguish. Now she wished she had brought him along to the opening—to distract the Toddler while she made her escape.

"Amn't I hearing an Irish inflection in your voice?" the woman from *The Times* now asked.

"Oh, aye," Biddy blurted out as she watched the gallery owner approaching the Toddler with a wide smile and both hands out; obviously the bastard had been in there before and bought something.

Biddy took two steps away from the critic, so she could see into the office and if there was a door into the alley that would lead where? Into Duke Street. The city, it was her one advantage. Having grown up in Dublin as a homeless waif, she had its streets and laneways etched in memory.

"Me mither is from Galway," she now added in an exaggerated brogue that the woman found amusing.

"Via?"

"Hunger and poverty, like others in the West."

After shaking the gallery owner's hand, the Toddler turned with his arm up, his index finger pointing, and his thumb raised. As though shooting the photograph, the thumb snapped down. And then at the next and the next. Three in all. Quickly the owner moved forward and placed a small red dot in the lower left corner of each, indicating that the pieces had been sold.

"What about your father? Is he Irish too?" The woman placed the nib of her pen on her notepad.

"Christ!" Biddy muttered. Should she bolt? How could she explain it later? A call of nature. Cramps. A panic attack, which would only be the truth.

But the gallery owner had turned and now had his own finger outstretched, pointing at her. That was it; she couldn't flee now. The Toddler would know. She'd have to face him down, but unlike him—she told herself—she'd changed considerably in the dozen years, having put some weight on her gaunt form.

Also, since her return to Ireland, she had taken the precaution of keeping her wavy blond hair dyed brown and cut short. She wore no makeup. After all the years that she had spent as a child out-of-doors, the skin of her face was creased and lined, like somebody much older. And she now only thirty-three.

Almost as though for practice, Biddy said in the best Surrey tones that she had learned from Cheri, "Actually, he was a Yank." Which was the truth for Beth Waters.

"Who met your mother where?"

Slowly, torturously, the Toddler was moving down the wall of photographs toward her. The owner—a tall, thin man dressed in a tawny stovepipe suit just the color of his hair— was bending to him, pointing to details in Biddy's work, which he was explaining. And praising lavishly. It was his job.

Biddy pulled in a large breath, squared her good shoulders, and let the air out slowly. Her bosom, which in her youth had been considerable, was now formidable and heaving. And suddenly hot, biting, visceral anger, which—she knew from her recovery program—was the flip side of fear, coursed through her.

To think of who and how many mainly young, confused, misguided, or simply—like herself—abandoned people he had ruined and killed. Quickly, like the man under the bus and Mickalou up in the tree. Or ultimately, like Beth Waters, who couldn't face a life without his drugs. Hundreds, no, *thousands*. He was a vulture, a viper, a prick.

And watching the miserable, round, little, bald fucker— drug pusher, multiple murderer—waddling toward her, Biddy's eyes snapped to the desk, looking for a letter opener or a scissors. Anything sharp.

She wasn't the same Biddy Nevins who'd allowed herself to be run out of the country twelve years earlier. She'd slit the bastard's throat right there in front of everybody and then tell why. She didn't care. She'd go to prison. Why not? Dublin and Oney, her daughter and her daughter's generation, would be rid of a death-dealing leech.

"In a pub," Biddy said to the reporter. "They had a pint; then they had each other in a snug. Nine month later there was me. It's why I feel so at home in bars." It was her standard brave answer, even though false. Biddy never went into bars. She was afraid of them, categorically. Alcohol, like the gear, could and would kill her. "We didn't see my father again, never cared to entertain the possibility. I hope we never will."

"Why's that?"

"I hate fucking men." The Toddler was nearly close enough to hear.

"Are you a lesbian?"

"Whenever I fancy a woman. Not often, mind. Not always. But you have a look about you, you do. Busy tonight?"

The reporter's pale eyes widened. She looked away, color appearing in her face. "Well, I fancy you too, but not in that way."

"Aw, shucks, and there I thought we might get something off tonight." In spite of her nonchalant pose, Biddy was feeling reckless. "You change your mind, give me a shout. You have my card."

"What about your mother?" the reporter managed.

"Was she a lesbian too?"

The woman shook her head slightly; it was not what she meant, but she would hear the answer.

"It would have been better had she been."

"Why?"

"Males suck. Which is the only good we'll ever get out of them."

The reporter's laughter was nervous. "May I quote you?"

Biddy nodded. "With your editor's leave. She a woman?"

Now the reporter was truly confused. "Where was I?" She consulted her steno pad.

"Me mither."

In tow with the gallery owner, the Toddler now joined them.

"Oh, yes—is she still alive?"

Biddy looked straight into the Toddler's face, making sure his hard black eyes met hers. "Thankfully she's dead as well. It's curious being dead, you're just never heard from again. It's like taking the ferry to England. But for keeps."

"Beth, excuse me, are we interrupting?" asked the gallery owner, knowing he damn well was but wanting to announce to the reporter that the photographs were selling briskly. "I'd like you to meet a patron of yours, Mr. Des Bacon, who just bought *three* of your prints. Des—Beth Waters."

The Toddler's hand came out, and for a moment Biddy only looked down at it, still furious, wanting to snub the bastard but knowing she would only be calling attention to herself. She touched her fingers to his, then glanced up at him again.

With a slight smile, he was studying her. "I'm a great admirer of your work, Ms. Waters. I'm only after telling Mal, here, that I wish I'd arrived earlier—so much has been sold."

"Well, there *are* several pieces left," the owner, Malachi Jordan, put in. "In particular there's the footpath shot, which I think is the most spectacular work in the show."

"I agree," said the reporter. "It's almost cubist, the way the footpath flags are arranged so that the images fuse into one another. Or is it a collage of those postcards you can buy in the Trinity College Library, Beth? The ones that are pages from the Book of Kells."

Biddy could feel her heart pounding in her ears as the Toddler turned and peered down the length of the gallery toward the photograph that she knew she shouldn't have included in the show. Her mother, Maggie, had said it was wrong. And Ned, her father, had advised against including the piece.

"Yeh just can't get over livin' on the fookin' edge" was how he'd put it, now that he had quit drinking and was "Mr. AA" and could suss out everybody's "motives."

And maybe to spite him—since she still had not completely forgiven him for kicking her out of the van when she was nine to be prodded and pricked by sharp and blunt instruments of every description and size—she had decided to hang the picture. But only in the back of the gallery, she had made the owner promise. "It's not really for sale. I'm just including it because it's so completely Irish."

"The Book of Kells, you say? That's always intrigued me. I must have a look." He turned and began making his way through the others in the room.

Jordan was right on his heels, saying, "I must tell you, Des, that Beth has said it's not really for sale. Hasn't even been priced. But I'm sure we can work something out that's fair to . . ."

It was as if an alarm had gone off in the Toddler's brain, louder with every step that he took closer to the last piece by Beth Waters. A large photograph, it pictured a footpath shaped like a vortex and flagged, supposedly, with other, smaller photographs of pages from the Book of Kells.

The closer he got, the more impossible it seemed that she could have so perfectly sized down the photograph of each flag that the illusion of a vortex was created. And utterly convincingly. Which would have taken—what?—something like a computer. Yet the Toddler could tell at a glance that the entire effort was traditional photography. After skeet and competition target shooting, it was Bacon's second hobby.

No. Removing a pair of reading glasses that had become necessary now that the Toddler had entered his forties, he saw instantly that the picture was not an example of rephotography at all. It was an artful deception.

Having been cut in diminishing sizes, the flags had then been arranged in a whorl, and the pages actually painted or drawn in with—he took a step closer and adjusted the glasses—yes, with pastel chalk. The entire composition had then been photographed from above by means of what, a crane? Or some tall building that did not cast a shadow.

But the precision of the drawings. Now that was something he recognized. There was only one person that he knew of who was capable of such fine detailing in chalk.

Stepping back from the photograph, as though to consider it from a distance, the Toddler felt as he had in Vietnam when he found himself cut off from his firebase. Suddenly he knew who Beth Waters was and why she had seemed so reluctant to shake his hand.

Gone were the long, brassy curls, the thick gold Tinker earrings, the fresh complexion from kneeling out on the footpath at the top of Grafton Street in every kind of weather. But he knew it was she from her height, which was tall, her build, which had been angular then but was now full and womanly, and her flat, distrusting, streetwise Tinker eyes. Back then one had been brown and the other blue. But the simple addition of a contact lens could change that.

"Do you like it?" Mal Jordan asked.

"Oh, yes, very much. How could you not?" The Toddler replied automatically, as he racked his brain to think of how he could deal with her and not compound the problem that she represented. Twelve years now and running. He had done everything he could to track her down, hired snoops, computer surveys, even paid government employees to search tax, dole, and public assistance records in Ireland and England.

With no luck on Biddy Nevins. Because—he now knew— she had been Beth Waters all along, which was a name he recognized from the past, of a doper who had done herself in. When? Around the time he'd had the trouble with Mickalou Maugham and Biddy.

Since then the Toddler had remained very much the Toddler, keeping himself feared and therefore respected in the Trade, as drug dealing was known to its principals. But gradually he had left the dicey realm of street-level dealing to become a wholesaler, often internationally on a scale that he would not even have imagined twelve years earlier.

In fact, the pains he had taken to buffer himself from any possible criminal charge extended to his staff. The Toddler no longer employed a single Irish national. Instead he relied upon ten, skilled operatives from Cambodia, where Lance Corporal Des Bacon had once survived undercover for almost a year during his sniper/scout days with the U.S. Marines.

None of his staff spoke English, making testifying against him difficult, and if some problem arose, the Irish government would probably just deport them as illegal aliens. Whereupon the Toddler would merely bring in some others—most likely their brothers and sisters or cousins or neighbors—as replacements with the next shipment of heroin. They'd do anything to get out of that hellhole, and what the Toddler paid was for them and their families a small fortune. Consequently, they were loyal to a fault and would do anything he asked.

Also, Des Bacon had become almost respectable, at least among the merchants and tradespeople who supplied the goods and services he required. Since his granny's death a decade ago he had moved out to Hacketstown in the Wicklow Mountains, where he now had a large estate, horses, a shooting range, and more Cambodians as staff and who thought him a god. And told him as much. In short, the Toddler had not been threatened by anybody—a rival, the police even—in so long he hardly remembered the feeling, which he now found . . . intolerable. There was no other word for it.

Scanning the vortex of pages from the Book of Kells, he suddenly panicked, imagining it sucking him down. But panic was good. It was what had kept him alive, scuttling on his belly through the jungles and rice paddies of Vietnam, and would here, could he just channel the fear.

It occurred to him that the biographical statement by the door said "Beth Waters" was an Englishwoman who now lived in Dublin. He would buy the photograph and pretend he had not sussed who she was. For the price, however, he'd get her address. The rest—how to take her out without incriminating himself—would come to him as it always did, as a fully formed plan of action. But it had to come fast. Maybe this time she'd go straight to the police, now that she was no longer just another Knacker wench out begging in the streets.

"So, d'you want it?"

The Toddler nodded. "I can't resist it."

Jordan's smile was triumphant. "Let me see if she'll put figure on it—one that's fair to both of you."

Which meant as high as he thought the Toddler would go, working, as he was, on commission.

Forcing what felt like a pleasant smile into his face, the Toddler slowly turned and glanced down the length of the gallery toward where the woman—"Beth Waters," née Biddy Nevins—had been standing. But she was gone.

That was it then. She knew he knew, and he'd have to act fast.

"I can't understand it. She said she was going to the loo, but she's not in there either. My assistant checked."

"Maybe she nipped out for a drink."

"Well"—Jordan glanced at the wine on the table in the center of the room—"I was under the impression that she did not drink."

"I wonder—would you have her address?"

The other man's brow suddenly furrowed.

"Not to worry, Mal; if I buy anything else, it'll be through you exclusively. I appreciate your thinking to invite me here and your concern for my collection.

"Now then—the address, please. I'm in a bit of hurry. And let me pay you for what I just bought."

The Toddler was carrying a weapon that he was never without. But it was small caliber, meant for defense only. And he'd have to drive all the way out to Hacketstown—twenty mainly mountain miles each way—to equip himself more completely. By then she'd be gone, he was sure.

Better to catch her now, before she went to ground. Given the chance, he'd take her with his hands and have done with the problem. But at the very least he'd know where she was.

9

SPLIT!

Biddy Nevins was shaking with fear and anger by the time the taxi dropped her off in front of her large Victorian house in Ballsbridge, and she could scarcely fit the key in the lock. Her eyes were blurred with tears.

Suddenly the door opened, scaring her more to think that the almighty Toddler might have beat her there.

"My God in heaven," said her mother, Maggie, "ye're a wreck, so. In bits." She craned her head to look beyond Biddy into the street. "Where's Mal? And the limousine?" The gallery owner had arranged for one to pick Biddy up and bring her back as part of the "show" of the opening. With the expense entirely justified by all the pictures that had been sold, was Biddy's bitter thought, as she stepped around Maggie and rushed into the house. And never again.

"What be the matter, child?"

Biddy stopped in the hallway, where the others, alerted by Maggie's voice, now appeared: her father, Ned, and Tag Barry, her young lover, from the sitting room. On the stairs above her stood Cheri Cooke. Even her daughter, Oney, now seventeen, came out of the kitchen and began moving up the long hall.

"I don't know how it happened," she said, her eyes searching the pattern of the Persian carpet on the floor. "But didn't the miserable, murderin', little bastard show up at the opening?"

"Who? The Toddler?" her father asked.

"Lookin' for you like?" Eyes wide, Maggie scanned the street before closing the door.

"Maybe it was by chance. But one thing's for sure, he'd been in there before, buyin'."

"But how'd he cop on to you?" Although only in her early sixties, Cheri Cooke was arthritic, and she now began hobbling down the stairs, her feet angled to the side, both hands gripping the rail. "Didn't you have your contact in?"

Disgusted with herself, Biddy swirled her head; nobody else was to blame. "Ach, wasn't it the bleedin' footpath picture?"

"The one with the pages from the book?" Tag swirled his right hand, which, as usual, clutched a bottle of beer. "Didn't I tell yiz all it was a fookin' mistake? How could yiz have let her put it in?"

Biddy glanced at the handsome young man, who was often mistaken for her brother or Ned's son, the three of them looked so much alike. Out the night long, Tag had not been back to stop her from taking the final picture as . . . an after-thought, she'd felt so confident of its merit. So much time had passed. And she had been so secure for so long in her identity as Beth Waters.

"But the pic was rapid all the same," said Oney, who re-sembled Mickalou more than Biddy. She was tall, thin, and dark with curly black hair and hazel eyes flecked with silver chips. Or so they appeared to an adoring mother. As Oney had begun to fill out, Biddy—with her artist's appreciation—had judged her to be one of the most beautiful creatures that she had ever seen. Which made Biddy fear for her child's future, and never more than now. "Deadly."

Precisely, thought Biddy. "Well, he knows, and now there's nothin' for it but to quit this place. Now."

Her eyes took in the lovely hall with its sculptured plaster ceiling and period furnishings. Even the Victorian wallpaper was special, made to a pattern that Biddy had copied out of a book and Cheri had commissioned a craftsman in Nottingham to make at great cost. "Nothing's too good for you," Cheri had said. Biddy might now be well off, but Cheri was rich.

Tag took a few unsteady steps closer, the bottle clutched to his chest. "But why, Bid? The fook does he t'ink he is he can roust people from their own bloody kips?"

Biddy had met Tag in Belfast only the year before, and although he fancied a drop, he did no drugs. When sober, as was now seldom, he could be good company. "I'll ring up some o' me lads on the Falls Road. We'll sort the shagger out!"

Looking at him, Biddy felt her nostrils flare. It would be one thing, did he mean a word of it—she might even let him—but Tag was all piss and wind, like the proverbial Tinker's mule. He would not stand a chance against the Toddler, who, if anything, was probably more powerful than he had been a dozen years earlier. Biddy thought of how . . . self-possessed he seemed and how easily he had purchased the three photographs, splashing out 22,500 pounds as if it were nothing.

No, there was nothing for it but to bolt. Again. Spreading her fingers wide. "If you tried that or anything like it, he'd only kill more of us. You don't know the man. He's hard and capable, and he'd snuff you, me, all of us without a second thought.

"Now then, we're leaving, and that's that. You"—she pointed at Oney—"you go with Maggie and Ned. Right now."

"Me? Why me? I've me friends and school and"—boyfriends was the next thought—"and can you not see you've allowed this man, this fuckin' *Toddler*—"

"Mind your mouth, you."

"—to control you and to control *our* lives from my earliest memory right up to this very moment."

Which you would not be knowing had his Bookends dashed you from the top step of the caravan that night in Tallaght, Biddy thought. She had been told of it by Maggie, to whom she now turned. "Do you mind?"

"Oh, aye, I mind. This place is heaven," said Maggie, her eyes wide with concern. In recent years her face had become a system of loose, sallow wrinkles from all the weather she had endured. Always thin, she was now gaunt, and dressed in Biddy's old clothes, which Maggie wore with pride, she looked rather like a scarecrow. "But I mind death more.

"Come you," she said to Oney. "And you too, Ned. The sooner we take to the road, the better."

"In the Merc," said Biddy. "It'll get you farther faster."

"No!" Cheri Cooke complained, finally having reached the bottom of the stairs. "My Mercedes? You won't take my Mercedes!"

Biddy spun around on her, suddenly hating the woman's niggardliness in spite of her millions. The only time Cheri opened her hand was when she saw some advantage with Biddy herself—to control her.

For no small time Cheri had been good for—no, *essential* to—Biddy, who wouldn't be where she was today without her, but in recent years her presence in the house had been . . . stifling at best. "Answer me this: Did I not buy and pay for the car myself?"

Cheri had never been a pretty woman. She was short, round, dumpy even with rounded shoulders and a pommel of flesh at the back of her neck that you could grasp, like a soft leather bag. With large, round eyes that always seemed to be brimming with wet and a mouth that curved down at the corners, she appeared to be what she had become in recent years: bulldoggish and severe. Her hair was cropped short. "Only to replace my own."

Biddy sighed. An argument was the last thing they needed. "But you'll be going with them."

Her liquid eyes swelled with resentment. "I'll be . . . what?"

"Going with Ned, so you will. It's how I want it."

Biddy turned to her father for his agreement, which she knew she'd have, since the power in the family had switched to her all of five years earlier.

"I will not. I'll be going with you wherever *you* go. It's where I belong."

Biddy shook her head. She'd be far better off alone, and certainly not with a carping, crippled old shrew. No matter her money. "Or to Reigate. Why don't you go back to there?"—where Cheri still had a house and family nearby. "If you leave now, you'll be safe there. I'll get in touch, I promise."

"No!" The flesh under Cheri's chin wagged like wattles. "I go where *you* go. That's what I said, what we agreed to years ago, and only what I'll abide by now. In spite of my sorry condition."

Which was martyr to their failed relationship, even more than her arthritis, which Biddy had always considered mostly a ruse. Cheri turned and began a laborious, puffing climb up the staircase to pack, Biddy guessed. But by that time Biddy would be gone, and Cheri would have to fend for herself. But she'd manage; she always did.

"Tag?"

"Me?" The beer bottle came out again. "I'll be humped if any . . . bullyin', pudgy scut who calls himself a Toddler will drive me from me digs." He glanced around at the others, obviously for their approbation, but they were staring at Biddy. "And you." Tag went on, touching the fist with the bottle against Ned's arm, man to man. "Don't tell me ye're pissin' off on yehr daughter's orders?"

Ned ignored him, moving toward the door, and Biddy wondered if she could ever have loved Tag Barry. Or had it simply been narcissism, since they looked so much alike? Or some attempt to regain her youth. Every now and then Tag showed the same joy and zest for living that Mickalou had, once he got off the gear. But Tag had none of Mickalou's kindness or his generosity and spirit.

"So"—Biddy turned to her mother and daughter—"you're off."

"Ah, no—Jaysis. This is shtew-pid and t'ick!" Oney complained in an argot that was part Dublin street slang and part the language of other young Travelers. For some reason unfathomable to Biddy, Oney had chosen mots and bowsies as friends when at school she had the daughters of the country's elite.

She supposed that Oney had to make her own mistakes in life, as she had herself, but it was a thought that only ever made her worry more.

"Wha' about the *shadog*, the one copper ye're only after tellin' me about, Granny? The one who took after the Toddler back then."

"And failed, it's plain." Maggie reached for Oney's hand. "Remember the name Archie Carruthers?" Maggie pulled Oney toward the door.

"The limo driver, the one who died in jail."

"No, the one who was *murdered* in jail. Now, since you do be lovin' the Travelin' people, here's your chance to live with them."

Biddy pulled Oney to her for one last hug.

"Isn't there any way we can stop him?" Oney asked in her ear.

"You let me manage that, darlin'. If there's a way, I'll find it, I promise." Which Biddy meant. In the twelve years that had passed, she had changed radically, and she'd sooner go out with a bang than a whimper. She thought of the gun she had bought years ago and now kept above the door inside the landing to the cellar.

Biddy held her daughter away and looked into her hazel eyes. "May God bless and keep you. Remember, your mother loves you, and you're to respect that love and love yourself. It's the only way."

Oney nodded, having heard the advice many times in the past.

Biddy then reached for Maggie. "Take care of yourself, Mammy."

"It's not me we're worried about, luv. Wherever will you go?"

"I haven't a clue," though she had.

"England again?"

Biddy only shook her head. "I'll be in touch through the Maughams," who, after all, were Maggie's family too and were a close-knit Traveling family. Biddy would only have to contact one of them for her message to be conveyed to Maggie via the "Traveler telegraph," as their way of communicating among themselves was called. They might even speak Gammon to make a conversation most private.

Biddy turned to her father. "Have you money?"

"Sure, is there ever enough?" By which he meant they'd make do. Ned Nevins had turned over a new leaf as he had aged and was now a careful, conservative man with a craggy face and dark hair that he kept short in a brush cut, like a teenager. He was wearing a good but rumpled gray suit, one of several that Biddy had given him. On his feet were a pair of good brogues; on his wrist was a Rolex.

"Are yeh comin', Tag?" he asked when Biddy had re-leased him.

They watched the young man's eyes sweep the handsome hall, then glance down at the bottle of beer that he wiggled and held up. Empty. But he had a dozen more longneck Bud-weisers—his drink of choice—in the fridge and boxes more in the cellar.

In his notecase Tag Barry could count maybe a thousand pounds that he'd skimmed from Biddy in the past month alone, whenever she sent him out on a message. Then there was the sex, which he'd been missing with her for a while now, only to have discovered that there were much younger and better rides in town for the taking with a few quid in your pocket. And now with Biddy gone and a "pad" like this? Why, he'd run through half the easy young women in Dublin.

All in all, it was as if he'd died and gone to desperado heaven. He'd ring up Belfast the moment she closed the door and bring down a few mates to share in the *cracque.* "Ah, no—thanks. Why don't I just nail down the premises like? Make sure nothing's carried away. By the Toddler. I get the chance—why, I might put an end to him as a problem." With index finger pointed and thumb cocked, he pretended to shoot the chandelier.

It was the same gesture that the Toddler had used in the picture gallery, thought Biddy. But from Tag only pitiable drunken bravado. "If you stay, you should mind yourself."

He stepped to the hallway mirror. "Whenever I'm lost, I'll only have to look there."

Cheri Cooke was now back on the stairs, dragging her traveling case down, step by step.

"Then we're gone," said Biddy to her family, pointing to the door. "You're first. He'll not want you, until he can't find me. God bless!"

"Ah, Mammy, can't we just stay?" Oney complained. But Maggie and Ned had her out the door and them after her.

Biddy turned and fled down the hall past Tag toward the back of the building. And the kitchen.

"What? No kiss, Bid?"

Kiss yourself, Biddy thought, now finally deciding that she was done with him. Stopping at the cellar door, which she opened, she reached up into the shadows by the transom and felt for the velvet-lined case that she had placed there as "insurance" against this day. She opened it to make certain it contained the thousand quid in fifty-pound notes and the torc that was worth much more. She placed it and the thousand quid in her purse.

Made of pure braided gold encrusted with diamonds and rubies, the torc was like something out of the Book of Kells, which was not the only reason that Biddy had bought it with nearly all her profits from her best year. It was her kind of "legs," as Mickalou had spoken of their bank account. Pawned, the torc would carry her anywhere in the world. Poor Mick. No—silly Mick to think he could trust buffers in a bank.

Reaching up again, Biddy removed a second item that was wrapped in an oiled rag that she had been told would preserve the thing. Beside it were two boxes, one of which she also took down.

"Wha' have we here, luv?" Tag asked. He was now standing beside her.

Biddy pulled off the rag, which she placed back on the

shelf, then carried the large, shiny object out to the kitchen table.

"Make me fookin' day—if it isn't Smith and fookin' Wesson. The two murderous Yanks. Where'd you get it, Bid?"

From an IRA gunman in Camden Town with the first paycheck Biddy had received all those years ago in England. It was what she wanted and needed. "Have you a target in mind?" the man had asked her. She had nodded. "I thought as much, so I filed off the serial numbers. Wear gloves. Then drop it. There's no tag."

Tag. His hand was now out. "Give us a look. That's the biggest, ugliest gat I ever fookin' seen."

Which was the reason that Biddy had chosen it—an immense, silver Dan Wesson .44 V with an eight-inch barrel that weighed nearly four pounds loaded and that at first Biddy could barely lift with her arms extended, much less shoot. But she had learned to, once a week with a shooting club in Reigate until she could hit a target at thirty paces with most shots, which was all she wanted from the thing. It was too bloody hard on her hands, arms, ears, and nerves. But it was nothing if not intimidating.

"What's the fookin' caliber?"

"Forty-four Mag."

"Janie, you could blow a hole in a Saracen with that thing."

Tag took another step closer to her. "I wish to Jesus yeh'd shown it to me earlier. Can yeh give us the feel of it?" His hand was still out.

Biddy flipped open the cylinder and slipped in a cartridge, and then another and another, six in all, until the weapon was fully loaded. Locking the cylinder back in place, she turned the barrel of it on him and paused a moment, until their eyes met. "I hope to God your seeing this convinces you how serious this is."

But plainly it didn't; he only wanted to get it in his hands.

Which she would not allow. Fitting it down inside her bag, which was large, she wondered if she should take the rest of the bullets. No. She'd need it only if he got close, where one would do. After placing them back on the shelf, she closed the door.

"For the final time: I'd leave were I you." And when you do, see that it's not with the silver, was her second thought, which, if said, might only give him a resentment and cause. Closing the bag, she fitted the strap over her shoulder and looked up at him. "Remember, now: I warned you."

"Biddy, you right bitch—wait!" Cheri was shouting from the stairs.

"But if I did, who'll look after yehr lover?" Tag winked, then showed her his tongue. "Or was it the other way round?" He raised a fresh bottle to his mouth and drank.

And his laughter—punctuated by Cheri's screams—followed Biddy out into the back garden to the gate in the wall.

10

WHACK!

 The Toddler had watched them pile out of the house on Raglan Road. He could tell from the way they moved—quickly, looking this way and that—they had been warned.

First came the old one, the Tinker woman from the camping site in Tallaght all those years ago. She had aged, but she was one of a kind and would never be able to disguise herself, no matter how she tried. Here with a stylish costume, layers of trendy rags. But her face was still the same old dried prune, her eyes big, round, and fearful. In her ears were thick gold Tinker rings.

After her came her husband, the Toddler judged by his age, his porter-colored face, and rumpled suit. Then the Tinker bitch's get: Beth Waters's or Biddy Nevins's daughter, who was—what?—sixteen or seventeen. That had to be her. Apart from the hair, which was longer, the girl looked just the way Mickalou Maugham had, right down to the loose-hipped way she walked. The Toddler wondered if she was on the gear yet, which was only a matter of time. Like father and mother, like daughter. He knew whole families that shot smack. She would have to try it only once.

Watching them climb into the Merc—not the stripped-down model but the big one with tinted windows and a V-12 under the hood—the Toddler reached for the cell phone on the console of his Land Rover. Punching in the main number of Garda Siochana headquarters in Phoenix Park, he waited until a prerecorded voice came on, advising him to toggle an extension or wait for an operator. He then added three more numbers, and the phone answered on the second ring.

"It's your mother's uncle Bill. I'm in a phone booth on a Callcard. Could you ring me back?"

"By all means, Uncle Bill. Good to hear your voice."

"Do I give you the number?"

"No need, Bill b'y. Don't I have it right here on me display?"

The Toddler rang off. Incoming calls to the police were automatically recorded; outgoing were not.

For the twelve years since the nearly disastrous night at the top of Grafton Street, the Toddler had handled all vital problems alone in ways that produced no witnesses like Biddy Nevins. But that did not mean he was unassisted. With wealth on the order that he now possessed, he had hired on retainer more than a few civil servants of one stripe or another who kept him informed, and warned and who—sometimes, as now—could act in his stead.

As the Mercedes pulled away, the cell phone bleated, and the Toddler held it to his ear. "I've got two favors to ask of you. The first is a car that I'd like followed discreetly." He then described the car and its occupants and read off the number plate. "Turning left now onto the Pembroke Road. Can we handle that?"

"I think so, once we locate it."

"Second, I have an address." The Toddler glanced up at the house. "Number twelve Raglan Road. I want it raided and tossed."

"On what grounds?"

"The usual." Once inside, the man on the other end would salt the house with drugs that the Toddler had already provided him. Everybody in the house would be charged, including the owner, and the dwelling closed up until a court determined it was no longer a hazard to the community. Which took years.

The law was new and a boon to somebody like the Toddler, who no longer sold narcotics at street level but from time to time had to punish those who did. Or who dared challenge him. It was all so much easier and less risky than the last recourse, which was still his Remington 700.

"How soon can it be done?"

There was a pause. "Sure, if the place is a pesthouse, as you say, then right away, Bill. This very instant. Sean! Dermot!" he barked. "Get in here on the double!"

"Good man, Paul," said the Toddler. "I won't forget."

"And the best of health to you, Uncle Bill!"

Ringing off, the Toddler slipped the phone into its yoke and started the large, powerful van, which was new and which he had ordered with special features at much expense. Wheeling out from the curb, he turned at the corner and sped toward Raglan Lane.

An alley at the back of a house was how Biddy Nevins had escaped twelve years before. Would she try it twice? Why not? Talent in art did not necessarily mean brains; witness her hanging the photograph of the painted footpath flags shaped in a vortex to represent what? Her past? Or his? What could she have been thinking? The Toddler would have picked the thing off had he seen it in a newspaper.

Slowing nearly to a stop, he nosed the large vehicle into the narrow alley and began counting the number of houses to hers. Eight.

That was when he caught sight of—could it be?—the bitch herself. Yes, he couldn't believe his luck. She was just stepping out into the laneway and reaching a key up to lock the back gate door again. She then turned and began walking straight at him. Tall, angular, but quick nonetheless. Wearing the very same metallic weave dress she'd had on at the gallery. From her shoulder swung a large purse.

It took the Toddler only a second to decide. Hit and run, it couldn't be better! He'd grind her right into the wall, then stash the Rover in a building that he owned in Ringsend only a mile or two away. There he parked a large articulated lorry that he sometimes used for big deliveries. Empty now, it would accommodate the Rover easily. For years, if need be.

Down came his wide, flat foot, slamming the accelerator to the floor. Tires shrieking, the Rover juddered and swerved, then bolted down the alley.

Biddy hardly had the chance to look up, but she knew

who it had to be, roaring down at her, all blazing bright metal and glass in the late-afternoon sun.

Snapping her head back, she saw that her own gate was too far to make. But maybe ten yards in front of her was the next back garden entrance, which, like all of them, was recessed a foot or so within the wall. Perhaps she could squeeze herself into the gap.

But her legs felt as if they were made of lead. Or—the thought flashed through her mind—her number was up. She was done, and it was the end of a life that had been brilliant in moments but filled mainly with fear and pain. So be it. At least now it would be over.

But she stumbled. In fact, she fell flat on her face, her bag spilling out in front of her. And the car, lurching down the laneway, kissed the wall about twenty feet from her, bounced off, and she could see the Toddler, throwing his weight against the wheel, trying to turn it back at her.

And did. The left front tire, skidding over her dress, pulled her into the path of the back tire that skinned the side of her face, her ear, the tip of her shoulder, before the car slammed into the wall again. The side mirror snapped off, and the sheet metal shrieked, as it slid down the rough rock wall.

The Toddler looked back. Had he missed her? Or just not hit her direct? She seemed to be moving still. He pumped the brakes once and then stood on them, and the Rover fishtailed to a stop.

Yes, he'd missed the bitch. She was crawling toward a gate in the wall. He reached for the Beretta in his jacket pocket. If he missed her with the Rover again, he'd jump out and do her with that. It was only a .25 caliber, but the bullets were hollow-tipped, and he'd pump all seven shots into her brain. The car then he'd take to the warehouse, as planned. And he'd be done with the only person who could still link him to a murder.

Jamming the stick into reverse, he tromped the gas pedal, and the Rover, skidding, leaped wildly back down the alley, rocking from side to side.

Biddy thought she'd been blinded. Her face was covered with dirt and blood. But catching sight of the bright stainless steel body of the revolver, where it had fallen out of her bag in front of her, she threw herself forward and snatched it up. Turning, she sat up, arms extended, the heavy gun locked in both hands. If he would kill her, she'd not go alone.

The Toddler did not know what happened. The rear window, which, like the others, was bulletproof glass, crazed suddenly into an opaque pattern of like crystals. He could not see a thing through it, and with the left external mirror now gone as well, he could not see her.

Twisting the wheel to the left, so he could, he lost control of the careering van, which slammed into the farther wall and nearly spun around. Like that he was straddling the alley. Where at least he caught sight of her again, just sitting there with something in her hands.

A bolt of flame spit from the thing and crazed the window of the passenger seat, sending a shower of glass slivers over the Toddler. And the next window on that side and the next, before he realized what it was and reacted. Christ, it must be a cannon, he thought. A second shot at any one of the frazzled windows would carry right through.

Spinning the wheel, he turned the Rover and aimed it

directly at her. Fuck it, he'd just run her down and chuck her corpse in back, then proceed as planned.

But the gun was still up, and the Toddler threw himself across the credenza and onto the shattered glass on the passenger seat, just as the windscreen exploded and the Rover crashed into the wall on the other side of the alley.

There was a pause of maybe four or five seconds—the Toddler would later think—as he tried to collect his wits, and he realized he could still hear the engine ticking over. Before the floor of the car—the only part of the Rover that wasn't armored—exploded right under him, smashing the credenza and sending a bolt of searing pain through his left thigh. Bits of frayed headliner sifted down on him.

Christ, he'd been shot. He'd even dropped the Beretta, which he now picked up again. She must be right under the car. He had either to kill her now or to get out of there. Or both. He pulled himself up, wondering if he could still walk. There was a chunk out of the fleshy part of his thigh the size of a tanner. It was bubbling blood.

Enraged now that she had actually managed to injure him, he jerked up the handle and threw the door open. He'd blow the bitch away, then get the fuck out of there and get himself some help. How could he have been so careless! He might even bleed to death from a wound like that.

But the door was wrenched out of his hand, and there she was standing above him all blood and dirt, some huge handgun pointed right at his head. She pulled the trigger. Nothing. And again. Only a click.

As the Beretta in his left hand came up, she smashed the

butt of the gun into his face, again and again. Then she spun and fled.

The Toddler roared. He bawled and spit shards of his shattered front teeth across the dashboard. His nose was broken, he could tell; there was a bright orange ball of pain right in the center of his vision; and his front teeth were ruined where the butt of the gun—some huge revolver—had punched into his mouth. It was filled with blood.

He spit again and tried to fight through the pain just as he had in Nam. He swung his good right leg out of the car and pulled himself to a stand beside the open door, which he would use as a firing brace.

But he'd only sighted the bitch in when she twisted her key in the gate latch and let herself into the back garden. And the three small-caliber slugs that he managed to squeeze off thwacked harmlessly in the wood of the closing door. Tasting his own blood, he fell back into the car.

He had to get rid of the gun, get himself to hospital, and get himself some other help before all this got out of hand. He'd call in favors, every one he could, he decided, finding it nearly impossible to drive with his left foot alone.

He'd put out a fucking dragnet for the fucking cunt—Beth Waters/Biddy Nevins. It wouldn't matter if it was known he wanted her, as long as he popped her himself. Discreetly. No witnesses.

The Rover jerked and bucked, as he pulled out into the Pembroke Road and headed toward the Royal Dublin Hospital.

Back in the house Biddy locked the cubby door, then

rushed through the kitchen to the cellar door, which she wrenched open.

"What—back so soon?" Tag asked from the kitchen table until he realized what he was seeing. "Christ, Bid, what happened to you?"

Cheri Cooke was sitting with him, beer in hand. "Didn't I tell you you needed me?"

Biddy pulled open the door and reached up for one of the boxes of cartridges. She'd been foolish to think only six shots would do. Now she might need an entire fifty. She'd leave the second there in case she had to return to the house, and then bullets were heavy. She could travel better light.

Snapping open the cylinder, she shook out the spent shells and quickly reloaded. That done, she poured the rest of the box into a pocket of her dress, dropping the empty carton by her feet.

The two at the table seemed dumbstruck until Cheri managed to ask, "And where do you think you're going looking like that?"

Said Tag, "Was that boomin' we heard yeh? Were you shootin' yehr six-gun out in the alley?" He shook his head in wonder. "Yeh should see yehr face. Yeh look like you just committed murder."

With any luck, she thought, tugging open the door and rushing out into the back garden. If he wasn't there, she'd find him somehow. Which should have been her plan from the start, way back years ago after he'd murdered Mickalou.

Opening the door cautiously, she stood where the wall would protect her, sticking only her head out into the alley. Once, quick.

But all that was left of him was the side mirror of his Rover, bits of shattered plastic and glass, and streaks of blue enamel down the walls on both sides of the alley.

"Are you all right, Miss Waters?" Her neighbor from across the alley asked, standing in her own back garden doorway.

Biddy concealed the gun behind her back. "Yes," she said.

"What was that anyway? I heard a fierce bit o' roaring and banging. It sounded like war." The woman stepped out into the alley to take a closer look. She picked up the side mirror. "Could it have been a car crash? And, look, here's a bag, a woman's bag."

Biddy glanced over her shoulder at her own house, where Tag and Cheri were now standing in the kitchen window, looking out. She couldn't go back there where the Toddler could find her; she had to be the one to dictate where and when and be ready for him. For the next time, which was inevitable.

Stepping out into the alley, Biddy closed the gate and advanced upon the woman.

"Oh, sweet Jesus, miss, you've been injured."

Biddy tried to smile. "I'm fine, really. Grand." She took the bag from the woman.

"Are you sure? Your face, now—it's all blood and dirt. Whatever happened to you?"

Opening the bag, Biddy tried to turn her body away, but the woman saw the gun. "Oh, my! Oh!" She turned and fled toward her open garden gate. "I don't know what went on here. But I'm ringing up the guards this instant. They'll sort it out, I'm sure."

Unsteady now, staggering a bit, Biddy made her way

toward the end of the laneway, her skinned scalp, face, and shoulder now paining her bad. If nothing else, she'd learned two things: She could get lucky, and the Toddler was not invincible. He made mistakes.

Maybe he was slipping. Maybe she could get him out of their lives the right way, the way that would matter to her most and pay the bastard back for Mickalou and all the others.

11
VICTIM

 Next morning Peter McGarr bumped through the swinging door of the Murder Squad office and made straight for his cubicle.

Twelve years had changed him little. Although short by the measure of younger generations at five feet ten and a half, McGarr still looked somewhat youthful. The hair that could be seen under a stylish trilby was brilliant orange and curly, and his eyes were clear and gray.

All that was different, really, were his posture, which was bit stooped now, and his gait, which had become more distinct. Called the Dublin trudge by his wife, McGarr's way of perambulating was distinctive. With hands plunged in his trouser pockets and hat still on his head, he traversed the office leaning forward. His steps were quick, seemingly purposeful, but also a bit harried, as though "carrying the weight of an improbable universe" on his shoulders. Her quote.

Which assessment was accurate at least this morning. McGarr's "form" was in no way good. Not more than a half hour earlier he had read an editorial in one of the morning papers that had made him angry. It contended that whereas Ireland could boast of one of the lowest per capita murder rates in Europe—lower, in fact, than Japan and Singapore, which were considered two of the safest countries in the world—the country's conviction rate was deplorable. Significantly below those two countries.

Granted, it was nitpicking at its worst, but the editorial went on to call for an inquiry into "Garda investigation priorities, techniques, and relevant personnel." Only in passing were government barristers mentioned, as though winning or losing in court depended solely on Garda evidence and not on the capabilities of prosecutors.

Nor was any mention made of the fact that a significant portion of Ireland's murders were political in nature and not pursued for political reasons. Or that those murders were generally not assigned to McGarr's squad or were taken away from him the moment progress was made.

Drug-related murders were another area that many politicians and even some of the police wished to play down. Probably a decade ago McGarr had heard a high-ranking guard say, "Why make an issue of them? Let the scuts kill each other off. And fair play to them."

Hands still in pockets, hat still on head, McGarr sat at his desk, beside which Detective Superintendent Hugh Ward was now sitting. He had replaced Liam O'Shaughnessy, who had long since retired.

With arms spread, Ward was reading a newspaper. "Gobshites, shooting from the lip," he said. "It's easy. A few pints of courage and a word processor. He's probably all the chat among his own kind. But safe, knowing we can't respond." Since it was Garda policy not to.

And they—the others in the journalist's *profession*, such as it was—would know that, McGarr told himself. But not the general public. Nor McGarr's superiors, who hated criticism of any sort. Nor his wife or young daughter and their relatives, who would take it personally. McGarr was in a foul mood.

A gracefully shaped hand now appeared in front of him, setting a large cup of steaming coffee on the blotter beside the sheaf of papers. Fully a detective inspector now, Ruth Bresnahan was no longer the least senior staffer, but she nevertheless performed the coffee duty whenever it required instant attention. Straightening up, she glanced at Ward, who looked away noncommittally. McGarr, however, had not moved, and she decided to chance it.

Bending, she opened the lower left drawer of McGarr's desk and removed a bottle of Hogan's Own. It was a single-pot-stilled malt whiskey that had been aged in sherry casks to impart a ruby color and a sweet-smoky bouquet. Although no longer produced, cases had been acquired by regulars, like McGarr, when Hogan's changed hands some years ago. He took a drop now and then, but only with cause.

Pulling out the cork, Bresnahan lowered the neck toward McGarr's cup and waited. When there was no objection from the seated, hatted, hands-in-trouser-pocketed one, she splashed in a dollop and waited again. With still no objection, she added some more. Finally she simply topped up the cup, then corked and replaced the bottle.

Leaving the cubicle, she heard the newspaper rustle, as Ward lowered it to watch her go out the door. There she paused and turned to him, knowing that the straps of her "braced" slacks were riding provocatively along the sides of her full breasts. These last were encased in a ribbed cotton spandex bodysuit. Having brushed her auburn hair off her forehead, she had arranged the natural waves to flow over her shoulders. Her eyes were smoky gray.

And his? Adoring, worshipful, conquered. Which was enough corroboration for the moment. She moved back toward her desk, fully believing she had heard a sigh, although they had parted intimate company only a few hours earlier. The man simply could not get enough of her, that much was plain.

Holding the cup in both hands, McGarr breathed in the evaporating malt before taking a wee sip. The cup would last him until noon. And should. Details and alcohol did not mix, but a "Hogan's coffee" could certainly improve an ugly mood.

Taking a second touch that seeped down his throat like a soothing balm, he began reading through the stack of police activity reports that had come in overnight. It was a ritual that he had performed every working day for the last nearly thirty years. And perhaps because of the editorial, one item on the second page jumped out at him.

It was the report of a gunshot wound. The name of the victim? Desmond Bacon. And there could be no doubt it was *their* Desmond Bacon who had virtually disappeared for years and was only rumored still to be involved in his former illegal activity.

In the margin Bresnahan had written:

Bulletproofed Land Rover left running outside the Royal City of Dublin Hospital on Baggot Street. Owned by Desmond Bacon of Hacketstown, Wicklow, but formerly of Coolock. Windows shot up & the interior. Tech Squad says three large-caliber gunshots entered from beneath the vehicle, wounding the victim, who, claiming shock, states he has no idea how or where it happened or who the perpetrator might be. Victim is in hospital and likely to be for some time. Please note the hour of his arrival at the Royal Dublin, then see pages 17 first, 11 second.

The time that Bacon had been admitted to hospital was circled in red pencil: 5:37 P.M.

McGarr set down the cup and followed Bresnahan's advice since she daily perused all police reports countrywide for items relevant to open cases. And she possessed a good memory and better analytical skills.

Page 17 said a woman had phoned in a complaint about what she first thought was a road accident in Raglan Lane but subsequently believed were also gunshots. After hearing the noises, she observed her neighbor—one Beth Waters of Raglan Road—with "a great shiny pistol." Waters placed it in her purse and walked toward the Pembroke Road.

McGarr glanced up from the activity sheet. Beth Waters: He'd heard that name before or read it. But where? He glanced back down.

A police patrol had been dispatched to Raglan Lane and discovered evidence of an automobile having struck walls on both sides of the lane. A side mirror from the car was later found that appeared to have come from the left passenger side of Desmond Bacon's Rover, as did paint chips taken from the wall. The time of the woman's phone call was 5:25 P.M. It too was circled in red.

McGarr turned to page 11. The item marked there said that acting on a tip, Chief Superintendent Paul Hannigan and his Drug Squad had raided number 12 Raglan Road, a residence owned by the same Beth Waters, and discovered a sizable cache of heroin, cocaine, and tablets of MDMA, the drug known on the street as Ecstasy.

Hannigan took two inhabitants into custody: Tag Barry, twenty-nine, originally of Belfast, and Cheri Cooke, sixty-one, who gave a permanent address in Reigate, Surrey. There was no mention of their having been arraigned, so they would still be in custody, McGarr supposed. The house itself had been sequestered.

Hannigan also issued an all-points alert for the owner, Beth Waters, who might also be a British subject. She was described as being in her early to mid-thirties, nearly six feet in height, of full build, with short brown hair and brown eyes.

"This much made *The Times*," Bresnahan had written in the margin. It was a paper that McGarr read mostly at night after supper.

The next sentence was circled in red and caused McGarr to remove his hat: "She also goes under the name Biddy Nevins and is known to associate with members of the Traveling community. She is armed and dangerous. If apprehended, she is to be remanded to Dublin, as per order of Chief Superintendent Hannigan."

The time of the raid on the Raglan Road house was also ringed in red 5:30 P.M.

"Now turn back to page 1 and read the 13th entry," Bresnahan advised in the margin.

It said that at 4:46 P.M. CS Hannigan issued an order that a four-door teal-colored 500 SL Mercedes-Benz sedan be followed, until a unit under his command could take over the surveillance. It was headed south on the Merrion Road. "The car is registered to Beth Waters," Bresnahan noted, "who is a rather well-known British artist now resident in Dublin. Yesterday was her first Irish opening."

That was where McGarr had seen the name: in the shop a few doors down from his wife's picture gallery in Dawson Street. McGarr reached for the phone.

"Our Toddler? Our Biddy Nevins?" Ward asked without looking away from his newspaper. "Together again."

McGarr consulted the phone listing taped to the writing slide of the desk, then dialed Hannigan's number. "Paul—Peter McGarr here." After pleasantries were exchanged, he asked, "The Raglan Road raid? Who gave you the tip?"

There was a pause before Hannigan said, "Er, why do you ask, Peter?"

Which McGarr found interesting of itself, one chief superintendent to another. He waited, and when no other answer was forthcoming, he went on. "Did you see the other report? The one that says Desmond Bacon, the Toddler, was shot in the laneway in back of the Raglan house just before you arrived there. Later a householder reported seeing Beth Waters with a handgun?"

"Janie, you don't say. The Toddler? And there we'd been hoping he'd dropped off the face o' the airth."

Hannigan was from Cork. Or Mars, thought McGarr, although he'd long ceased speculating on who got promoted to senior Garda positions and why. Even he, who handled homicides, knew that the Toddler was still active in the more concealed aspects of the drug trade—as financier and importer, having sold off his holdings in Coolock and removed himself to an estate near Hacketstown. He worked seldom, it was said, and in volume only.

" 'Twas an informant, Peter, to tell you the truth. But keep that to yehrself."

Dead easy without a name. In his mind's eye McGarr pictured Hannigan: a large, gruff middle-aged man with a shock of steely hair, a lantern jaw, and jowls the color of iron filings. It was said he'd been a hurling standout in his youth. Or was it Gaelic football?

Now Hannigan had a great protrusive belly that he made a show of at CSA (Chief Superintendents' Association) banquets, patting it, while saying, "Ann-y day now. Anny-y day." Or, "Beep, beep, here come da fudge." Or, "The missus won't do the Lamaze with me. She's afraid me water might break, and she don't swim a stroke."

"Was it the same informer who put you on to the Mercedes on the Merrion Road?"

"Well . . . now that you mention it, we've had the woman in our sights for quite a while now, and when I heard she was about to scoot, why, I gave the order to move in. You know, man, woman, and a young one all pilin' into the car and lashin' off just when we were about to lift her. Why, I thought she'd been tipped, and I had to do somethin'."

"Did you get her?"

There was another pause. "Get who?"

Christ, was he speaking Swahili, or was the man simply an eejit? "Beth Waters."

"Nah. Jaysis, I tell yeh, the lads they're just not up to it at all these days. Not like when we come in. Lost her, the car, whatever packet she had on her somewhere around Greystones. Said, once on the dual carriageway, she put on a great burst of speed and was gone. Car like that bein' as quick as a cat."

McGarr leafed through the activity sheets, noting that if the car left the Raglan Road house at 4:46 and was followed as far as Greystones, some twenty miles south of Dublin, Beth Waters (or Biddy Nevins) could not possibly have been seen in Raglan Lane sometime before 5:25, when the neighbor phoned in about the gun. Or she was not in the car.

"What about the Biddy Nevins alias? Where'd you get that?"

"Er, the others. The suspects. The ones we lifted from the house."

McGarr read the names. "Tag Barry and Cheri Cooke."

"That's them exactly."

"In statement form? Signed?"

It was as if there were a screening delay on the line with all Hannigan's dead air. "Presently. We're about it now."

"You'll send me copies."

"I will, sir. As soon as we've got them transcribed."

"What do you make of the Toddler being there, just as you were raiding the house?"

"Well . . . years ago now, when he was circulatin', he was a scourge, so. But a capable scourge, if you know what I mean. Beat us at every turn. And clean as an effin' whistle. There was nothin' we could do to put him away. Nothin'.

"Now . . . what gives between him and this Waters woman, I have no idea, and to be frank, I could not care less. Let the bloody scuts kill each other off, says I. The more, the merrier. I only wish her aim had been better. If it was her, and not some shower of . . . ambitious louts. Can I tell you something, Peter?"

McGarr grunted; it was Hannigan he had heard all those years ago.

"In the drug line there's only one motive: greed. It rules one and all."

"Thank you, Paul."

"Ann-y time, Peter. I'm here for yeh, lad!"

McGarr rang off, waited a moment, and dialed his wife's picture gallery, which answered, as usual, after an eternity of ringing. "You were?"

"Up the street."

"At Malachi Jordan's gallery."

He heard a small cry of pique. "Are you having me followed?"

"Haven't you learned by now—I'm omniscient? You and Malachi were . . . *discussing* Beth Waters, for want of a more accurate term."

Like most born-and-bred Dubliners, Noreen could not resist the many stories that the Dublin gossip mill churned up daily, and she spent the early hours of most workdays engaged in "chat." A kinder view, McGarr supposed, would be to contend that Dublin, a metropolis of some half million, enjoyed what few cities of size could claim—a strong sense of community—and such *discussion* was its glue, its running historical narrative.

"What about Beth Waters?"

"How she left his gallery, just walking out of the opening. Know why?"

There was only silence on the other end.

"Because Beth Waters is really Biddy Nevins, the former sidewalk artist who did the Book of Kells bit at the top of Grafton Street. And when Desmond Bacon, who is the Toddler, came in, she panicked."

Now the silence was stunned, he imagined.

"Beth Waters/Biddy Nevins repaired to her house on Raglan Road, told her parents and maybe some others in the house that they were in danger, that the Toddler would soon be arriving, and they left in the Mercedes, heading south along the coast.

"Beth/Biddy herself stayed behind, at least long enough to equip herself with a large-caliber handgun. The Toddler caught her coming out the back into Raglan Lane and tried to run her down. She pulled out the gun and managed in some way to put several shots up under his otherwise bulletproof Land Rover.

"He's in the Royal Dublin now with a thigh wound. Biddy's missing. But Paul Hannigan, it seems, had been watching her house for drug activity, and when he saw the Mercedes leave, he moved in and raided the place, finding a large amount of drugs and taking two people into custody."

McGarr waited for a reply. "Are you there?"

"I am—yah."

He imagined the multiple revelation was nearly too much to take in, all at one go. But it was definitely one of the "perks" of having a cop for a husband.

But she managed, "If you're so percipient, Superchief, why are you calling ignorant me?"

"Two questions you're to put to Malachi Jordan. Ask him if the Toddler asked him for Beth Waters's address? Second, was alcohol served at the opening?"

"Wine, I'm sure. You know Mal."

Who thought a cup an excellent catalyst for buiness, McGarr concluded. "Ask him if Beth or Biddy took any."

"Do I ring back?"

"No, I'll wait."

"Why? What's the rest of it?"

"Please, it's urgent."

Some minutes later Noreen returned to say, "Desmond Bacon asked for the address the moment he saw she had left. As for the alcohol, Beth told Mal to pour her only a little since she did not drink and was only going to hold the glass for form's sake. Mal fancied she was a Pioneer or in AA or something. And would be, if she's Biddy, after Mickalou and all her own trouble with . . . substances earlier on. D'you know what I just saw in Mal's gallery?"

McGarr had no idea, but he was desperate now to make another call.

"A photograph of footpath flags with chalk drawings of pages from the Book of Kells."

Then it *was* Biddy all right. But how had Paul Hannigan known that unless—"Thanks, you've been a great help."

"Oh, no, don't even think of ringing off without telling me the rest."

"But I don't know the rest yet. Tonight."

"Ah, Jesus, Peter—after sending me up the way to Mal and—"

"Bye." McGarr rang off and turned to Ward, who'd been listening. "What's the name of our contact in Drugs, the bloke we had with us in Coolock that time?"

"Lyons. Tom. He's a desk sergeant now."

McGarr sighed. Ten years ago, maybe even five, he would have remembered. Was it just his age, or was he losing his yen for the job? "Rut'ie!" he called out the door of the cubicle.

He had her ring up the Drug Squad, ask for Lyons, and ask him to phone back. When he came on, McGarr took the receiver. "Tom—Peter McGarr here. I have a few questions that won't compromise you there but could be helpful to us."

"If I can't answer, I won't. That's all I can promise."

"That's all I ask. Have the two you picked up in the Raglan Road house made statements?"

"Not a word. He won't let any of us go near them. Says he'll take their statements himself, and so far he hasn't." There was a note of disgust in Lyons's voice.

"What about the raid itself? You'd been watching her—the woman Beth Waters—and the house for—"

"Not at all. Not once. We never heard a word of the place until he shouted out the address, saying he'd lead the raid himself."

"And he made the discoveries once you were inside." Of the drugs that were found, McGarr meant.

Lyons paused. Then: "I think I know what you're aiming at. Around here it's known as the Hannigan factor."

"It's happened before?"

"Now and then. Once a year, maybe twice. Usually it's known trade, to give him his due. Some people here think it's what makes him chief. It's got to be different where you are."

Murder not being as easy to manufacture, McGarr guessed he meant.

"Come here," Lyons said in a lower tone, sounding as if he'd wrapped a palm over the mouthpiece of the phone, "can you tell me something, Chief? Are yeh plannin' to *do* somethin' about this, or are yeh just checkin' up like?"

Which was *the* question, although there was only one way to know for certain. "You'll know the answer to that one way or another. And soon."

"Then I'm glad I could help. It's been a long time coming."

McGarr hung up and turned to Ward. "How's our credit with the telephone monitor?"

"The bunch that records incoming calls?" Ward shook his head. "They keep changing people there. Transfers. It's boring and gets old fast. And you'd want to deal with somebody senior who could look at records without being questioned."

It was not what McGarr wanted to hear. "You mean Pauline."

Ward nodded. "She runs the show, and she's helped us before."

But not without emotional cost to McGarr.

"I could go over there myself. Maybe she'd check for me."

McGarr reached for the phone. "Nah, Jesus, it's your day off. Get out of here now. And thanks. I appreciate your showing up this morning. Give my best to Lugh." Who was Ward's son, whom he visited on his day off.

Passing through the office on his way out, Ward heard, "And to the missus. *My* very best to her. But remember, *not* yours." It was Bresnahan, who remained jealous of his relations with his son's mother, in spite of the fact that Ward had only just been made aware of his fatherhood. Up until a few months ago he hadn't seen the woman in fourteen years.

And the "missus" business—it was just plain low and off the mark in every way.

12

SNAKE

 No more than ten minutes later Hugh Ward arrived at the shop in back of which his son and his son's mother lived in the Coombe. It was a narrow through street that followed the hollow created by the River Poddle and was now almost exclusively a commercial area in the Liberties, one of the oldest sections of the city. And certainly not a place to hang your hat.

But looks could be deceiving, he thought, as he approached the two modest windows that said SIGAL & SON, ANTIQUE JEWELRY, OLD GOLD & SILVER and a battered oak door. It opened before Ward could knock, and he stepped into what he always thought of as a museum of the way Dublin used to be. Or at least a vast warren of low rooms with tin ceilings that were filled with things from the Dublin of old.

Nearby were glass cases filled with pocket and brooch watches, antique jewelry of obvious value, gold-headed canes and umbrellas. But beyond—in fact, way beyond the cases— there was a light source that seemed leagues distant. There, Ward knew, was a spacious and well-lighted modern apartment with every convenience that even possessed an unusual view of the Poddle's narrow valley.

As Ward's eyes adjusted to the light, he was amazed, as he always was, by the aisles upon aisles that were packed with old pianos, musical instruments, clocks, chandeliers, and candelabra, others with brass sconces, spittoons, vases, and an immense collection of newel-posts that had been in the collection of Leah Sigal's father. Not having said a word, she was standing beside Ward now, in the near darkness. The door was closed.

He could feel her there. More to the heady point, he could smell her—some arousing, exotic perfume that flared his nostrils and, he struggled to deny it, made his groin tighten. And he could only see her silhouette!

Granted she was a diminutive woman, but she possessed both an ample hourglass figure and a way of carrying herself that suggested she was bearing a gift beyond compare. Which wasn't far wrong, as he remembered. It had something to do with the movement of her arms and the grace of her walk. And her legs. Leah Sigal had excellent legs at once thin, shapely, but strong too. He remembered that.

Unfortunately it was what Ward remembered of her most—the physical Leah—although he knew—and had acknowledged he knew all those years before—that there was much more. Too much; evidence their child. In matters intimate (or *possibly* intimate) Ward knew himself. Visual images ruled. Utterly.

Which was more than enough to test him now. *Why*, when he was in love (or believed he was) with somebody else? Namely, Ruthie. He drew in a breath and let it out. It was a bitch being a man. Or, rather, a bastard, a word that he no longer used now that he had sired a son out of wedlock. By her. Leah.

He could feel her move a bit closer to him. "Lugh is waiting for you in his room. He has something to show you. But I thought we might chat for a while."

Like that? They were buckle to buckle. And had her hand reached for his hip? Ward felt something there, but he dared not check.

Ward had met Leah Sigal fifteen years prior, during the only year that he had spent in university. Always interested in history, Ward had sat a course at University College that focused on the origins of ancient Northern European societies. The lecturer was well regarded, but not nearly so much by Ward as one of his graduate student assistants, who was pursuing a Ph.D. at the time.

She was older than he by five years, and her name was Lee Stone since she had been married at the time. Dark like Ward, she had raven hair, dimples, high cheekbones that looked like chiseled knobs, a classic retroussé nose, and starburst blue eyes, to say nothing of being well formed otherwise. She once said that when she met him, it was as if she had met her "literal other." Apart from the eyes, they looked like perfect, complementarily sexed clones of each other. Ward's eyes were brown.

At the time Ward did not know what "other" meant, but it had led to an explanation and yet another session of passionate lovemaking. And the statement "All love is essentially egocentric. You are trying to find yourself in the other person. The closer, the better. Whether you know it or want it or not, we are the match of our lives." Which she proved by leaving her husband.

And still believed, he could tell, standing as they were in the deep shadows, their bodies nearly touching. It made Ward feel rather hopeless, as though he had suddenly been stripped of his free will and his life were determined and preordained. He had felt the same back then, as though they couldn't help themselves, that it was all somehow out of their . . . hands was not the right word at all. For they had gone at each other wildly, destructively almost: in her office, his digs, an alleyway, her car. It didn't matter if they might be discovered. They were all that mattered. Together.

But six or so months after they had met, Ward's father had died, leaving his mother and five younger children with no means of support. As the eldest Ward left university to seach for a job, sitting the exam for the Garda Siochana and recording the highest marks of that year. He saw Lee Stone only once again, when they said good-bye.

Fourteen years later during another investigation, Ward had come to the Sigals' shop seeking some advice about a piece of old jewelry, never suspecting that Leah's family—and now Leah—owned the business. A few weeks later she had revealed who she was and that her son, Lugh, was also Ward's.

Then she had seemed rather dowdy and plainly . . . well, old at thirty-eight. But now, looking down at her as his eyes accustomed themselves to the shadowed darkness, he could only agree with Ruthie, who had been along with Ward on that first visit to the shop. Bresnahan had said, "That woman's a well-preserved thirty-eight and not a day older. With a little care and that haughty nose and those eyes, she'd look like a younger, thinner, and"—she had swirled her hands in front of her chest—"more attractive Liz Taylor than Liz Taylor was at that age. And that's going some."

Now those eyes were looking up at him, and Leah looked anything but dowdy, wearing a bright red and fitted chenille cardigan with a scooped neck and pearl buttons down the front. Her slacks were black and tight, and the little bit of gray that had been left in her wavy black hair was becoming.

But Ward only waited. He had not moved after stepping in the door. Farther into the shop he could hear clocks ticking off the moment, myriads of them, all over the vast interior. "Where's Lugh?" he managed to say.

She did not answer; the clocks ticked on. Traffic kept passing in the street. Ward kept smelling her perfume and whatever good shampoo she had used in her hair. Did she have hold of his hips?

Yes, both hands. She pushed him back into the door, then lifted her face to his.

"Come 'ere, Hughie. Come closer now." Which was impossible: They were as close as they could be. "Tell me somethin'." She was employing the heavy Liberties accent that of course, she had grown up with and could mimic flawlessly and Ward found fetching, knowing who she was otherwise: Ph.D. historian, art and jewelry expert, and as sophisticated a person as he had ever met. It was her playful, flirtatious tone of voice, which she had used with him all those years before.

"Can yeh not kiss me? Have yeh forgot how? And who's to know, so? Here in the dark." Leaning back, she was pressing her hips and pelvis against him. And her thighs. Which felt . . . well, too good entirely. For a man committed to somebody else.

"Is it too much to ask? Or could you be"—she paused and smiled in a way that made her dimples pucker, her eyes devolving on his lips—"afraid?"

Now they could hear some movement off at the back of the shop. It would be Lugh, their son.

She raised her face to his. "Quick now, before Lugh comes."

When their lips met, Ward thought he felt a shock—and did he see a spark?—before she was in his arms, and they were, well, engaged.

It was as if they had never parted. The years fled. They were together again, and Ward felt suddenly immortal, as though he were a god simply because she thought he was and would affirm it time and time again. As she had for—how long had it been? a little fifth-column voice asked in the back of his mind—fifteen years, was all. Ah, not much of a test. Give her fifteen more, and see how she feels.

"Ma, was that Hughie?" Lugh called into the darkness as he moved toward the counters.

They broke from each other breathless, and Ward caught a glimpse of Leah's face that he knew he would never forget, as she turned and walked in that direction: blue eyes glassy, her smile masklike. The expression? Bemused but confidently so. As though she had reaffirmed that she had not been wrong in what she had said all those many years before.

On Ward's part, he felt a mix of emotions: deep, traumatic guilt that his emotional focus, which had remained fixed on Ruth Bresnahan for the past nearly ten years, was by one kiss alone now blurred. But also a kind of joy that was founded in lust, since now—his eyes following Leah's . . . voluptuous (was the only term for her) form toward the lighted cases—he conjured up in a flash every heady, heart-stopping detail of how they had been together all those years before. Ward had then only just got to know women in an intimate way, and Lee Stone—older and married—became his "Aphrodite," she called herself. And the lessons were utterly unforgettable.

Now he wondered how she had managed to keep her waist, which had been narrow then and was narrow still. Could she be wearing a girdle? He reached for her waist, and she stopped and turned to him, the same curious smile still on her face.

"Know what I'd like?" she said in a whisper. "Just one more session with you."

When he began to object, she placed a finger on his lips.

"I know, I know. You have your Ruthie, who's beautiful, bright, and young. But"—her blue eyes cleared and fixed his—"would it be too much to ask for us to have, say, one final weekend together?"

When Ward opened his mouth to object, the finger traced his lips.

"A wee, wild fling is all I ask. And no more."

Ward took her finger. "And a wee babby?"

Her smile did not diminish. "Would that be so wrong? I have time and money, and I love children." She pulled her finger from his hand, then tapped his chest, turning the nail this way and that into his skin. *"Our* children."

As if they were married in some alternative way. There was a lot of that going on in Dublin these days, thought Ward, and there, although unknowing, he'd been a part of one for fifteen years.

Because—adding to his burden of guilt was the probability that for all those years Lee Stone/Leah Sigal had been faithful to him, whereas he had used her lessons in love only to conquer as many women as he could before Ruthie. Who had conquered him. And who was very much in his life.

"And I'd hazard Lugh has turned out well."

Who was watching them from the open door of the living quarters and doubtless wondering what his mother and father were discussing with obvious passion out of his hearing. Ward could only agree. Lugh Sigal/Ward, as he now chose to call himself, was a fine lad in every regard: taller than either of them, darkly handsome, bright, and perhaps a better athlete than Ward himself, who had competed in the Olympics and won several European amateur boxing titles in the seventy-kilo weight class.

What could Ward say to her? How should he reply? "I'll have to think about it."

"Oh, do. Do!" There was a pause, and then, in a lower voice that was laced with ardor, she added, "And think about this: You can kiss me anytime. Anywhere. Your choice. You have my number, just ring me up. I'll make time or meet you anywhere. Or you can come here. Lugh's in school most of the day. I love you, I've always loved you, and I've loved only you. But just as I was when I gave birth to Lugh, I won't intrude on your life in any way. I just want you to fill me up again. *Please.*"

She then turned from him and walked smartly toward their son, leaving Ward feeling as if he'd just been mugged emotionally. Watching her, knowing who she was and how much they had loved each other and how they'd been together, Ward wondered how he could possibly refuse her request.

It would change things between him and Ruthie, who did not want to get married or have children. At least not yet. She was only thirty. Ward's past amorous betrayals had proved fatal to the relationships he'd been in, not because the other party found out but because *he* knew. Somehow it just took the edge off everything, and then a kind of fatal emotional rot set in.

Ward held out his hand, and Lugh took it in both of his. "Dad, good to see you. What was that all about?" It was the first time that he had seen his parents touch.

Ward shrugged. "I dunno. I was just trying to see if your mother's wearing a girdle."

Leah's smile was suddenly brilliant. "Like Aphrodite? You remembered."

How could he forget?

"Well, I'm not telling, not even you." She turned and walked toward the kitchen. "It's my secret for the moment." Which would be revealed the moment Ward acted on her request, of course.

"Would you like to see my new model?" Lugh asked.

Ward had to think: Model *what?*

"The Blériot."

"Ah, yes, the biplane you're building from scratch."

"*Built* from scratch."

"You mean it's finished already? You're a genius and take after your mother."

Who, with her palms propped on the counter behind her and her glorious bosom wrapped in tight-ribbed red chenille prominent, now regarded Ward as he followed their son to a workroom that functioned as Lugh's studio.

Her expression? That same masklike smile but with a slight difference. Now it seemed contented. Or was it smug? As though having satisfied herself on one score, she now knew something he did not. Or refused to acknowledge.

That she was fighting for his affection and had now planted what amounted to a snake in his mind? That it was inevitable and determined and they would have their session. It was as good as done.

Having to pry his eyes from hers as he closed the door, Ward felt as if it were.

13

HANG

 By half twelve in the afternoon Peter McGarr was ensconced in Ryan's Pub not far from Garda headquarters in Phoenix Park. It was a handsome old bar made of mahogany and rosewood with tall Victorian mirrors and frosted glass in the doors of its several snugs.

The one McGarr chose was at the very back of the pub, and he positioned himself on a banquette where there was no possible mirrored view of him. Ordering three large whiskeys and three larger glasses of iced water, he waited as the popular pub filled up with a lunchtime crowd, loud talk, laughter, and scurrying barmen.

More than a few times the intricately paneled door swung open and a head appeared. But seeing McGarr and the other glasses on the table, each invariably muttered, "Sorry," and departed.

At length an older woman peeked in and, seeing McGarr, entered. "Ah, so there yeh are, and in the usual company I see. Is it for me you bought one o' them?"

McGarr shrugged. "All of them, if you like. As I remember, it's what you drank the last time we met here."

"All of a dozen years gone January and on the very same matter, it turns out."

McGarr's head came up. She had something for him. Pauline Honan was in charge of Administrative Services, and the last time they met it was to discuss how the Toddler could have obtained official Garda uniforms, badges, and even handguns. For the Bookends, whom he had just murdered.

"But I have me knittin' to do this after'. Not like some. Johnny!" she called to a barman, who had only to see her to know what was wanted: a large pot of tea and a plate of salad sandwiches.

"What about you?" she asked.

McGarr flicked a finger at his glass. "I'm fine."

"No, you're not, silly man. Didn't I predict you'd end up like this? All glass, no food—it'll be the death of you yet." She carried the pot of tea over to the table, then returned for the plate.

Pauline Honan was a thin, diminutive woman in her early sixties. With a round face, large brown eyes, and an aquiline nose, she looked not a little bit the way McGarr himself had before his own nose had been broken and canted off to the side. In fact, she and he had been an item, once upon a time some twenty years earlier, before McGarr had met his wife.

"So, how's the child bride?" Like a slap, her eyes met McGarr's once, hard, before angling off. She set down the tray and sat. "And now the child. It must be grand being a daddy."

McGarr knew better than to reply.

Her age, which was ten years greater than his, had always been a sore point for her. Somehow she blamed him for the difference, as though they should have met or he should have been born earlier in life, and he could have made it happen.

Which was the problem between them. There always seemed to be something about him that she found wanting in an essential way and she could correct, according to her agenda. McGarr had stopped seeing Pauline Honan when, one day over a quiet drink, he realized that she simply did not approve of him. He now reached for his glass.

As though having read his thoughts, she seemed to collapse against the cushions of the banquette. "Ah, Peter, I don't mean to seem so bitter, here not seeing you for all this time. But it's just every time I do, I'm reminded."

Of how she had thrown her life away on him? Hardly. She was fully forty years old when he met her.

"Do we get this thing over with, over so I can enjoy me lunch?" "Now that you find me useful again after a dozen bloody years," went unsaid.

And how to reply? McGarr held out his hand. When she took it, her body shook with a sob, and tears burst from her eyes.

McGarr moved closer and wrapped an arm around her. Pulling her close, he held her until she stopped crying.

The barman, passing to the kitchen, stopped. "Are yiz right?"

Well, they weren't wrong.

"Pauline?"

"Thank you, Johnny."

After a while she pushed herself away from McGarr and turned to a wall mirror. "Will you look at me?" She reached for a serviette. "Just a bitter old bitch, when what I wanted to say was different."

McGarr poured her a cup of tea and added milk and two sugars. He placed the cup in front of her.

"You remembered." But she reached instead for one of the whiskeys.

"Is it here I'm supposed to say, 'I'll never forget'?"

She waited a long moment, regarding him. Then: "I ought to get up and walk out."

But she knew he had meant it, which was enough.

She blew her nose so violently and at such length that even the barman reappeared.

McGarr sought relief in his glass.

"Now—do we deal with Hannigan, yehr other bastard? And a *right* bastard, so. Look at this." From her purse she removed some printouts.

"The computer with the search function only goes back seven years. But on every occasion—nine in all—that Hannigan was rung up by his 'Uncle Bill,' the voice calls himself, didn't Hannigan bust some poor drugged-up divil and polish his reputation for clairvoyance.

" 'Not at-tall, not at-tall,' " she mimicked in an exaggerated Cork accent, "he's only after saying to me yesterday when I congratulated him on the Raglan Road arrests, " ' 'tis just plain, old, dogged police work, Pauline. I'm knackered from it, to tell you the truth. 'Bout ready to pack it in altogether.' The gobshite.

"Now here's what Uncle Bill had to say just before the Raglan Road bust." She flipped to the last sheet and pointed to the transcription, which McGarr quickly read. "Odd, what? The voice is stranger still."

Again she reached into her purse and pulled something out: a small tape recorder that she placed on the table. She picked up a glass and drank off a whiskey, before punching down the play button. "Sedative, don't you know? For the ears. His *uncle* Bill! From the bleedin' States no less."

Said the voice, *"It's your mother's uncle Bill. I'm in a phone booth on a Callcard. Could you ring me back?"*

And Hannigan, *"By all means, Uncle Bill. Good to hear your voice."*

"Do I give you the number?"

"No need, Bill b'y. Don't I have it right here on me display?"

McGarr had to hear only two words to know who it was. "Desmond Bacon," he said.

"The Toddler? Didn't he just get shot in the laneway behind the house? It must have been slightly after. Not even an hour."

McGarr nodded, pleased to learn somebody else read the dailies closely. And could think.

"And did you hear Hannigan's happy, thievin', treacherous reply? Could he have kissed Bacon's arse right there and then, he would have. He should hang." The recorded conversation was over; she punched off the machine. "Care to hear the earlier calls?"

McGarr shook his head; there was no need. "What about the number?"

"That the Toddler called from? Cell phone billed to a business on the quays that's owned by another firm in the Liberties that has an address on the Isle of Jersey."

With privacy laws more confidential than those of Switzerland, McGarr knew from other investigations.

"So, we have a dilemma," Pauline Honan concluded, reaching for the last full glass. "There's nothing in that conversation to incriminate Hannigan. Even if pressed to produce 'Uncle Bill,' he can always say he's just a concerned private citizen who made Hannigan swear never to give up his name. And we both know Hannigan. He could retire and play the crusading but persecuted policeman right into the Dail. 'Sure, Oi've busted too many drug dealers for the liking of' "—she swirled a hand—" 'Garda power brokers.' That class of rot.

"But you know, I've given this some thought. There is something we *could* do. Hannigan, it seems, is a great one for the cell phone. Carries one with him wherever he goes. And his use of it? Shameless. He's broadcasting most of the day." Opening the sheaf of papers, she showed McGarr page after page of numbers called. "That's just in one week."

"Where'd you get that?"

Pauline Honan glanced up at McGarr; her smile was mirthless and predatory. "Where I could get his conversations were I of a mind. Easily and by meself on borrowed equipment. No risk, no worry.

"And you—let's think of what you could do to like check and see if we're right about this, and it *is* the Toddler who's Uncle Bill. Done right, it might even make charges and tri-

bunals and a court unnecessary. And punishment. I can imagine a scenario in which Hannigan could get the max, and you
and I would know why."

Turning to McGarr, she waited until their eyes met.

McGarr nodded.

"You'll do that?"

He nodded again, and Pauline Honan's hands jumped for
his face, which she pulled toward her and kissed on the lips.

Releasing him, she blushed scarlet. "Now, leave me to my
lunch. And I hope to see you again before I die. You're a rare
brave and foolish man."

Hugh Ward and his son, Lugh, were bench-testing the four-
stroke 2.5-cubic-inch Saito engine Ward had bought him for
the Blériot biplane he had built when a knock came to the
door of the studio. Leah looked in on them, and Lugh had to
shut down the roaring engine so she could speak.

"Sorry to disturb you. This could be nothing. But didn't I
read a piece in *The Times* today about a house being raided in
Ballsbridge owned by a woman named Waters?"

Ward stood up.

"I think she's out front, wanting to pawn an ancient torc
with sapphires and rubies. She has a provenance in her name
that's legitimate. I just got off the phone to England. It's
worth"—Leah hunched her shoulders—"maybe fifty thousand
quid, I'd hazard. At least I know I could sell it for that quickly.
Says she needs forty and will be back soon to pick it up.

"We settled on thirty by my personal check, and the balance in hundred-pound notes." Leah raised a large money bag.

"Knowing about the check means she's dealt with us before, which is probably why she's here."

Sigal & Son was probably the only jeweler in Dublin who would deal with an item so valuable, Ward knew.

"But I can't place her. And she's a Traveler, I'm sure, in spite of the way she looks, which is . . . chic. I can tell by the way she haggled. The patter. Like she was selling swag." Meaning the sewing needles, cheap jewelry, and trinkets that Traveling women used to sell door to door to farm wives.

"You can see her on the television monitor in the kitchen."

Looking down at the screen, Ward saw a woman of size standing at one of the counters out front. She had dark hair cut short and was dressed in a rather formal-looking costume, like something she might wear to an opening. And dark glasses.

Also, many Travelers did not trust banks and might typically possess some object of value that could be pawned in an emergency. Or sold outright.

"She have an accent?"

"British, but she's Irish too. Or was."

"Is there a way I could get out front before she leaves?"

"You mean, you're going?" Lugh was plainly disappointed.

Ward pointed at the screen. "Yesterday evening that woman shot the biggest drug dealer in the country, who twelve years ago murdered her husband. It was self-defense, we think. Actually he was trying to kill her too, and he will again if he gets the chance. Best case?"

Now Lugh was plainly impressed; his eyes were fixed on the monitor.

"We follow her until the Toddler—that's his name—tries again. Then we lift him and put him away for a long time."

"But how will you know he's trying to kill her until he actually makes the attempt?"

Ward shrugged. "If she were worried about her safety, shouldn't she have already contacted the police?"

"But don't Travelers fear the police?"

Ward nodded; it was true. And in Biddy Nevins's case for good reason. "But she's made her choice, and think of the benefit to society if we could put the drug dealer away."

"So, you'll do what—follow her?"

"If you're game."

Lugh swung his head to his father. "You're jokin' me."

"Not if your mother agrees."

"Oh, I don't know," Leah said, her brow suddenly wrinkled. "Will it be dangerous?"

Ward shook his head. "Car work mainly. If I have to get out, Lugh can handle the radio."

They waited while she plainly struggled with the decision. "Well, all right. I trust you two. But you take every care and caution, now, and get back here safely. And phone if you'll be late."

"Take your time with her," Ward advised. "Count out the money slowly or something. My car is a few streets away, and we'll want to set up a few others."

Plainly over the moon at the prospect of being out with his father on an actual murder investigation, Lugh Sigal/Ward led his father down through the building to the yard and car park. Then out through the gate onto the street.

14

CRUSH!

McGarr found the Toddler standing by a window in his private room in the Royal Dublin Hospital, staring down at the traffic along busy Baggot Street two floors below.

There were crutches under his arm, a plaster across the bridge of his swollen nose, and both eyes were blackened, making him look owlish and haunting. He was holding a cellular phone to his ear.

A dozen years had changed him otherwise as well, McGarr judged. Desmond Bacon looked older, balder, smaller in height, larger in girth than when he had ruled Coolock. And—could it be?—a bit frightened? Or was he just wary? Back to the wall, he had placed himself between a large oak armoire and the door, where he could scarcely be seen.

Catching sight of McGarr, he switched off the phone and

slid the antenna back into the body. "There's Chief Superintendent McGarr," he said as though speaking to a third party. But softly. His lips were split both upper and lower. He looked back down into the street. "Fancy the irony of his coming to see me in the hospital. With me the victim. Is it *attempted* murders he's doing these days? Or the old ounce of prevention routine?"

The hospital and *routine* were Americanisms that rather revealed Bacon's history. Pity McGarr had discovered it only after the man had dispatched the Bookends that night at the top of Grafton Street. Not that knowing about Bacon's U.S. Marine sniper/scout background would have mattered, given his alibi of having been shooting skeet with Corny Duggan, the now-vanished solicitor. And his prowess with a weapon.

McGarr made a show of looking at the door to the room. "I beg the Toddler's pardon. I must have the wrong number altogether. Sorry to give your Todship a fright in your reported distress. I was looking for Uncle Bill. Or, rather, your mother's uncle Bill."

He watched as the Toddler's slight smile muted.

"No, that's not how it goes. How is it now? You tell me where I'm wrong. Let's see. Ring-ring, ring-ring. 'Hah-low.' That's Hannigan. Cheery fella, what? Always up for whatever's on. I'd say he's a man who can take instruction and the odd backhander. Or do you have him on retainer?

"Now, this is you. 'It's your mother's uncle Bill. I'm in a phone booth on a Callcard. Could you ring me back?' Here's Hannigan. 'By all means, Uncle Bill. Good to hear your voice.' 'Do I give you the number?' 'No need, Bill b'y. Don't I have it right here on me display?'

"You were calling from your cell phone in the Rover where you were parked on Raglan Road outside Biddy Nevins's house. Oh, pardon me. I shouldn't have divulged that. There I go, giving everything away. Poor Hannigan. Could he soon be dead because of me?

"Or was it the same cell phone that's in your hand: four-four-eight-nine-five-one-six? Did you just get off the phone with him? We're to see each other this evening. Some scoops, a little chat. Trust me to be wired. Oh, but now you'll tell him that. My, but I'm careless."

Slowly, calmly, with learned patience, the Toddler turned his head and looked back down into the street, where the more immediate threat might just have appeared. He had been in crisis before, and he knew how to act. Hannigan would be dealt with in due time. It was the woman who was the continuing problem, as she had been now for a dozen years. He'd been watching her for longer than he should—while she tried to park an obviously new green Volvo she was obviously not used to.

Finally she just quit a foot from the curb and got out: dark glasses, what looked like a babushka tied under her chin, a big spray of flowers in her right hand, and the same purse she'd had over her shoulder the afternoon before in the alley. The one with the large-caliber revolver in it that must be a magnum of some kind. The Toddler had only been nicked, but the chunk it had taken from him was as if he'd been gored by a bull.

What had changed her from the timid, terrified, illiterate, Tinker junkie that she'd been when she was shooting his gear? he wondered as she waited for traffic to pass before crossing the street to the hospital entrance. The success she'd had in London? The money? In his experience, people with something to lose were more cautious, not less. But here she was: a big, comfortable-looking woman, graceful even in the way she carried herself, now tripping through the slow-moving traffic in a kind of disguise, with the flowers and gun to kill him.

Cop or no cop, it was time for him to leave. But when he turned his head, he found himself alone. Why? Because the cop was just dropping the dime on Hannigan, as was said in the States, and wanted him dead too. He had his own plan and had already put it in motion. Reaching for his bloodied jacket, he let the crutches drop from under his arms. They clattered to the floor.

It wasn't as though he could not walk without them, but that it was painful, which was good. He had used pain before to keep himself alive, when the VC, enraged by his long-range assassinations, had tried to hunt him down. Pain had kept him alert and alive. Now he'd use it again.

By the time the Toddler fitted his jacket over his hospital smock and got to the hall, sweat was beading his brow, and he felt vaguely nauseated. And defenseless. Not wanting to be charged with a weapons violation, he had shoved the Beretta down the sewer in front of the hospital, never imagining she would come for him here.

Anger, he knew, was bad. It blinded you, made you make mistakes, like the one in the alley that had landed him in this cockup. But the Toddler was angry now, all the more with the pain that was galling him. He'd make her pay in a way that would matter to her most—with the daughter first. "And then the whole fucking family," he muttered, stumping down the hall. He'd wipe them out. "Every last lovely one."

And his teeth were bloody ruined. Maybe that bothered him most, being something he'd never get back. Every time he spoke or took a sip of water, pain coursed through his cranium.

Biddy made straight for the reception desk, knowing he was still in the hospital. She had her own contacts, especially now that she'd returned to being Biddy Nevins, wife of Mickalou Maugham, who was still revered in the Traveling community. His music—on tapes and discs—was still played.

It hadn't been hard finding the bastard since shot and bleeding, he'd had little choice but to get himself to a hospital nearby.

"I've flowers for Des Bacon," she said in her best British accent.

The woman consulted a list before glancing up at her. "If you leave them here, I'll see they're taken to his room. He's not allowed visitors."

"Not even his sister? I've come all the way from London."

The woman shook her head. "I'm sorry. Doctor's orders. There's nothing I can do. But I'll see they're delivered to his room."

Biddy knew even then that she'd get at least part of what she wanted; she had not begged and survived all those years on the Dublin streets without learning her craft. "But can't you just check? I'm next of kin. He has no wife, no children, no family but mother and me. Would it say that? Would it say no visitors apart from immediate family? Mother's elderly and frail, and she's worried sick. She made me promise to see him myself. Would the doctor be about? Might I have a word with him? Could you check and make certain. Please?"

Why not? she could almost hear the woman thinking. *Anything* to get rid of you.

The woman's finger descended the patient list again, stopping at Bacon's name and following it across the page to the number 117. She then referred to a clipboard that was thick with yellow copies of doctors' orders. Pushing those back with the eraser of a pencil, she finally came to the instructions for patient Des Bacon. "No, I'm sorry. It says nothing here about next of—" She glanced up, but the tall woman with the sunglasses and scarf over her head was gone.

Biddy made for the stairs. Lifts took too long, and somebody might question her while she waited. Also, she had to dig the gun from her purse and conceal it in the paper wrap of the flowers. That was not easy, especially when she had to open the door onto the first floor.

After that it was two hands, and she felt her heart quicken at the prospect of finally settling with the bastard, of blowing him away right there in his bed. She'd fire the entire cylinder, reload, and fire again until she was stopped. And damn the consequences.

She'd tell the truth, all of it—about the gear and Mickalou and the others she knew he'd killed—every chance she got, and her people, the Travelers whose kids the son of a bitch had preyed on, would make their voices heard. And at least good rough justice would be served. Whatever happened to her as Biddy Nevins or Beth Waters was unimportant. She could die even, happy.

She dropped the flowers as she entered the room, locked the pistol in both hands, pointed the barrel at the bed, then swept the room. "No!" she shouted. The fucker was gone. Utterly. No clothes, no shoes, no sign of him. Had he been watching? Had he seen her?

Biddy rushed over to the window and looked down into the street at her new car, the Volvo she bought with some of the money she'd got from pawning the torc. If he'd been here—she looked down at the crutches on the floor—he would have seen her. Spinning around, Biddy pulled the scarf off her head, wrapped it around the gun, and rushed back into the hall.

So, she'd come up the main stairs. Would he have taken the lift? It would have carried him right down to her? There had to be another way out

"Nurse! Nurse!" she called to a woman in uniform walking up the hall. "I'm desperate, so. In a panic." Now her voice was pure Tinker. "I'm after seein' my da, who's dyin', and I'm like the black sheep o' the family. They're comin' now." She waved the scarf in the direction of the lift and the main stairs that were side by side. "And I'd rather not see them. Would there be another way out?"

The woman's eyes swept Biddy, her nostrils flaring in contempt. A hand flicked out dismissively. "End of the hall, through the door, take a right."

Biddy flew down the hall, thinking: He's hurt, he must be limping, he dropped the crutches, his car was towed away by the police, and the "girlfriend," who's something like Cambodian—was out in the country where he was now getting the gear—and she did not drive. Biddy'd found out all that and more in Donabate last night, where she'd camped with some Traveler cousins who'd kept tabs on the Toddler. He had nearly destroyed their lives too with his dope.

I'll never get this chance again, she kept telling herself, once he gets back to his place in Hacketstown, which was wired and guarded by dogs and like a fortress, one cousin had said. "Didn't he put a bullet through me engine block when I tried to look in there with binos? Must've been a mile away. I didn't even hear the shot."

Lowering her shoulder, Biddy burst through the door, turned right, and took the stairs down two at a time, realizing—as she got to the ground floor—that she was following a small trail of blood, which gave her a thrill. The bastard was bleeding to death. It was his blood there at her feet.

Suddenly she was flooded with recollections of how the Toddler had sent some of his gearmen, as he called his stone-cold junkies, out to the dump in Ringsend where all the Traveler kids were camped and trying to live through the winter. Three that she knew of did not, because of the Toddler.

"Free dope for all. Weeks and weeks' worth," was the cry. "Sure, don't all the rock stars shoot it? Ye're not a man or a woman 'til yeh've tried. And come closer while I tell yeh: Get on it good, and you'll lose the hunger." At that time Biddy would try anything that was free and would rid her of the cramps she'd get when she had nothing in her stomach.

She became a woman fast: gang-raped by some friends of

the gearmen when she was nodding off after her first injection, then living for years on heroin, sweets, and whatever money she could make turning tricks for old men in a quayside walk-up that the Toddler owned.

One dirty fucker knocked her out, then tied her facedown by the wrists and ankles to the four posts of the bed. She nearly died, hemorrhaging from the rectum. One of her friends was found floating in the Royal Canal, her body dumped there after her throat had been slashed during a snuff movie. The other two just died of the effects of little food, great cold, and bad gear.

And now here he was. The Toddler himself up ahead of her scarcely halfway down the alley—squat legs showing beneath the smock, flat-footed and gimpy, toddling toward Baggot Lane. Slow.

Biddy sprinted forward, wanting to catch him before he got to the end of the alley, eye to eye. It would be no good killing him from afar. She wanted him to know she was the one. She'd shoot him someplace foul—the cock, the balls. She'd shoot him up the hole, so he'd know how it had felt.

She was dizzy, heady, wild with her hatred of the man and the chance for the only revenge that mattered: a painful, ugly death. The pavement, the buildings, the cars passing at the end of the alley swam before her eyes. Bearing down on him and taller than he, Biddy raised herself up and, with the gun still wrapped in the scarf, slammed the butt down on his bald head.

But he didn't go down right away. Staggering, he swung around in a piece and slammed his right leg into her stomach.

It felt like the kick of a mule, and suddenly she was off her feet, on her back, the gun clattering over the cobblestones and bouncing into the wall.

Making for the weapon as well as he was able, the Toddler knew what it was even before he picked it up: a Dan Wesson .44 Magnum with an eight-inch barrel. He had one just like it back in his armory in Hacketstown, which he had concealed in a way that nobody would discover, the Cambodian mules who had built the magazine having died in defense of the secret.

Stumping painfully toward the revolver, the Toddler thought: Somebody in the cars that were stopped in the traffic at the end of the alley must have seen her attack him. He was obviously injured; he could pick up the piece, pretend to fall, and put a bullet through the side of her head, no problem. They were that close.

Maybe a few people would swear he'd been attacked by her, that he'd gone for the gun just to pick it up but had lost his footing and the gun had gone off. A firearms accident, he—and some of the press, whom he could pay—would say. She having attacked him for the second time and provided the weapon.

Shiny and massive, it glistened against the dark cobblestones and sooty brick of the alley. But in reaching for the thing on the one leg, the other stretched stiff and bleeding, the Toddler lost his footing and fell heavily, his head striking the wall.

•   •   •

Hugh Ward had been surprised when he saw the Toddler appear in the alley. He had been following Biddy Nevins/Beth Waters with his son, Lugh, now for several hours.

She had taken a taxi to a bank, then to an automobile dealer in Blackrock, where she bought a new Volvo, and finally she had driven here to the Royal Dublin.

Not finding a parking place, Ward had pulled his car up onto a footpath near the corner across the street where he could survey every exit of the hospital and still maintain radio contact with Murder Squad headquarters and the other sur-veillance cars that had been assigned the task of tailing the woman.

His first impulse was to follow her into the hospital, since he could think of only one reason why she had come here: to finish what she had attempted in the alley behind her house on Raglan Road. But he'd been told by Bresnahan that McGarr was presently in the Toddler's room. Lowering the volume on the radio so Lugh and he could converse with some measure of privacy, Ward had settled back to wait.

Then suddenly there was McGarr, coming out of the main door of the hospital, and the Toddler with his nose bandaged and his eyes ringed with bruises was limping up the alley from the rear with Biddy behind him. Moving fast.

Before Ward could react even, she was upon the man. The Toddler's kick was savage and practiced, like something out of a kung fu movie. As the Toddler began hobbling toward the gun, Ward threw open the door and hopped out of the car, saying to Lugh, "Stay here. If there's shooting, get down on the floor."

"Be careful, please," Lugh blurted out, scarcely able to speak the words. He was excited—no, astounded actually—to be along with his father on such an adventure involving a known criminal and the woman whose husband the man had murdered, Hugh had told him. And now her attacking him and the drawn gun. But at the same time he was shaking with fright, and he feared for Ward.

Pulling the gun from the holster under his jacket and holding up his laminated Garda ID to oncoming cars, Ward jinked through the traffic, hoping he could reach the alley before the Toddler could get to the gun, some large, nickel-plated weapon.

He arrived there just as the other man was lowering himself on his stiff leg toward the handgun. Blood was oozing through the bandage on his thigh. The hospital smock was carmine and wet.

But the Toddler went down, his forehead banging off the wall, his body now limp on the cobblestones. Staying well away from the man, who was obviously some sort of martial arts expert, Ward grasped his own Beretta in both hands and aimed it at the head. Behind him, he could sense that the woman was coming around, stirring, trying to raise her torso up.

"You!" he said to her. "You stay where you are, stay down. You're a right bloody fool to go after him. He's a trained killer. Why the Christ did you not pop him when you had the chance?"

"I want him to see me," she managed to say. "I want him to know it's me."

"What?" Ward redirected his aim on the Toddler, who had

stirred. His face was streaming with blood from the gash on his scalp. "How will that matter to him dead?"

She pulled herself to her feet. "To me it matters. It matters very much indeed. And I'll be taking that now." She pointed to the gun that Ward could see at a glance was a .44 Magnum Dan Wesson with an eight-inch barrel. It was a huge thing, a veritable cannon.

"No, you won't." Ward stepped by the Toddler and picked the gun up. He thumbed open the cylinder and shook out a cartridge that was jacketed, the bullets filed flat. They were Speer Gold-Dots packing a full three hundred grains of powder, announced an inscription on the case head.

Designer bullets and exactly the kind of round that could have punched through the floor of a Land Rover. Had one of them struck the Toddler's leg directly, it would have taken it off.

The Toddler now pushed his back up against the wall, his face a ghastly wash of blood.

"Look, you'd be better served going home, where we can protect you. I can promise you that. You go back to Raglan Road, and I'll see you're looked after."

Using the wall as a brace, the Toddler now got up in one smooth motion, his eyes moving from Ward and the guns to Biddy. Blood was dripping from his chin. "I'm going to leave now, Detective Ward. I think you know I was attacked by this woman. That—" he pointed to the weapon in Ward's left hand—"is hers, not mine."

Ward felt almost cheated, as though there had to be some way that he could turn the situation against the man, make him break a law or rush him so he might do what was necessary, which was to put the bastard down. Ward had been forced to kill before; it had not been easy. He suspected this would be different.

But traffic had stopped in the street, and he could now see faces in some of the hospital windows, watching the altercation.

The Toddler read his eyes. He pushed himself away from the wall and began hobbling toward the footpath. "It's not my gun, and I can prove it. It's hers. You must have seen her. She tried to kill me."

"Did she shoot at you?"

The Toddler only continued to put distance between them.

"Will you swear out a complaint?"

The man stopped and turned his head back to Ward, a contemptuous broken-tooth smile flickering across his bloody face, as though to say he handled his own complaints. Then he was gone around the corner of the building.

Stepping to Ward, Biddy held out her hand. "Let me have it back. I think you know I need it."

Ward did indeed. In fact, if she wouldn't submit to being protected, he wanted her to have it and to continue to hunt the Toddler. Or he her. Eventually the man would make a second mistake, most likely in killing her, and then they would have him. At last. She was a fool to go after him; she wouldn't be lucky a third time, he was sure. But it was her decision.

Still, Ward could not be seen simply handing it back. "You come with me." He took her by the arm, but she pulled away.

"In jail I'm dead. Like Archie Carruthers. It's what he wanted with the raid on my house."

Ward took the arm again, this time more firmly with his thumb on the pressure point just up from the elbow.

She howled in pain and roared, "Yehr another fookin' Hannigan!"

That interested Ward. "How long have you known about him?"

"Christ, doesn't everybody? But not you, no. Being on the pad too."

"Take it easy," he said in an undertone. "You'll get in the car with me. I'll drive you around the square, and then it's back to the Volvo *with* your gun. And come closer while I tell you and you're to listen." He pulled her into him, walking her to the curb. "You're a right bloody fool to go after him. The man's a killer."

"Do *I* not know?"

"You'd be better off telling us about the man he put under the bus that night at the top of Grafton Street."

"And then what? Get shot like the Bookends. Or spiked like Archie Carruthers?"

"Not if he's in prison."

"For how long? There's no death penalty in this country. When he got out, I'd be dead. Or before. He has bags of money from the drugs. He'd pay somebody to kill me and my family. As a lesson. He's big on lessons. And what if he gets off? Everyone else who was there that night is dead. My only chance is for him to not know where I am. And for *me* to jump *him*."

Ward shook his head. She'd had her chance and blown it. If he knew anything about the Toddler, the man would now regroup, call in his markers, wage a kind of vicious war against her and her family. But plainly she had already decided what course to take.

Ward made it look official, as if he were arresting her. Lowering the tall woman into the back seat of the car, protecting her head, he muttered, "I won't say this again: You can't win this."

"Then I'll lose, but I'll take him with me. Now give me me fookin' gun."

After Ward got in behind the wheel, he reached back and placed the immense pistol on her lap without letting it go. "Do me a favor. If you survive, you had two of these. This never happened. I never gave you this back."

Their eyes met, and Biddy nodded. "Thank you, sir."

Ward released the gun.

Said Lugh, after she had left the car, "Why'd you give her back the gun? She attacked the man; we saw it ourselves. And isn't it illegal to own a handgun in Ireland?"

Ward nodded. "And what I did was illegal. But she poses a danger only to him, and that's good. Without that gun she's dead." Although he suspected she was anyway.

"But what about . . . protective custody?"

Ward glanced over at his dark, young son who was nothing if not . . . "precocious" was a word he disliked, but certainly it fit. "For how long? It's been twelve years since he last tried to kill her. In twelve more, he'll try again, I've no doubt."

Lugh considered that for a moment, then said, "Isn't there anything you can lift him for? Hasn't he broken any law?"

"It's a good bet all of them. But he's careful. We've no proof."

"But if he's been dealing drugs for so many years, how careful can he be?"

"Well . . . practice makes perfect." Ward was peering into the rearview mirror. Having pulled the unmarked Garda car into the curb, he was waiting for Biddy to wheel the Volvo out into traffic. Since she now knew his vehicle, he'd follow her for a while until some other car in the team picked her up, then make a point of turning off where she could see.

But as far as he could tell, now checking in both of the side mirrors as well, there was nobody in the Volvo and no sign of her on the footpath or in the road.

Ward tugged open the door and again got out of the car. No. She was not in the car that was parked half out in the street. Nor anywhere that he could see. Back in his own vehicle he reached for the radio and punched up the volume. "She's gone. Skipped. Tall woman, broad. In her thirties. She might be wearing dark glasses, a white sun hat. The dress is . . ."

But Biddy was already a quarter mile away, having walked right by the Volvo and boarded a bus that had come to a stop at the corner near the car. Once inside she had dropped a coin and pretended to search for it until they were well beyond the car of the guard who had saved her, God bless him.

And beyond the cars of any other guards who might have been with him. It was yet another lesson Biddy had learned as a child: how to avoid the police.

Later she'd send some of her cousins to collect the Volvo. The *shadogs* wouldn't watch it forever.

"What now?" Lugh asked in the patrol car, plainly disappointed at how his father had performed the first time he had observed him in action.

Ward pulled out his billfold and handed the lad a five-pound note. "Can you find your way home?"

"What about you?"

Ward pointed to the Volvo. "The situation's not as bad as it seems. She'll send somebody to collect the car, and that person will lead us to her."

Sooner rather than later, Ward hoped.

15

THE FIRST FREEDOM!

 Like a politician working a crowd of voters, Drug Squad Chief Superintendent Paul Hannigan began pressing the flesh from the moment he walked into the Horse & Hound, shaking hands with this one and that as he passed down the bar.

It was a neighborhood pub on the Merrion Road across from the Royal Dublin Society Horse Grounds in Sandymount, a much more acceptable section of Dublin than Rathmines, where McGarr lived.

Earlier McGarr had driven by Hannigan's large Edwardian house with colored leaded glass windows and plenty of gingerbread molding that must have cost a "bomb," as was said.

Which McGarr was about to drop on Hannigan, the house, his family, his life and prospects in a figurative way.

And better by far than the punishment the Toddler would most likely dole out. Hannigan deserved at least a warning

"How ya, Donal? How's t'ings?" said Hannigan. Then: "There's Jack. How's Jack keepin'?" And "How yiz, gir-ills? Yeh're in great form altogether. How long have I been keepin' yiz waitin'? And there yeh've bought me five drinks."

When Hannigan reached for one of their drinks, he was smacked smartly on the hand. "Ooo, now, that's the class of abuse I crave." All was said with a rough, gravelly but infectious bonhomie, such that other patrons in the lounge turned to the man with the absurdly protuberant paunch, and they smiled.

Why? Because of his position, who he was. It was a small country, and people in his local had to know who Chief Superintendent Hannigan was in the way that McGarr was known to many as well. But it was the look of Hannigan too.

At once pigeon-toed and bow-legged, Hannigan moved with a quick, rolling gait that made his stomach sway. His face was saturnine, his complexion high, his dark hair flecked with gray, and his eyes were some deep shade of blue.

The suit he was wearing was costly and had been tailored to make the man look less comical. But there was nothing that could hide that belly. Shaking hands with McGarr, he eased himself down onto a stool across a low table, and his stomach—THE STOMACH—distended, like some third presence, between them.

McGarr averted his gaze, wondering how his own not inconsiderable belly appeared to some other party—namely, his wife, who was twelve years his junior and still looked like a comely adolescent, at least to his eyes.

But Hannigan's position on the edge of the low stool said something else: that he would be staying for only a short wet, even though he was a fixture here. McGarr had spent the last few hours on the phone, learning everything he could about the man. Yes, the Toddler was a scourge; Hannigan was, on the other hand, an abomination, given how long he had abused his position while the Toddler's gear had spread among the young and the foolish.

"Lawrence of Arsippe!" Hannigan bawled at a barman, then swirled a finger to mean another round, even though McGarr had a full glass before him. "Classical literature, it's gas, what? Of all the shite we were made to read in Synge Street, wouldn't I remember the one writer? It's shameful."

More so the ruse. The school in Synge Street that was famous for its rigid discipline had produced a good number of graduates more notable than McGarr, but Hannigan had not gone there. McGarr had checked.

"Well now, Peter—Jaysis, how long has it been since we had a wet together? One on one, like they say."

An operative phrase, thought McGarr, smiling slightly. If he could frighten, then turn Hannigan into providing evidence, maybe a court might jail the Toddler for enough time to put him out of business. It would be a meager victory, given all the people he had killed. But gratifying nonetheless.

"What's up?" Hannigan asked after the drinks had been placed on the table.

"The Raglan Road house. I'd like to go over that with you if I could."

Suddenly Hannigan's smile seemed forced, and his eyes were wary. "Certainly. Surely. Christ, anny-thing for you, Peter. Still no luck running her down. And the bitch is big time, I tell yeh. Been into the gear since she was a wee lass, nine or ten. Can yeh imagine? Then twenty year ago or so they packed her off to a rehab—at our expense, mind—and didn't she turn around and start peddlin' the shit herself? To other kids. And her own people." Hannigan drank from his glass.

McGarr waited, suspecting what was coming.

"Fookin' Knackers, is what. Mickalou Maugham. The busker who was chained to the top of the Cliquot tree? But you'd know that, of course, having found him. She had a child by him. You'd think she would have learned from his example, where all this leads." Another sucking swallow.

That was when Hannigan's cell phone began bleating. "Ah, Jaysis, they never leave yeh alone." He pulled the device from his suit coat and extended the aerial. "Now what?"

In the pause his eyes darted at McGarr. "Uncle Bill! Hasn't it been a dog's age. No, well, I'm rather in company at the moment with a colleague." Another wait. "Yeh say ye're on a Callcard, yeh haven't much time."

Hannigan cupped the receiver and raised himself off the low stool. "It's me uncle Bill. Haven't heard from him in a month of Sundays and probably won't again. He's up in years, yeh know. D'yeh mind, Peter? I'll leave you to yehr drink. It won't take but a sec'."

McGarr nodded and reached for his glass, hoping Pauline Honan had already initiated the tap.

Hannigan was gone all of ten minutes and seemed less full of himself than he had been earlier. Knocking back what remained in his glass, he called to Lawrence of Arsippe for more. "Where were we?"

"Raglan Road. Biddy Nevins."

"Or Beth Waters," he put in with a knowing wink. "A slippery one, she is. All those years in England, the artist's cover and all. The young lad from the North for a lover when she needed to get off with a man. And didn't she have the old one, the Brit, when it was a woman's touch she fancied?

"Know what? I've a feelin' them two'll walk. Both has sworn they knew nothing about the dope themselves, and they let us draw some blood. They're clean, the both o' them. And the gear and all was all found in her room—the Biddy's."

"In the house."

Hannigan nodded.

"By you."

Again. "I have a nose for the stuff, I swear. Like instinct or somethin'."

Exactly, thought McGarr. Or somethin'.

More bleating broke in, this time from McGarr's jacket pocket.

"Your turn," said Hannigan. "It's gettin' fookin' ridic'lous, so. You'd want to be on the moon to get shed a the thing."

"And not even there," said McGarr, hearing Pauline's voice on the other end. He slid across the cushions of the banquette and stood. "Remember, 'One small step for mankind' and the golf and all? The only sound we missed was the club on the ball."

"No word of lie in that."

And therefore the first truth uttered between them. "It's the missus," said McGarr, adding to the plenum of falsehood. "Sure, I'll have to take it outside." He pointed to the cell phone. "Mine's older than yours and not up to the walls of a lounge bar."

Hannigan seemed relieved.

McGarr waited until he got out into the car park. "Fire away, Pauline."

"You're with him?"

"That's right."

"Think of that—why?"

"To turn him, of course."

"You mean, you've already spoken to the Toddler?"

"Yah—this after' at the Royal Dublin." It was no time to tell her what Ward had witnessed in the alley behind the hospital, which she'd learn of in the morning, given her *connections*. "Before he checked out."

"Good man. And thanks for the promotion."

McGarr waited for the slag; after all, it was Pauline.

"To missus, or are yeh just rubbing it in?"

To which there could be no reply. Still, she sounded up-beat.

"So, mister—earlier in the day, when the Toddler was still in hospital, didn't Hannigan ring him up? Says Hannigan, 'The missing persons in the Mercedes from Raglan Road? They're in Cork, in a Traveler campsite on the N-twenty-five between Midleton and Youghal. You can't miss it, it's the only Knacker lay-by between them two places.' The Toddler thanked him and rang off.

"And just now it was Uncle Bill again. Same voice, same Toddler. After the initial hello, et cetera, they fell into an encrypted mode, but nothing that couldn't be cracked."

By the computers that had been acquired to defeat the

scrambling and coding devices now being used by drug dealers, criminals, and the IRA, McGarr knew.

"On came questions, the Toddler asking Hannigan about
the two who were lifted in the Raglan Road raid."

"Tag Barry and Cheri Cooke."

"The same. He wanted to know what they were, how they
related to Nevins. Hannigan had all the answers since he said
he'd questioned them himself. Alone. No witnesses. The Toddler liked that.

"He said Barry was the lover and Cooke the lesbian lover.
Both fairly well past tense, though she wouldn't put them out
on the street unless they did drugs.

"Hannigan laughed over that, but the Toddler cut him off,
telling him to take them back to the Raglan house and put
them in there. 'You tell them it's house arrest.'

" 'What?' says Hannigan. 'I can't. Only a court can do that.'

" 'I don't fuckin' care about any fuckin' court,' says your
man in a broad Yank accent. 'Just fuckin' do it. You tell them
you made a mistake. You say they had nothing to do with her
drug trade. They were—*are*—innocent houseguests. You fill in
the blanks; it's what I pay you for.'

" 'And another thing: If you find her and lift her, put her
in there too.'

" 'What? The house? *Why?*'

"And here's the truly curious part. He adds, '*With* the package I'm sending you. It should be at your house now. I want
you to get it, place it in the freezer compartment of the fridge,
and then go back to Mount Joy and get them released.

" 'Once they're inside, you put a car in front and another
out back in the alley.'

"There was a pause. Then Hannigan says in a low, like defeated voice, 'What? Why? What will I tell my staff about that—that they're waiting for her? Like that? Out in the open?'

"'No, asshole—to keep them *in*. And when the woman, Biddy, shows up there, which she will some time or other, you're to tell the men to let her in too. But anybody else, even McGarr or one of his staff, no. You're to keep them out.'

"'I can't do that. What would I say?' Then, '*Will* I say?' You know, now with a bit of fear in Hannigan's voice.

"'Think of something: you're staking them out again or protecting them or . . . it's your bust, your territory, your turf. You'll handle it yourself.'

"'McGarr won't believe any of that.'

"Then there was a pause before the Toddler says, 'When I asked you along for the ride, Paul, what did I say?'

"'Ah, er'—how many jars have yeh give in him, Peter?— 'that there might be a bump.'

"'That's right, but mainly we'd be cruising. Well, the cruising is over. This is the bump.' He rang off."

McGarr wondered what the Toddler had in mind with the package. A bomb perhaps? Did he intend to blow up the place when and if Biddy returned and blame it on Tag Barry, who was from Belfast and had a Republican connection through a half brother? McGarr had checked his background too.

With the allegation of drug dealing and then a bomb, people would assume it was some rogue, gangster element of the IRA that either blew themselves up or were blown up as an example to others who would deal drugs. To send a message.

But a bomb was not the kind of message that the Toddler had sent in the past. His had always been more inventive and personal than that.

"What will you do?" Pauline asked, now that turning Hannigan into a tout would prevent the Toddler from acting on whatever plot he had in mind.

Would the Toddler involve himself? was the question. It was the only sort of message that meant anything to him. Alone meant no witnesses. Look at the lengths he had gone to eliminate the only witness who could link him to a murder.

"Nothing. He decided to 'cruise' with the Toddler. Now we'll let him feel the bump."

"Good man. I knew you'd say that. Whatever he gets, he deserves all of it and more. What about the other bit—the three in the Mercedes down in Cork? Will the Toddler go for them?"

McGarr had no idea, but it was a possibility, either to use them as hostages to exchange for her life or to punish her indirectly for wounding him. The latter, McGarr decided. Hostages were again too complicated and messy for the Toddler.

"I've put out a cot to stay here overnight. If I hear more, I'll be onto you."

"Thank you, Pauline."

Walking back into the lounge, McGarr again considered about Maggie Nevins, her husband, and their granddaughter down at the Traveler encampment in Midleton in Cork. And what the term "guard" should mean in the strict sense.

If the Toddler made a try for them and, being "guarded,"

they escaped, he'd realize that Hannigan's calls had been compromised. And the chance of trapping him would pass. But at least they'd be alive.

McGarr studied the dark, devious Hannigan, who was staring down into his whiskey, as though trying to divine some secret in the bottom of the glass. Flushed, sweating, *bumped* in every way.

He had chosen his path over at least the last dozen years, not just once but day in and day out, and McGarr would not keep him from his fate. He walked back toward the car park.

16
SMACK

Oney Maugham immediately took to life in a
Traveler camp. After the distant, impersonal, up-
market neighborhoods of Reigate and Ballsbridge,
where she had passed most of her girlhood years, the warmth
of the greeting that her grandparents and she received at the
Traveler encampment in Cork seemed magical.

Didn't everyone revere her father, Mickalou? Wasn't his
music playing on one of the many boom boxes that were
constantly blaring there even as her grandparents and she got
out of the car? It was as if they were expected.

Immediately they were surrounded by interested, adoring
people. "Yehr da, now," said one woman to Oney, "he was
brilliant, he was. The best of our people, going away."

"And don't she look the spit and image of him?" said *the*

McDonagh, the patriarch of the large Traveling family that had always been close to the Maughams and now proved it.

Her grandfather was given the use of a large, new caravan that had every amenity—toilet, shower, kitchen with microwave, the lot—"For however long you stay, Ned. And please God, may there be no end."

Tea was laid on, and the entire experience was like a revelation to Oney. She could not imagine any one of their neighbors in Ireland or England ever doing or saying such things. In those places her mother and she had remained at best curiosities, at worst probable Tinkers.

"I can tell from her blather she's a Knacker," Oney had once heard the Irish mother of a classmate say about Biddy while they were living in Surrey. "Worse still is her two-color eyes what come from incest." Oney had not told Biddy about that; for some reason she couldn't.

Instead she had carried the shame until now, when she decided that since they *were* Knackers, she would accept and be proud of it. At least here she belonged—in a caravan at the side of a road with her grandmother snoring in the bunk next to her. Feeling a contentment that she had never known, Oney slept soundly the night long, even though she knew the door was unlocked.

"It's a tradition," her grandmother had said. "Travelers never lock their doors against other Travelers. And we don't knock coming into another house. We've nothing to hide or fear from ourselves," which also seemed like a marvelous practice to Oney.

In the morning even the pervasive litter of old cars, scrap

metal, discarded toys, and just plain rubbish seemed to her like a necessary component of the community. And the continual noise: shouts, curses, music, dogs barking, people arriving and departing, and the whoosh of cars speeding down the motorway.

And over a "nice fry cooked out in the open so ye can taste the woodsmoke," Maggie went on. "Travelin' people is the best people. The old ones, the ones like McDonagh here, the ones that was reared up in the country and not nigh some city slum. They're the real Irish people. Good-hearted, open-handed, and they remember always who is who and all the closeness of the past.

"Sure, we were poor. *Are* poor. What's this"—Maggie cast her hand at the Mercedes, which was now covered with a tarp to conceal it—"but something that will soon be that?" Her hand moved to a pile of scrap not fifteen feet from the bumper of the expensive automobile.

"It's got no life. Not what you or Biddy have, or your handsome, brilliant father had which is still alive. List'." Maggie held a gnarled old hand to her ear, and they could hear a Mickalou tape playing deep within the camp. Maggie was wearing a red and white bandanna around her head that made the thick gold bands in her ears look like hoops.

"That's joy, music is. And spirit and divilment. Both your parents had loads o' that. And you too, which is nothin' to be ashamed of. Not at all. No. Just be careful when you let it out—for yourself and for me, since I love you."

Which was when five girls, all around Oney's age, approached the caravan. "How yiz?"

"How's yehrselves?" said Maggie, tilting her head back to assess them, dressed as they were in various conditions of outrageous.

The one who had spoken was a probable blonde with a green Mohawk haircut and rhinestone acne up the side of one nostril. A black spandex-like bandolier had flattened her breasts against her chest in a way that looked painful. Otherwise she was wearing a dungaree miniskirt and hobnail boots.

Most of the others had visible tattoos on their hands and arms, and many had the same one on their ankles—of a red spider, fangs showing, in the center of a pink and blue web.

Another one had what looked like a silver bone through her nose.

"We're wonderin' if yehr young one there would like to come out with us."

All for it, Oney smiled, put down her plate, and began to stand. She had never met people like this, although she had secretly wanted to. And after all, they were hers now, and she theirs.

"Out where, if ye don't mind my askin'?"

"We're goin' into Youghal to a meetin' and then shoppin', and dancin'."

"Dancin' where?" Maggie's hand came out and eased Oney back onto her chair.

"In a pub near Cork City. It's safe. Loads of kids go there."

"And this meetin' now. Who you meetin', if it's not too much to ask?"

"NA," said another one.

"And who's NA when he's at home?"

"Narcotics Anonymous," the Mohawk one said. "We go there every day."

Maggie's head went back, and she blinked, remembering. NA and AA and the Catholic Pioneers, who also swore off drink and drugs and were maybe the only reason her Biddy was still alive. All the meetings she had attended, all the support she had received. For Maggie, NA was golden, a miracle, and this girl could not have mentioned a better meeting, harrowing sight that she was.

"Go," said Maggie, pushing Oney up. "And have fun," which was what she needed to keep her mind off her mother. "Do you have any money?"

"Will I need any?"

Maggie had second thoughts, considering how naive and protected Oney had always been. Sure, compared with the others, she looked like a babe in the woods with her long, wavy hair, fresh complexion, and thin limbs. Yet she was fully a woman with good breasts and hips.

"You take this, and if you see somethin' you like, buy it, but don't tell your grandfather where it come from."

Maggie gave her an even hundred pounds, thinking she'd see some of the togs the others were wearing, which would help her blend in. And should. Her with a Traveler pedigree better than most.

"Don't be showin' how much you have," she whispered in Oney's ear as they kissed. "But if ye glam something you like, buy it for yourself. You should look the way you want."

• • •

Twelve hours later Ruth Bresnahan was still tailing the clutch of Traveler girls who had forayed into Youghal in an ancient and battered Bedford van that was easy to follow. The tailpipe gave off clouds of black, sooty, and foul No. 2 diesel smoke that had been banned by the EU.

It was the least of their illegality. The tags on the car actually belonged to another vehicle that had long since been scrapped, Bresnahan had learned after radioing in the number. Also, the tax stamp was missing. Alone the violation was enough for the vehicle to be seized, had it belonged to somebody else.

But Bresnahan could imagine some *shadog* at a road check simply waving the wreck on, loaded as it was with its fright of Tinker young ones, whose raucous chorus of explanation and/or complaint could make several hours of a guard's life unbearable. The assumption being, of course, that Travelers were incapable of obeying the law and didn't know any better.

From the vantage of her "plain brown wrapper"—as the squad's beige unmarked Toyotas were sometimes called—she had watched the girls visit the basement meeting room of a church where an NA placard had been hung in a window. Outside, a motley collection of mainly young and proletarian-chic people were smoking cigarettes and chatting. There was the odd older person—a dowdy housewife, an aging hippie, or an artist or a dated rocker with his long hair tied back in a ponytail. He had climbed out of a new Jag, and Ruth wondered what *his* story was.

An hour later and the meeting over, Bresnahan followed the girls back out onto the highway. They drove west through Midleton to a mall on the outskirts of Cork City, where they cruised the shops in an intimidating punker clutch, helping Oney Maugham select jeans, tank tops, and a few pieces of necessary jewelry—spiky earrings and a dog collar to match. But in the way that they established themselves—at doors, at windows—it was plain that they had been given the task of protecting the lass.

After that Oney was conveyed to a hair salon. Bresnahan nearly intervened, thinking that the girl's rainbow black, wavy tresses would be cropped. Instead she came out with her hair frazzled—tweaked into long, thin, curled spikes as though transformed by electroshock—that were arrayed to make her look much older and dangerous and not a little bit sexy. The earrings and dog collar only added to the impression. And given the tank top that all but exposed her shapely breasts and thin waist, Oney Maugham was without a doubt the most attractive one among them.

A pub—of all places, for recovering addicts—came next. But the large car park out back was filled with cars, and hearing music, Ruth assumed that the young Traveler women militant were there for dancing. Deciding to change into appropriate vestments that would make her appear a bit different and like part of the crowd herself, Ruth moved to the back seat. After all, she was only thirty and young-looking, if she did say so herself, and she would have a better view of Oney Maugham from the bar.

It was while she was scrunched down in the back seat of the Toyota, changing, that the windows were raked by head-lamps and a large American-type car pulled in beside her.

Lowering herself deeper into the shadow of the front seats, Ruth realized that she had even failed to lock the doors, feeling—as she often did—that nothing could happen to her since after all, she was a guard. And there she was in only a bra and knickers.

What to do? Nothing, at least for the moment. She'd wait for them to go into the pub or drive away.

Men—she could tell from the voices as the doors opened—stepped out, speaking in the always recognizable pancake accent of Dubliners. Now lying on the floor of the small car, Bresnahan tried to make herself as tiny as she could.

"Remember you, you two-eyed junkie. Yeh fook dis oop, yeh're dead. Now, what's her name?"

"Get out of my face, will yeh? I know what I have to do." The second voice was different, at once country but somewhat refined. But it also sounded tired or resigned or disconsolate in some way. "I'll do what you want."

"I asked yeh, what's her fookin' name?"

"Ah, fuck off! And get your hands off me!"

Bresnahan heard a sharp crack, like from a slap, and her car rocked as somebody fell against it. And another crack.

"It's Oney, for Chris' sake. Oney!"

"Don't," a third voice said. "You'll ruin his looks, and where will we be?"

"I don't care. Once a junkie fook, always a junkie fook. He browns me off."

"Well, you leave him to me now. Get back in the car. You'll want a bit of a rest if we're to do the job at the camp and get back to Dublin by morning."

"Knacker scut," the second man muttered, evidently climbing back into the car. A door clumped shut.

Then in a low, confiding voice the third man, who

sounded much older than the other two, said, "You should know this, Sean, since your life depends on it. You're not doing this for me. No. Who you're doing it for is bigger than me, much bigger, and if you fail him, you're dead. You hear me?" There was a pause, then: "I want you to say that you've heard me."

The first man, who was much younger and wearing a white shirt—Bresnahan could see—grunted. All she could see of the other man was a swath of jacket, dress shirt, and stylish tie.

"I realize you don't feel good about this, nobody does. But we've been given orders, and this is who we are, you and me. What we chose, years ago. Maybe it was a wrong decision then, maybe it's still wrong now, but we've no choice but to go through with it. You carry it off no hitches, I'll take care of you. I promise. That means, out of that horrid halfway house you're in and out of the country, if you like. Madeira, the Canaries. You name it.

"Or back to university. You want that, it's yours. If you want back on the gear even, it's yours. Your choice. Now, then. Tell me what you have to do."

The boy sighed. "Get her to come out here with me. Get her into the car."

"Where we'll take over. Then what?"

"I walk away, down the road to the next pub. I wait in the bar. When I see you, I come out to the car and take her into the lounge. I order two lemon sodas and sit with her. I make sure she sits upright, doesn't nod off. If need be, I walk her around. You show up, we leave."

"Good lad. Remember now, this could make you or break you. I know it's distasteful, but it's probably the most important thing you've ever done in your life. And like me, you've no choice, really, but to do it right. Now, off with you."

As the boy walked away, Bresnahan got a look at his face, which looked enough like Oney Maugham to be her brother—or Mickalou Maugham's son—apart from his two-colored eyes. They, of course, were like Oney's mother. And while somewhat gaunt, the boy—Sean by name—was squarely built with narrow hips and long, thin limbs. And he was handsome in the extreme.

When the man opened the car door to get back in behind the wheel, his passenger said, "At the Traveler camp, when we do them other Knackers, that scut is mine."

The car door closed.

Reaching between the seats, Ruth Bresnahan slowly pulled her clothes and her purse toward her. The leather bag was heavy, weighted with the 9 mm Glock that she kept in a zippered side pocket. She might still be unclad, but she no longer felt naked.

Oney Maugham could not believe what she was seeing when the boy walked into the bar. It was as if the clock had been turned back: Her father had been cloned but given her mother's two-color eyes.

Otherwise the boy looked in size and shape—his face, his hair—like the very same Mickalou Maugham who had peered out at Oney from album covers for all of her sixteen years. Those were the only good images of her father she possessed, all that she remembered of him.

Then, then—come here! Oney could have died happy

right there. Wasn't this boy one of them, a Traveler? And not like the other Traveler boys at the bar, who were either too shy to dance or into the drink, which was unacceptable in *her* crowd, as Oney now thought of the girls she was with.

No. This boy was different. Hands in pockets, not caring that he was being stared at, which he was, he came right over to the table. And he was gorgeous, there was no other word for him: dark with chiseled facial features, square shoulders, and a nice tan that was set off by a fresh-pressed white shirt with three buttons open.

Oney peeked into the vent; yes, he had a hairy chest. When she glanced up at his face, those eyes that were so different yet so familiar were staring at her. Blushing, mortified, she wrenched her own eyes away.

"How yiz?" he said in a low, subdued, and (to Oney) very romantic voice, his eyes still taking them in one at a time. "How yiz feelin'?" It was an NA set phrase. And then, turning to Oney's new friend with the Mohawk: "There's Rita. How's Rita?" She was like the leader of their pack.

"Sean McDonagh," Rita said, studying him for a while before moving over so he could sit beside her. "Still in the Hope House?"

He nodded, his eyes again moving along the line of young women.

"Still clean?"

Again.

"How long is it now?"

"Eleven months. Plus the detox. Make it a year."

The girls thumped the table. "Good man," said one or two.

"How do you feel?"

His two-color eyes swung to Rita, and he tilted his head slightly to the side to mean not good, not bad. "Real, I guess."

"What's that supposed to mean?" Rita demanded. "What's wrong with real? Sure, you're not thinkin' of going back out and using again?"

Sean McDonagh—who could only be one of the McDonaghs who were now being so helpful to Oney and her family—shook his head. After a while he added, "It's just . . . my life is missing something. I dunno what."

Oney was not the only girl there who had an idea of what. Again she had to pull her eyes away, just to gather breath.

A barman now appeared, and Sean McDonagh placed a twenty-pound note on the table and ordered a round. "Whatever they're having and some crisps. Or a menu? Are yiz hungry, girls? I am. Order what you like."

He seemed so calm and casual and open-handed that Oney couldn't take her eyes off him. Nor could she speak when he pointed at her and said, "You?" as the barman was taking their food order.

She only waved a hand, blushing again. Eat? She'd choke if she tried.

They spoke of this and that—the "program," people they knew, places they'd been—waiting for the food, and Oney tried to control her emotions. She'd had crushes before on boys in school, but the way this came on, how she was attracted to him, was something almost scary. Just glancing his way made her heart race.

After they ate, the band began playing, and most of the girls got up to dance, mostly with each other, and Oney kept hoping that Sean McDonagh would not ask her to dance, since she couldn't. Or at least couldn't dance like the others out on the floor.

But he didn't either. Or wouldn't. And Oney began praying that there'd always be somebody else at the table and not just her. But after a while they found themselves alone.

"You have a name?"

"Oney," she managed to say. Now she couldn't look at him, and she looked everywhere but.

"Oney what?"

"Maugham." It sounded like a cry for help.

"Any relation to the Mick?"

Her eyes flashed at him. "My father."

He straightened up a bit and smiled. He had a nice smile. "You're jokin'."

Oney shook her head; she could feel the bright patches on her cheeks. They were burning.

"Then you're Princess Oney."

She cocked her head and chanced to look at him directly, put out now that he seemed to making fun of her. "Excuse me?"

"Well, if your mother and father were the King and the Queen of the Buskers, I'd say that makes you a princess. Unless, of course, you're trying to remain anonymous."

"Are you having me off?"

"Not that I know of. D'you dance?"

Oney panicked. A slow song was just being played, and she'd hate herself—tomorrow, the next day, for the rest of her life—if she said no, and he never asked her again. She managed a shrug.

"Want to dance?"

She shrugged again. But when he took her hand to lead her out of the booth, she felt dizzy. And her body, like a traitor, was actually shaking and stiff when he put his arms around her.

"Are you cold?"

She pushed him away. "If you make fun of me, I swear, I'll walk away and never speak to you again."

He waited for a moment, regarding her, then said, "Relax. We're only having a dance. It's simple, like floating. I won't bite you."

Yet, thought Sean McDonagh, again taking hold of her and beginning to dance. Already he was hating himself for what they would do to her the moment he got her to the car. Which was what?

Shoot her up, whack her with a bolus load, and then fill her clothes with more to carry on. It might take hours, but they'd hold her down and force a little on her first, showing her how it was done: the spoon, the match, the needle. The mix they'd use would feel like sex but better, and they'd jack it in and out of her until she nearly passed out.

But the feeling, the euphoria, the ecstasy would be retained in memory, never to be expunged, and she'd go back to it again and again and again, trying to recapture that first high and never succeeding. And given her parents and who she was—a susceptible Tinker, like McDonagh himself—there'd be no going back until she bottomed out or died. More probably the latter. One way or another, intravenous drugs were mostly fatal to beautiful women, since few men ever wanted to hear them say no.

And no woman she. Yet. She was still a child for however

long it took him to get her out into the car park. Which is what drugs did: relieved you of your youth, your innocence, your joy and spirit.

Why her? he asked himself as he felt her warm, soft, young body relax and move into his own. Because somebody in her family had offended some Dublin dealer or gangster, Mc-Donagh assumed, having seen it before. It was punishment of the dirtiest kind, meant to send a message to others who would brook their authority.

Gearmen were sent out, dope laid on, mounds of it if necessary. And then withdrawn, only to be restored for *considerations*. He could only imagine what they would be for the person in his arms. Up until her early death, which at least would be a release.

They had come for him particularly. "It's you," the Monck had told him. "Nobody else. He wants you."

"He? He who?"

With a backhand swipe, the Monck had knocked Mc-Donagh to the floor of the halfway house that he and Baileys—they called the larger, older man, like the liqueur and the pub—had barged into. "He who a junkie fook like you need never know, that's who."

"But why me?" he had complained. "Why not somebody who's out there?" Using, he meant. And you could control absolutely. "I'm clean. It's over for me. I want to stay clean." And return to health and life and maybe even university. Someday. He didn't have to rush. And couldn't, not having the money.

"Because I say it's you, you Knacker scut, and if you don't, I'll fookin' kill yeh myself."

And would, Sean McDonagh was sure, the Monck being responsible for more than a few deaths of people he'd known.

Dancing on, now with the girl's lovely head against his chest, he asked himself if he'd had any options really. Not then, not with the two of them standing by the door and the Monck with a gun under his jacket, McDonagh had been sure.

Or even later in the car, say, when they'd pulled up at a light. He might have hopped out and run into a field, but how long could he keep that up with no money, no clothes, and his two-color eyes, which would give him away no matter where he went?

Which thought made him realize suddenly the whys and wherefores of the situation. The big man, the "bigger than me"—Baileys had said—was the Toddler, who had murdered Mickalou Maugham, it was said in the Traveling community, and had tried to murder Biddy Nevins because (it was further said) she had seen him murder another man at the top of Grafton Street.

And here was his daughter in Sean McDonagh's arms. Why? Because—he leaned back so he could look down on her; he smiled, and she smiled back—he looked so much like her father with her mother's two-color eyes. McDonagh had long known of that too, the families being close.

The Toddler, who was the worst of them all, which explained the fear that he had felt in the Monck and Baileys. It was said not a gram of heroin was sold in Ireland that the Toddler hadn't brought in and that he was one with the police.

McDonagh eased the girl's head down on his chest and twirled her around. Once, twice. He was a good dancer, and it was true, he could float.

Mickalou Maugham. When he was a child, McDonagh's mother and father could sing his songs, verse after verse after verse, and the old mainly instrumental music that Maugham had saved and recorded from the Gaeltacht and other Gaelic-speaking areas of Scotland, Cornwall, and Brittany was always playing in their caravans. He'd even visited them once, when McDonagh was maybe six; Sean could still remember the crowd that had surrounded the tall dark man and the hooley his music had inspired.

The music had stopped, yet they were still holding each other. The other girls, Rita and the other young ones she had come with, were looking at them. Watching, waiting maybe for something like a kiss. Then, of course, he could take her outside. Without them.

Instead McDonagh lowered his head to her ear. "Tell Rita I told you the Toddler knows you're here. He sent some men down here to shoot you up."

She pulled away from him. "What d'you mean?"

"Just tell Rita, she'll know. But tell her as well she's to do nothing stupid, that I'll take care of it if I can. And if I can't, she's to know it's the Monck and Baileys. Acting for the Toddler. Got that?"

She blinked. "I think so. Are you jokin'?"

He shook his head. "And also you're the finest Traveling girl I've seen in many a long day, and I hope to see you again."

Her face darted at his, and she kissed him hard on the mouth. Even their teeth clashed. Before she turned and rushed back to the others, who clapped, applauding her derring-do.

Passing by the bar, McDonagh found a large, heavy, empty whiskey bottle in a litter bin and made straight for the back door. It had been awhile since he'd been in a serious fight, but the other two were old, heavy men, and during the last year McDonagh had regained most of his strength. And his quickness. He was quick if nothing else.

Also, he'd have the advantage of surprise. They'd never think he'd have the courage to attack them—skinny, junkie Knacker scut that he was.

The Monck would have a gun for sure, he decided, walking across the dark parking lot toward the car on an angle that would keep him from being seen. Baileys maybe not. He'd whack the Monck in the face, then gouge him and try to get his gun. And if he did, he shoot them both, right there. No questions asked.

The rage that he thought he'd come to terms with—at himself and his addiction and all the years he'd wasted and been exploited and conned and abused—now boiled up in his throat. Why hadn't he considered fighting back before? Why had he accepted the lie that they were powerful and he weak, just because he had succumbed to an addiction over which ultimately he'd had no control once the stuff was in him?

Holding the heavy bottle by its neck behind his back, McDonagh wrenched open the passenger door of the large American car, frightening the Monck. "Christ, the fook you doin' back here? Where's the girl?"

When the Monck leaned out to look toward the pub, McDonagh whipped the bottle with all he had, dashing its square corner against the Monck's forehead. It bounced off and did not break. Again. It did. Using the jagged end, he then chopped down again and again, gouging, hacking, twisting, digging it into the fucker's fat face.

Who roared and batted at the bottle with his left hand, his right jumping into his jacket for—McDonagh saw the handle even before it was out—a large black automatic.

He gouged again, but still the gun came up. Which was when the Monck's head exploded and something struck McDonagh's chest, knocking him right off his feet and up against the next car. He couldn't see; he couldn't stand. He slid off the car onto the macadam, and everything went dim and grainy.

Ruth Bresnahan had to leap over him. Bending at the waist, her Glock in both hands, she shouted, "Drop the gun!"

But the car lurched forward, then swung around, spilling the dead man from the passenger seat. It bolted across the parking lot, scattering the girls who had been running toward them. And Bresnahan dared not fire. The car jounced out onto the road and disappeared into the night.

One girl screamed. Oney Maugham threw herself down on the young man who'd been shot and was covered mainly with the other man's blood.

"Call the guards, call an ambulance!" another shouted, as she ran toward the crowd that was now gathering in the car park door of the pub.

The girl with the bright green Mohawk raised a boot and began stomping the gory head of the dead man. "Fookin' fucker fook!"

Remembering what the two men had discussed earlier, Bresnahan pulled her away. "What's the fastest way to your camp?"

The girl looked down at Bresnahan's gun, as though seeing it for the first time. "Who are you?"

"Guard. Can you take me there? The quickest way."

"Why?"

"Because those men were also planning to murder Ned and Maggie Nevins. For the Toddler." And the survivor now could not very well return to Dublin having accomplished nothing. The Toddler would not allow it.

The girl blinked, then spun around and dropped down by the dead man. She pulled the gun from under his jacket.

"I'll take that," said Bresnahan.

"The fook you will."

Bresnahan did not hesitate, feeling incompetent that she had let the shooter escape without at least firing at him. Like a club, her free hand came down on the girl's wrist, the gun clattering on the tar. Howling, the girl crumpled to her knees.

Bresnahan snatched up the weapon. "Now, get in the fookin' car and show me the way." When the girl hesitated, Ruth grabbed the green mane and pulled her to her feet. "In!" She shoved her into the passenger seat, and slammed shut the door.

"The rest of you, help him!" She pointed at the courageous wounded boy.

Reaching the Traveler camp, Baileys knew what he had to do and where. He had scouted the place earlier, paid fifty quid to a Traveler drunk in the nearest pub for the information. Unlike the Monck—whose plan Sean McDonagh and the dance had been—it was how Baileys worked: efficient and informed.

And he hardly slowed down, since he had long ago

learned there was only one way to approach these people. Hard set and dead on. They respected nothing and nobody— not bureaucrats, not the police, not even priests anymore. Only superior force, which he had in the boot of the car.

He didn't even much care if he was seen; at least then he'd have to be identified, captured, charged, and tried. But if he came back empty-handed, he'd be dead, summarily, the Toddler having made it plain. "I haven't asked much of you ever, my man," he had said from the Royal Dublin Hospital two days ago. "It's all been one way, me providing you. Now there's something you and the Monck can do for me. Yourselves, since I want it done right."

Wrong. But at least he could put the blame for the mistake on the Monck and McDonagh, since with any luck at all they were dead. And he could always do the girl again. Himself.

After skidding to a stop in front of the caravan with the tarp-covered Mercedes by it, Baileys jumped out and moved directly to the boot of his car. A collection of maybe a dozen men and boys were sitting around a campfire about a hundred feet off with bottles of Guinness in their hands, watching him now. Closely and intent.

Not moving when he pulled the Steyr Aug Bullpup assault rifle from the back of the car and slotted in a clip of forty-two rounds, slipping another under his belt. And still not moving when he closed the lid of the trunk and made for the stairs of the caravan, holding the stubby gun down by his side.

It was a high-tech–looking thing, a sweep of cast alloy with a stubby barrel and a long silencer that made it sound as if it were blowing bubbles.

Baileys's real name was Donal Davies. Wearing his usual

dark business suit, shirt, and tie, he was a hugely built, balding man who at forty-eight had run to fat. He had been a drug dealer since his days at Trinity College, where he discovered that he really didn't care for mindlessness himself, while others would pay anything for a steady supply of hashish or heroin flown in via the diplomatic pouch of his addict brother, who was the Irish consul in Istanbul.

With profits always over 1,000 percent, he could think of no other career as rewarding. But now rich beyond his wildest college dream, he should have got out years ago, retired to the Maldives, and lived like a pagan prince, he realized as he climbed the metal stairs of the caravan.

The door, when he tried it, was open. Stepping in, he could hear snoring. "Maggie?" he called into the deep shadows. "Ned? You there?"

He heard a grunt and then a cough, and a figure moved in one of the bunks. The snoring was coming from the other side of the narrow caravan. Which was enough for Baileys.

"What is it?" an old woman's voice asked. "Do I know you?"

"No. But I have a message from the Toddler." Baileys raised the stubby gun to direct a burst of high-velocity 5.56 mm fire at the old woman.

But something flashed in the darkness—again and again and again—driving him back to the door, over the metal strap, out the door, and then off into the night, sailing back, arms out, where he landed in a heap in the dirt and mud at the bottom of the stairs.

With curious dispassion and little palpable pain, he tried to place the stocky older man who now appeared in the doorway, gun in hand. He'd seen him before, but where?

And the woman he could see getting out of a car a few feet away: tall, red. He'd seen her before too. She also had something in her hand, and he could see up her skirt, which caused him to smile slightly. The absurdity of noticing that when he was dying.

When he tried to raise his body and reach for the Bullpup, which had fallen a few feet away, the man made no attempt to rush down the caravan steps and prevent him. Instead his gun came up and flashed once more.

Bresnahan paused, her own gun now pointed at the man on the ground. But it was over, McGarr's final shot having struck Baileys in the middle of the forehead. Cleanly, the wound looking like the smudge of absolution given on Ash Wednesday.

Straightening up, Bresnahan tried to act calm, composed, as if it were all in a day's work. Which it had been of late. But her voice was reedy and forced. "Who is he, Chief?"

Or was he? thought McGarr as he moved slowly down the stairs, ejecting the clip from his Walther and slipping it into a jacket pocket. McGarr had always told himself he never liked this part of the job, and he didn't. But somehow this was different, the dead man at his feet having made himself eminently executable. Killing the Toddler might even prove pleasurable, he imagined. And think of all the others he'd save.

"Baileys, he's called. One of the Toddler's 'independent producers.' "

"And a fookin' scut!" said a girl with a chartreuse Mohawk rushing around Bresnahan. When she raised a boot to stomp the fallen man's head, Ruth grabbed the back of her denim jacket and spun her toward the gathering crowd.

Said McGarr, "I'll need some names, some statements." As to how the dead man was reaching for the assault rifle when McGarr dispatched him.

Bresnahan nodded and reached for the Bullpup. "And after that?" Should she go back to Dublin? she meant.

It was strangely quiet, given what had happened. McGarr scanned the crowd, who were speaking only in whispers, regarding him with a mixture of fear, awe, and gratitude.

McGarr turned his head to Ned and Maggie Nevins above him in the door of their caravan. "You should shift now." As they had discussed when McGarr had first arrived. "And you with them," he said to Bresnahan. "Don't ring me up at the office with your new position." In case Hannigan was more adept than he seemed. "Phone Noreen at the picture gallery."

"Rita, where be Oney?" Maggie demanded of the girl with the Mohawk.

"Back at the dance."

McGarr walked toward the crowd which broke before him. His personal car, which was a Mini-Cooper.

"Where you off to, Chief?" Bresnahan asked to his back.

"Dublin." And the Raglan Road house that now had the "packet" in the freezer and two of Hannigan's guards posted out front, all at the Toddler's request.

Why? Because the Toddler knew Biddy Nevins/Beth Waters would return there eventually. And how did he know that? Because he would make sure she did by—McGarr had no clue, only the feeling that he should get back there fast.

How long would it take? Dublin was 140 miles away by the best highways, and his car—small, agile, and fast—could top the ton (100 mph) on straightaways. Two hours with a portable dome light spinning on the roof, he decided. And no tie-ups.

17
BANG! BANG!

Catching the final few rays of the setting sun, the
complex of new buildings off in the distance
looked more like the nest of an eagle than the lair
of a Toddler, thought Hugh Ward. Hanging well back, he was
following Biddy Nevins in her new Volvo across the treeless
expanses of the Wicklow Mountains.

In Baggot Street near the Royal Dublin Hospital, Ward
had waited nearly ten hours before a speedy Ford stopped at
the rear bumper of the parked Volvo to block traffic. A car-
rot-headed passenger hopped out, key in hand. In mere seconds he was behind the wheel, had the engine started, and
was out in traffic, almost before Ward had his own car ticking
over.

And then they were off to the races, the Volvo and Ford

jinking in and out of traffic, around buses and lorries, and nipping between lackadaisical, homeward-bound commuters. They even drove up on a footpath for a while, losing Ward completely.

He wasn't worried. The general direction was south, where he alerted all available traffic gardai, and the Volvo and Ford were passed from picket to picket until they were observed pulling up in front of a bus kiosk. There a woman got behind the wheel of the Volvo. Ward asked the next picket to stop traffic, until he could catch her up.

Now he was tailing her across a barren ridge a few miles beyond east of Hacketstown. In the near distance was the Toddler's estate, glowing like a castle in the air, and Ward imagined that any visitor or threat could be seen miles away around a full 360 degrees of the compass.

Fenced all around with chain link and razor wire, the estate had great chrome steel gates by the road with flooded bogs, like moats, to either side. From there the drive was straight and open across maybe a quarter mile of bog, until it struck the flank of the mountain and began switching back and forth. Small structures dotted each corner.

Sentry houses? Or pillboxes with gun slits? In the failing light, Ward could not make them out exactly, but the place had the definite look of a fortress

Maybe a half mile away now, he slowed, then stopped to watch Biddy turn her car onto the drive, where another car was parked, as though the driver—having failed to open the gates—had walked around them and then up the long drive to the house on the crest of the mountain.

But Biddy hardly glanced at it. Instead she backed across the road to the far margin of the opposite shoulder, which was a sloped hillock of maybe twenty-five feet. Ward shook his head, knowing what she would do.

How far did she think she would get, given the Toddler's prowess with a rifle? And the complaints—never proven—that he had not hesitated to fire at other intruders. In the past few days the squad had dug up everything possible—official and otherwise—about the man.

Yet the sparkling green Volvo shot forward, off the hillock, across the road, and straight toward the bright metallic gates that flew up in the air when the car struck them. But held.

Whole seconds later the harsh metallic sound came to Ward.

Yet undaunted, Biddy reversed and again crossed the road to the hillock, the grille of the Volvo spewing steam. And again she shot forward, this time bursting through the barrier, sending one of the gates bouncing across the top of her car that careered down the long dirt road toward the mountain.

Ward began moving forward, thinking he should at least be a bit closer, when suddenly the Volvo jerked or halted or staggered momentarily, before lurching forward for another hundred yards and rolling to a stop.

Only then did Ward hear the noise—a sharp crack followed by a howling roar that echoed through the mountains—and could be just one thing: the report of some large-caliber weapon.

• • •

To Biddy it felt as if the car had struck a boulder. Or a small tree. The force of the collision threw her against the steering wheel, and the air bag deployed in her face, knocking her back against the seat.

Then the windscreen on the passenger side exploded, and the headrest burst into a cloud of leather and stuffing. Biddy only just managed to open the door and roll out of the car when the window above her head shattered.

She threw herself off the drive and rolled down the grassy verge to conceal herself in a depression in the bog where peat had been cut years past and the water was only ankle deep. The car suddenly exploded in a stunning fireball that singed her eyebrows and hair. And even through the roar of the blaze the howl came to her: of a rifle.

Which discouraged her. Utterly. She felt weak, powerless, dead. How could she hope to challenge such a man who could strike her from such a distance? She'd been a bloody eejit to try. Even the bag that she had strapped across her chest was a burden too great to bear, weighed down as it was with the handgun.

She had to get out of there and move away from the bright light of the blazing car. If she kept herself low in the peat trenches, she might make the road, where she would hail the first passing car. Or—she now remembered—boost the car that was parked there, which gave her some hope.

Yet feeling more terrified than she had in all her born days, Biddy set out. The *shadog*, the one who had told her to go back to her house where they could protect her, had been right. She'd do that now. She might even ring him up and tell him, so that the police would be in place when she got there.

• • •

He—Ward, the *shadog* who had warned her—was out of his car, having determined the position from which the rifle was being fired. It was not from the house. In fact, it was beyond the fence of the Toddler's estate on top of another ridge that was rather close to Ward's car.

It could be dangerous traversing a bog at night. But Ward had lived near one as a child in Waterford, and he had a feel for the terrain. Also, he was approaching the sniper on a flank from his target, Beretta drawn.

When Ward got closer, he could see two figures that looked like children and seemed to have abandoned their attack. Or counterattack. They were standing away from their weapons, which were now plainly visible on two three-legged stanchions. Hands folded at their waists, they did not move as Ward approached.

The weapon, he guessed, was an M-1 Garand equipped with a night scope. The other stanchion supported a large complex-looking spotting scope that, given its bulbous shape, was probably also enhanced by infrared.

The shooter bowed to Ward when he announced himself, then placed her hands together in a position of prayer or supplication. Both she and her spotter were pretty, doll-like Oriental women dressed in tight gold dresses with high collars, ornamental headbands, and slippers to match.

Ward lowered his eye to the nightscope of the rifle and peered into the smoldering cinder that was now Biddy Nevins's automobile. He then glanced at the Garand, which was both an antique and unusual in Ireland.

But he knew it was one of the most accurate and powerful combat weapons ever made, especially when shooting—Ward picked up the box of cartridges on a camp stool between the stanchions and played the beam of his penlight over the label—.300 Winchester Magnum shells with 176-grain Sierra bullets. High-priced, specialty ammunition, perfect for target shooting. Or assassinations.

Ward dropped a shell into the breach and shoved the bolt forward, locking it into the chamber. Through the nightscope, which made everything appear green, he sighted in the bonnet ornament on the burning Volvo that was maybe a thousand yards away.

Ward wasn't an expert shot by any means, but he was adept in most things that required hand-eye coordination, and he rather enjoyed target shooting. Touching his cheek to the rifle stock, he pulled in a breath, held it, and waited until he could assess how the beating of his heart affected his sighting in of the bonnet ornament. But the stanchion was sturdy and the movement slight.

Was there a crosswind? No, it was virtually still now that night had come on.

Slowly he squeezed the trigger, the stem of which had been filed and oiled to reduce friction, he could tell. Without the slightest errant movement, the pin snapped down on the case head of the cartridge, firing the gun. Even the recoil seemed muted against his shoulder.

When Ward brought the scope down onto the target

again, it was gone. Gun and scope were perfectly matched; the shooter could not have missed Biddy Nevins with that weapon fired from this perch.

Straightening up, he said, "You weren't trying to kill her?"

The woman, who was standing in back of the gun and must have been the shooter, shook her head. "Scare her," she said in barely intelligible English.

"Why?"

"So she go home. Please excuse." From the sleeve of her dress she pulled out a slip of paper, on which the other woman, who was much younger, trained the beam of a pocket torch. The older woman read, "My name Lo-Annh. This . . . my nice"—she glanced up at Ward—"Hon-Soh."

"Niece," he corrected.

She bowed slightly before continuing. "Cambodia staff Mr. Bacon. We hereby request"—there was a pause—"political asylum." She glanced up at Ward, her pretty dark eyes triumphant.

But when Ward got the two women down to his car and the lights switched on, he could see that the other car, the one that had been parked by the now-smashed gates and still-burning Volvo, was gone. Taken, he assumed, by the only other person in the area who had ever boosted cars.

He reached for the cell phone to ring up his office.

The car that was parked near the Toddler's gate had been unlocked with an ignition key in the switch. A note taped to the steering wheel said, "Miss Waters, You should take this car straight back to your house. I have guards posted front and back, and I guarantee your safety." It was signed "Detective Superintendent Hugh G. Ward."

Biddy folded it carefully and placed it her purse. She didn't know how he'd anticipated her coming there, but he was a genius. And a savior.

Biddy had turned the car directly toward Dublin.

18

LOCK OUT, LOCK IN

 Foolishly, since the Toddler had established himself in her Raglan Road house whole hours before Cheri Cooke and Tag Barry were brought back by Hannigan. And before guards were posted outside.

He'd even had time to wire electronically front and rear doors, a small red and a green light on a monitor strapped to his left wrist informing him whenever either was opened.

Also, he had conducted an exhaustive search of the place, attic to cellar, where he discovered a coal chute that had been used in earlier times. He had slipped the latch and worked it open to provide himself with an avenue of escape, should he need it. It was there he remained—deep within the coal bin of the basement—until his cell phone rang, the sound muted in the pocket of his black pile combat jacket.

But once Hannigan informed him that he "had it on good authority—the bloody *best!*—yehr woman is headed back to the house there. Ward just called it in. She should be arriving within the hour," the Toddler moved up the stairs toward Tag Barry, who was maintaining his own beery vigil at the kitchen table.

Bottle in hand, a television blaring on a counter by the fridge, he'd been ensconced there since his return, getting up only for further drink or the jakes. The Toddler despised drunks even more than he did junkies, alcohol being an even sloppier addiction than dope.

"Who's that?" Barry asked, not bothering to turn to the cellar door that the Toddler had opened. "You, Cheri? Sit yehr sorry arse down here and have a beer. It'll do ye a world of good. Ye're an old, gone cow, and you should get used to it." All said in a sloshy northern accent.

"Or is it you, Bid? If it is, you listen good. I've got somethin' to say." He paused dramatically, a drunken edge to his voice. "You'll want to be speakin' more respectful like if I'm to stay here."

"I really don't think she wants you to," the Toddler replied, walking past Barry to the fridge. "You should read her diary. The spelling's wild, but one thing's perfectly clear. You've slipped from prince to putz. She now hates your ass. Big time."

The Toddler opened the fridge door, pulled out a long-neck Bud, and pried the cap off.

He set the bottle in front of Barry. "Drink up. It could be your last."

The young man's eyes remained focused on the Toddler's hands and the whitish condom-looking rubber gloves he was wearing.

From the freezing compartment the Toddler removed the packet that Hannigan had placed there and would link the Garda chief superintendent to whatever transpired in the house, in case there was a cockup.

Pulling open the tie string of the package, the Toddler dumped the Dan Wesson .44 on the table, then stuffed the waxed wrapping paper with Hannigan's fingerprints, gun oil, and gunpowder all over it into a pocket. Hannigan, who was despised by his staff and whose usefulness to the Toddler was now over.

Next he pulled a box from the pocket of his tight black shooting jacket—the Biddy's flat-nosed shells that he had found above the door leading down into the basement. Like the very best of omens, the discovery had pleased him greatly. The entire operation was falling into place with a facility that was almost artful.

Flicking open the cylinder, he loaded the immense weapon that was every bit as powerful as it looked.

"That Biddy's?" Barry asked.

The Toddler shook his head. "But the nice part? It's enough like hers to be hers, if you know what I'm saying. Right down to the ammunition. And guess what?" He clicked the chamber shut and glanced up at Barry. "I'm going to make her a present of it. I plan to leave it here when I'm through."

"And take hers away."

The Toddler's eyes widened. "Very good! Very good indeed, Mr. Barry! For a drunk like yourself. But I can imagine you're now suddenly sober."

Barry had no reply. He was still staring at the gun. After a while he asked, "Are yeh goin' to shoot me?"

"Eventually, but not for—oh, fifteen or twenty minutes, I'd hazard. You've got time. Drink up. You know the saying: Sure, he died, but he died drunk and happy. So, drink."

Barry's head turned to the two bottles in front of him, one half empty, the other full. "Are yeh not havin' one yehrself?"

"Poison. Never touch the stuff. Only fools do."

Barry took that in for a moment or two. "What if I was to say, I never would either? Again."

"I wouldn't believe you, and you wouldn't yourself. So, go on. Enjoy, while you can."

Barry shook his head. "I can't. I've lost me taste for it."

"Then stick out your neck."

"Stick it out how?"

"Like you're showing me the label at the back of your collar. And not to worry. You'll hardly feel a thing."

"Will I, like, come to? Sometime?"

The Toddler canted his head, considering. "After a fashion. But not like your old self, since my plan is to have you stay right here at this table until I need to have you dead."

Barry's eyes were now roaming the kitchen wildly, his brow beaded with sweat. "What if I said—I mean, I *promised*—I would? Stay right here until—"

"I wouldn't believe that either, nor do you."

Barry nodded; it was the truth. Given an opening, he'd bolt. And should have with Biddy when she left. Why hadn't he heeded her warning? He glanced down at the bottles and knew why. "Then I'll be dead after I stick out me neck?"

"No, I didn't say that. I said you won't be dead until I shoot you, which is some minutes off."

"I suppose I don't have a choice in that either."

"Not unless you like pain, which I can and will supply if you resist. But do what you will. You're the boss."

With a drunken sigh, Tag Barry wagged his head from side to side, muttered something like "Just me fookin' luck," and stuck out his neck. Chopping down with his free hand, the Toddler broke it for him, fracturing vertebra C-4. It meant that while still alive and able to breathe on his own, Barry had suffered instant paraplegia. He would definitely stay put until the Toddler was able to return and make noise.

Catching the head before it could thump down and topple the bottles, the Toddler laid its cheek on the table. That eye was still open. "Blink if you can hear me."

It did.

The Toddler stepped back quickly to keep the urine off his shoes; it was spilling over the front of the chair and pooling on the tiles around the table, as the young man's muscles lost the signal from his brain, and all the beer leaked out. "Good lad. See, I wasn't lying. I'll be back for you in a bit."

Taking the stairs up to the second floor two at a time, the Toddler moved right to the master bedroom. There Cheri Cooke was sleeping in the Biddy's bed, hat on and snoring at the ceiling, like a spinster out of an old movie.

After carefully lowering himself down, the Toddler slid under the bed to wait for the old woman's erstwhile paramour. Who might be arriving sometime soon. Listening to the old woman's noisy rumbling only a foot or so above him, he felt suddenly elated in a way he hadn't experienced for a long time, not since the night of the Bookends, when after he'd killed them, McGarr had visited him in his granny's kitchen.

And he wondered if all along it wasn't the killing that he enjoyed most but rather the idea of taking revenge in a way that left him blameless. The art of it, the process.

But the little red light now began flashing on the monitor that was clasped over his left wrist, indicating that somebody had opened the back door of the cubby.

From under his belt, the Toddler pulled the long barrel of the Dan Wesson. He then heard the interior door open, and the Biddy—it could only be—utter a little cry of pique on seeing the mess that was Tag Barry.

The Toddler smiled. Payback time being only minutes away.

19

HIT!

 "Tag! Tag Barry, you sot," Biddy Nevins said when she stepped into the kitchen and saw the young man sprawled on the kitchen table, the bottles spilled and piss pooling around his chair.

"Look what you've done. You're a lazy, boozy piece of work, and I want this cleaned up and you out of here by morning." It was then that she noticed his eyes, which were open, blinking wildly.

"What?" she demanded. "Are yeh conscious? Can ye not even speak?" She waited for a moment, before turning away in disgust and moving toward the hallway. "You're a loss, Tag. A dead loss."

Exactly, thought the Toddler, now able to hear her. And you will be too, my dear, sooner than you think. He thumbed back the hammer of the Wesson.

Biddy could scarcely climb the stairs, she was so tired, beaten and bruised from her encounter with the Toddler earlier in the day and then having to throw herself out of the car before the force of the explosion blew her down into the wet bog. And simply from the stress of it all. She almost wished the whole thing were over, one way or another.

But when she entered the bedroom, she stopped suddenly.

From under the bed the Toddler could see her legs silhouetted against the glow from the chandelier in the hallway that could be controlled by a rheostat on the wall by the door, like a kind of night-light. The Toddler had discovered it on when he entered the house. And had left it dim, just for this purpose.

"Ah, Christ Almighty, the inmates have taken over the asylum. Cheri! Cheri! Get yehr arse out o' me bed this instant. I'm hammered, destroyed. And I need to sleep. Cheri!"

Little could she know how destroyed, thought the Toddler. But he would wait to fire his own minicannon at her in the very same way that she had fired at him: up from below when she was least expecting it. Which was the reason he was under the bed.

And low. He'd whack her someplace low so she wouldn't die right away and would know it was him.

"*Cheri!*" she bawled, advancing on the bed and shaking the older woman. "Up! Up!"

"Biddy, you're back," the woman managed to say in a groggy voice. "You're back. Come to me. You don't know what I've been through: the police, a jail cell. Give me a kiss."

"What? What *you've* been through? Don't bother me with

that. Just get up—git, git—and go. I must sleep, and I don't want you hanging all over me."

"I can't and I won't." The old woman's tone had changed; it was now petulant and whiny. "I'm after taking a tablet, and I dreamed I heard a man's voice speaking to Tag. I'm frightened, I need you. Look, I'll move all the way over here. You can have as much of the bed as you please. I just want to be *near* you. That's all I ask."

The Biddy sighed audibly. "What in God's name could I have done to deserve this! So help me, Cheri, if I feel you touching me in any way, I'll give you the thumpin' of your life."

"Yes, dear, I understand."

With his eyes focused on the bottom of the mattress that he could see through the springs, the Toddler watched as the lump that was Cheri Cooke slid over to an edge of the bed.

At the bottom of which the Biddy was disrobing, kicking off her shoes, dropping her slacks over them, peeling off her stockings, her jumper, her blouse.

In her underwear—the Toddler could see when she walked down the length of the long bedroom and snapped on the light—she entered the toilet, the gun (*her* Dan Wesson) in her hand. She placed it on the back of the commode, while she ran water into the basin. Bending at the waist with her back to him, she began washing her face.

And could be taken like that, since he had a clear shot. But the Toddler was bemused by how handsome she was with long, straight legs, good hips, and daunting breasts. She was just at that stage—what? near forty—when a big woman, such as she, looked just a bit overripe and truly voluptuous.

As compared with how she'd look in only a minute or two, when the filed and jacketed three-hundred-grain round fragmented through that body.

Straightening up, she dried her face, then, reaching behind her, unsnapped her brassiere and removed it. When she turned toward him to move back into the bedroom, her pendant and heavy breasts wagged, the nipples a deep rubicund color, like blood.

After switching out the light, she walked right at him in the dark and climbed into the bed only to discover that the other woman had moved.

"Cheri, I told you!"

The mattress above the Toddler jounced, the springs squeaking as the Biddy either hit or tried to move the older woman. "Now, get over there!"

"Oh, Biddy, please. I just want to feel you again, to know you're there."

"No—over. Now!"

There was a pause and then: "Well, if you won't, I will, and if you so much as touch me, I promise, I'll beat you." The mattress rocked; the springs squeaked again.

But the older woman said, "No need. If that's how you feel, I'll maintain my distance. I know when I'm not wanted."

"Ah, don't give me that. *You know when you're not wanted!* I could puke."

"What's that?"

"What's what?"

"That cold thing there in your hand."

"My pistol—what did you think it was?"

"I don't want that in bed with me."

"Then get out."

"You know I can't. You're just being cruel. As usual."

"That's it! I've had enough! Here you either move or I move, and if I have to move you—"

"No, no, like I said—"

There was yet more violent movement only a foot above the Toddler's face. When the springs stopped rocking, he waited for either of them to speak again, so that he could determine which protuberance in the mattress was the body of which.

But neither seemed to have any more to say, nor did the old one begin to snore. And it was while he was waiting for a sigh or a cough or whatever, the Wesson locked in both hands with the barrel pointed at the lump that the Toddler believed was at last the Biddy, that the red light on his wrist monitor came on. Followed almost immediately by the green.

Which meant? That two people had entered the house nearly simultaneously, who could only be the police with Hannigan's men posted outside. But not Hannigan's men since they were under orders to remain where they were.

It was McGarr then. With help.

But how much?

Calmly—in spite of the adrenaline that had jolted through him—the Toddler reset the monitor, in case others arrived. He still had a way out in the basement if he could complete the hit and create enough chaos to make his way down there.

It was time to act. Hearing no noise on the stairs, knowing that he'd need maybe five seconds to get out from under the bed and leave the room before the two came running, the

Toddler took aim at the deepest protruberance of the deepest lump—the Biddy's pretty arse, he assumed—and fired. The report was deafening in the confined space, the gun blast torrid on his face.

And when he tried to swing the barrel toward the second shape, the eight inches of steel snagged in the springs, the front-sight blade catching a coil. Tugging hard, again and again, the Toddler finally pulled it free. But the second lump was gone.

The doorway. He could see legs. Throwing his right arm down so he could fire out from under the bed, the Toddler had only touched off another round when a second, nearly simultaneous explosion occurred there and a bullet smashed into the wall near his head.

He fired again and again, wildly, not caring where, knowing he was now a fixed target, knowing his only means of escape would be to scare her, to make her run.

And it worked. Or he'd shot her. The legs were gone.

But there were the two intruders now to worry about as well. Pushing himself out from under the bed, the Toddler got to his feet and looked down at the bed.

The old woman, now dead, was on her back, her eyes open, a red wet wound in what had been her lower stomach. There the blankets were frayed, the blood already having blotted through the material. Even the tall ceiling above was splattered with blood. Drops were falling.

At the door he scanned the large square front hallway that was dimly lit by the chandelier that could be controlled by the rheostat near his hand. There was another down by the front door. But would either of the two cops know that? Not likely, only having just arrived. It would give the Toddler the edge he needed.

Where could she be? In any one of the bedrooms or the boxroom, the door of which was open a crack, where the Toddler now saw the glint of silver appear. It was a tiny room on a landing on the stairs and was used for storage, he knew from his earlier reconnaissance. He pulled his head back into the bedroom.

"Hughie?" a man's voice called out from somewhere near the bottom of the front staircase.

"Here!" That voice was very close and somewhere in the hallway of the second floor, not far from where the Toddler was standing. McGarr must have come in the front and stayed there, while Ward entered the back and then, hearing the shots, mounted the back stairs to drive him down.

What to do?

The Toddler scarcely had to think. The situation could not be better: two cops in a poorly lit house searching for an armed perp with, now, a terrified victim cowering in the box-room. And also armed. Which was the key.

The Toddler reloaded the gun from the Biddy's box of cartridges in his pocket. Then back at the bed he pulled down the covers and climbed in with the old, dead woman, tugging wet bloody blankets over himself, making sure that her corpse with its gaping wound was exposed but that the frayed and bloodied covers obscured his own body, making him look as though he too had been shot.

He even plucked off her night hat and fitted it over his

bald pate, then pulled her head and neck over his chest, as though while dying or being smashed by the force of the bullets, she had fallen across his corpse. The gun—his Wesson—he kept under the covers, pointed at the open door.

Would the cop, Ward, switch on the light? If he did, the Toddler would have to shoot him, which was not on his agenda. But if he was forced to, it would leave only his target, the Biddy—and he knew where she was—and McGarr, who would then have to die as well. The Toddler did not doubt he could hunt him down and kill him, one-on-one.

He'd then do Tag Barry at the kitchen table, switch guns with the Biddy's corpse, and leave via the coal chute, while the other cops stormed the doors.

"Miss Waters? Biddy Nevins?" the same older voice called out. "It's Peter McGarr. Can you hear me?"

There was no answer, of course, the Biddy not wanting to give up her position, which the Toddler already knew. Stupid woman—it would cost her her life.

"If you can," McGarr went on, "stay where you are. We're going to sweep the house. We've got the exits covered, more help on the way, and the building surrounded."

Which the Toddler rather doubted, unless McGarr meant Hannigan's men, who would be inexperienced at this type of operation. But he believed the rest.

And there was Ward in the doorway, glancing in and stepping quickly across to peer in from the other angle with the wall for protection. Gun out, pointing with it. Cop style.

He stepped into the room, pushed shut the closet door and twisted the key in the lock, then moved to the toilet. But it was in leaving the bedroom that Ward stopped suddenly and turned his head to the old woman and the Toddler, whose eyes, of course, were open. Since he—or the corpse he was simulating—was dead.

There was a long moment in which Ward's life hung in the balance, before he passed to the doorway. "There's two in here, Chief—both dead."

"Women?"

"Yah."

"Then it's him. Watch yourself."

Ward scanned the hall, then moved off quickly toward the next room, continuing his sweep.

The Toddler pushed the gruesome old woman off him, pulled back the covers, and climbed out of the bed. He advanced on the doorway slowly, as quietly as he could. In the distance he could hear sirens. Claxons. They were closing in on him surely.

Yet at the doorway with one hand on the rheostat and the Wesson pointing at the door of the boxroom, the Toddler waited patiently for Ward to reappear from the other bedroom. How long could the search of one room take? It all reminded him of Vietnam, of waiting by the side of a trail while a small army moved by you, so you could assassinate the general in the jeep at the back.

And there finally Ward was, out of the room and moving down the staircase on the far side of the square hallway toward the little room, the boxroom. There too the door was open again, a crack. He could see the glint of silver at the level of his tall Biddy's shoulders.

The Toddler exulted. A zero-sum solution? Better than

that. It would be a negative sum. He wouldn't slaughter her. No. He'd let them do it for him.

When Ward moved beside the door, ready to kick it open, the Toddler took perfect aim. He then waited the requisite full second for his sighting to pulse in, before squeezing off two quick shots at the heavy edge of the door.

The first smashed it open. The second swung it past the Biddy, who stood there, gun locked in her hands.

Ward with his gun out too now rushed the door, ready to fire.

With the heel of a fist, the Toddler punched out the rheostat, dousing the chandelier. The hall was suddenly pitch-black.

Pop! Pow! The first report Ward's, the second her gun, the big gun. The force of it was unmistakable.

Then Pop! Pop! Pop! Pop! from below, as McGarr fired up into the boxroom at what little he could possibly see of the person who had fired at Ward.

Sprinting as well as he was able, the Toddler rushed down the hall toward the back of the house and the stairs that would take him to the basement.

Pausing at the kitchen table, he placed the barrel of his Wesson at the weal of bruising at the back of Tag Barry's neck. And fired. The bullet nearly severed the head.

Down in the basement he took time—less than a minute—to reload, his eyes on the stairs leading down from the kitchen. If McGarr materialized there, he'd have to kill him, which would ruin everything. If he didn't, it could mean only one thing: Ward was in a bad way, and McGarr was tending to him.

No McGarr. The Toddler allowed himself a thin smile.

Loose ends? Only one: the guns. It would have been better to have exchanged his for the Biddy's. But now if his were never found, why, he'd walk away from any trial guiltless, he was sure. No proof, no guilt, no problem. Which would be theirs in even getting him in the dock. He'd hire the best legal help obtainable; he'd spare nothing.

At the back of the coal bin the Toddler slowly and carefully opened the hatch of the chute and then waited with what he thought of as sublime patience, given the situation. Hearing nobody, he pulled himself up into the window well and closed the hatch after him. Again he waited, listening, lifting his head just to the level of the grass to scan the side lawn.

There was a light on now in the front of the house, and he thought he could hear a man's voice, speaking brusquely. McGarr, it would be, calling for emergency services for Ward, his protégé, or for the Biddy. Or both, the Toddler hoped. The operation had been brilliant altogether.

Only then did he push himself out of the window well, a bit at a time, keeping himself well concealed in the shadows. Quickly, expertly he crawled the twenty-five feet to the wall, where a mulberry tree helped him to the top. There he paused briefly to admire the effect of the dome lights of the police cars in Raglan Road, splashing bloody light on the Edwardian facades.

And again when having traversed the wall of three other back gardens, he let himself out the final gate and arrived at the rental car he'd parked by the curb that afternoon. A flying squad was racing by, sirens and claxons blaring. Lights blazing.

"What's the fuss?" a man on the footpath asked as the Toddler fitted the key in the lock.

"Beats me. Tea time? Coffee break?"

"Or false alarm."

Hardly, thought the Toddler, driving away.

20

STAKE!

 The Toddler had seldom felt such elation when he arrived at his warehouse in Ringsend only a mile away from the house on Raglan Road.

Here in the fortieth year of his life he had been challenged by the one problem that could have destroyed everything that he had ever worked for. In fact, the problem that had nearly killed him.

He examined his leg, which was now paining again, as he changed clothes and disposed of them and the gun at the bottom of a deep vat. A century ago the building had been a brewery. Later he would retrieve the items and make their disposal more complete.

And then there was Cork. He'd have to ring up the Monck and Baileys and find out how that had gone, though he wasn't finished with the Maughams and Nevinses. He wouldn't let any of her Knacker family off; he'd put a curse on them all. To make an example, to send a message, to enhance his rep, which was his stock-in-trade and would now be revived. To the max.

Back in the car, it took the Toddler a full hour to climb the Wicklow Mountains, careful not to call attention to his driving. But rounding the final bend, he caught sight of his mountaintop estate, lit now at one in the morning in welcome for his return, and he relaxed. More when he glimpsed the burned-out shell of the Volvo by his shattered gates. And he congratulated himself for having trained such an excellent team. Cambodians, he had long thought, were a dutiful and eminently educable people. Here was proof.

He would throw a party, he now decided as he traversed the switchback road up to his aerie. Champagne and caviar for the staff, and a hot Jacuzzi for himself and the new girl that Lo-Annh had just brought over. Her niece, he thought from the little he knew of their language.

A pretty thing, how old? It was difficult to tell with those people, but young. "Gorblimey!" the Toddler said to the windscreen, remembering his Gibraltar years, the lessons of which had served him so well.

But there was no staff lined up in the hall, as required to greet him with their hands together, bowing, their eyes lowered. Subservient. And the computer at the security control panel in the kitchen reported only one breach, which would have been the Biddy at the gate. He scrolled back through the day.

There was the report earlier in the evening of Lo-Annh and the niece, Soh, having left on his orders but not yet having returned. But if the four others were gone as well, why was there no record of the chip that they carried on their employment IDs logging them out?

Could Lo-Annh have turned on him? he wondered, she having been in his employ long enough to have figured out how to defeat the system.

"Hell-low, anybody home?" he asked through the electronic pager that projected his voice into every one of the twenty-eight rooms and twenty baths, the garage, the gymnasium, the solarium, the pool, the shooting range, and the library. Not to mention the eight rooms in the servants' quarters. Echoing around all the stone and tile, nothing but the best.

"If somebody's here, please respond immediately."

The Toddler waited. But nobody buzzed the control panel, as he expected at least of Lo-Annh, who managed the estate when he was away and was responsible for the rest of the staff. She was always on call. Maybe somebody had reported rifle fire, and she had been picked up by the police, which would be unfortunate for her. He couldn't have her telling stories in or out of court, say, for a long-term visa or Irish citizenship. And the business of the others being gone without the computer recording their identities and times of departure was disturbing, no two ways about it.

He pulled himself out of the chair and moved to the gun locker in a kitchen closet, where he removed a twelve-gauge Benelli 90 automatic shotgun that he kept fully loaded with sabots that could punch through steel. With a short (twenty-inch) barrel, it was an ideal close-quarters weapon.

He locked the gun case and left the kitchen along one of

the several converging hallways that joined a central atrium, like spokes in a wheel. He peered into the rooms he passed to see if anything was amiss. But all was normal: spotless, neat, in place.

Taking the lift to his personal quarters on the third floor, he decided that it was rather a good thing that the girls weren't there. The wound in his leg was now calling attention to itself, and he'd jack up the heat in the Jacuzzi to some barely tolerable temperature, then lace the water with an antiseptic he'd used on other wounds in Vietnam. And let it soak.

He'd close his eyes; he might even sleep some before ringing up the Monck and Baileys for the report on Cork. Talk about a day at the office!

Over an hour later Peter McGarr pulled his Mini-Cooper into the lay-by that the Cambodian woman Lo-Annh indicated. It was about a mile from the Toddler's house.

"Why are you doing this?" he asked her.

"He kill me if I don't."

"Has he killed others that you know about?"

She nodded. "Six."

"Cambodians?"

"He say they go back. They no go back."

"Do you have proof of that?"

She shook her head. "Mr. T very careful."

Which was a point for McGarr to observe as well. He reached across her and opened the door. "You're on your own now, you and them. You've never seen me, spoken to me, or ridden in this car."

She nodded. "And you help me be citizen."

McGarr nodded, which was the only part of the deal he liked. But the whole thing of bringing the Toddler to justice— of any sort at all—had been necessary now for at least a score of years. Waiting another would only produce more corpses, and the woman beside him might easily become one. With Ward in hospital fighting for his life and Biddy Nevins dead, he'd settle for it.

Done right. "You should be on your way."

She touched the back of his hand, her pretty almond eyes fixing his. "Thank you."

"Godspeed. Remember, the van is big, old, and loud. You'll hear it before you see it. Don't show yourself to any other car. They'll be going slow, looking for you."

The woman got out of the car, shut the door, and, lifting her tight gold dress high on her thin legs so she could walk, moved quickly up the road toward the house.

McGarr knew what he should do from a self-interested perspective: leave the area immediately. His old car was distinctive, and later there might be some question about what he was doing there.

But he couldn't just abandon the group of women to the Toddler. Lo-Annh had said she had disabled the security system, told the others of the staff to flee, and then switched the grid back on before leaving with her niece. And before Biddy had arrived there in the Volvo.

Which might lull the Toddler and make him believe that his staff had been lifted by the police and that was the extent of the damage he had taken that evening.

On the other hand, he might have some backup system

that she did not know about. Or missing her and the rest of the staff, he might now suspect that something, like what was about to occur, was afoot. Against a high-power weapon, the old van with its thin sheet metal sides would not stand a chance. Or anybody in it.

Finally McGarr could not expect the women in the van— some of them hardly that—to take a chance that he wasn't willing to take himself.

After backing the Cooper as far off the road into the bog as possible, McGarr got out, a pair of binoculars in his hand. He positioned himself behind a hillock of turf where he could see but would not be seen from the road. And where he could sight in the Toddler's mansion on the hilltop.

As he scanned the veritable fortress, the lights in the top-most floor—his living quarters, the Cambodian woman had said—switched off, leaving the entire building dark. Could it mean that the Toddler had gone to bed?

Why not? thought McGarr. After his . . . coup of the night the man must be tired. And certainly the compound would be locked and secured by sensors, although—again—the Cambodian woman claimed she could defeat the system.

It was chill, where McGarr was standing, and blear, a wet wind sweeping off a bog lake in the distance that was a shimmering expanse of silver in the moonlight. Overhead the sky was clear, the stars myriad and deep, and McGarr said a silent prayer for Ward, hoping the man's youth and strength and all the conditioning he had put himself through over the years would carry him through.

"If he survives," the surgeon had said, going into the operating theater, "he'll have limited use of that shoulder and lose whatever lung that's been damaged," the .44-caliber, three-hundred-grain bullet having struck him in the upper chest. Just missing his heart.

McGarr again thought back on Ward's decision—reported to him by phone—to return the gun to Biddy Nevins, there at the Royal Dublin Hospital, where he was now himself. It had been courageous but foolish. But McGarr would have done the same himself, since they could in no way have guaranteed Nevins's safety in jail, save placing a squad staffer in her cell around the clock. For how long?

Nor could they have protected her in her house, as it turned out, the Toddler having acted fast even to supplying her with a car and a note from "Ward." It had been discovered in her purse by one of McGarr's detectives. No, there could only be one solution for the Toddler, and McGarr now hoped he could help supply it.

Headlamps had appeared on the road maybe three miles off but visible across the treeless mountain bog. McGarr raised the field glasses. Then . . . two pair of headlamps, the second hanging well back. It would be Bresnahan, as they had discussed.

McGarr waited what seemed like another dog's age, until he could hear the clacking engine of the old Bedford van, and he lowered his head behind the hillock. The fewer who knew of his presence, the better.

But once it had passed, McGarr returned to his Cooper. Rolling forward to the edge of the road, he waited for the second vehicle, which was indeed Bresnahan. She pulled her "plain brown wrapper" into the lay-by and joined him.

"What do we do?"

"Wait," said McGarr.

"In case they don't come out?"

McGarr nodded. "He's a jackal if there ever was one." Their one hope was that the Toddler's pride in his stealth, his deceptiveness, and his killing prowess—pride of the sort that McGarr had glimpsed in the granny's kitchen the night after he'd shot the Bookends—had impaired his caution, at least for the night.

Would he be expecting the police? Probably. But the security system that was already in place could deal with that. A direct, personal attack? Probably not so soon after Biddy Nevins's death. Travelers were nothing if not a traditional people, and they'd want to mourn and bury her first. And only then seek revenge.

"I only hope the Cambodian woman knows what she's about with the security system. We'd better make sure." He started the Cooper and moved forward, toward the house. Headlamps out. Driving by the light of the moon.

In his Jacuzzi on the third floor of his manse, the Toddler was reclining in the swirling hot water at an elevation of exactly two thousand feet, announced one of the digital readouts on the security control panel that was only a reach away. As was the Benelli shotgun.

The view out floor-to-ceiling double-glazed windows was not diminished in the least, however. In the darkness the Toddler could see all the way to Wales, sixty or so miles away.

Granted, the lights were dim, but they appeared to him like stars that had fallen into the Irish Sea. Gemlike and sparkling. The sight always soothed him.

See? No monster he. Desmond Bacon, the Toddler, was capable of—in fact, all too vulnerable to—finer thoughts and higher emotions. Witness his taste for photographic art that had reintroduced him to Biddy Nevins and had nearly got him killed.

But his great strength, which was cheering, was in never overestimating the worth of disinterested observations and sentiments. Because survival was the only impetus to be observed through every waking moment and protected by all means available. Again he glanced at the phosphorescent digital display.

In her own way—the Toddler continued to muse—the Biddy had known that. It was why she had run there at the top of Grafton Street all those years ago. She knew who he was and what had happened. How she couldn't live, having seen it. It was also why he had not forgotten.

And the biggest lie? The preposterous idea of civilization that we lived in something other than a state of raw and vicious nature. But spread abroad—he supposed, smugly, reaching for a can of Diet Coke—the deceiving notion only made life (lived clearly and fully) easier for somebody like him.

The Toddler had laced the water with antiseptic that was now soaking into the wound in his leg and galling him. Nevertheless, pain was good and both a lesson and a promise: that he should exercise greater caution and cunning in the future and that he'd survive.

Leaning his head back against the lip of the Jacuzzi, Desmond Bacon closed his eyes. After a while the pleasant, steady rush of the water and his own endorphins, kicking in to assuage the pain, lulled him, and he nodded off.

How long the Toddler slept, he did not know. But it must have been some time, because what woke him was a draft on his forehead and face, the only parts of his body that were not immersed. Opening his eyes, he closed them, then lurched up onto the next shelf in the pool.

"Something wrong with this picture?" a voice asked.

It was still dark in the room, but the Toddler could make out the shapes of maybe two dozen people squatting and standing around the sides of the Jacuzzi with things in their hands. Craning back his head, he saw somebody right above him with something big, like a slane, in her hands. "Move, and I'll split yehr fookin' head in two."

The lights flashed on, blinding him momentarily.

The voice said, "Bet you know why we're here."

When his eyes cleared, he saw that she was young with a bright green Mohawk, rhinestone studs up one nostril, a black swath wrapping her breasts, and a bare midriff. Her denim jacket was frayed, as were her jeans. Squatting on the edge of the pool, she was holding a hurling stick in both hands, the shaft resting on a shoulder.

The Toddler surveyed the others, who had clubs, iron pipes, two of them even long brush knives the size of machetes. His eyes rested on the one with the pruning sheers. It was the Tinker bitch's get, the young one. Oney, she was called. Something had gone horribly wrong down in Cork.

Why hadn't he phoned up? What had made him forget?

The Benelli 500 shotgun was where he had left it, right

by the boots of the Mohawk one on the edge of the tub. Seeing his eyes light on it, she kicked out, and the gun slipped into the swirling water. "Oops—I hope that doesn't ruin it. But you've got others."

Behind the girls, the door to the drying room was open, which was the cause of the draft. In it stood Lo-Annh, smiling.

"Go ahead," the Mohawk one insisted. "Take a guess why we're here. No invite. Didn't even fookin' knock." She shook her absurd head. "Fookin' Knackers, no fookin' manners." Her green eyes were bright, but her smile the Toddler recognized, having smiled it himself on occasion. No mirth, no warmth. It was the smile of cold control.

He shrugged. "Does it matter? You're trespassing. Get out."

The Mohawk one closed her eyes and laughed a bit. "You're gas, you are. Whoever said you were clever? Here's another. See if you can answer this. Know what those are?" She pointed to the shears. "We thought we'd use these"—from her back pocket she pulled a pair of surgical shears of the sort that were used to castrate rams—"but we took a vote: too good, too fine for the likes of you." She tossed those in the tub too.

In spite of himself the Toddler felt his gonads tighten yet more. He smirked. "You can't. You won't."

"Why not?"

"Because the police must know you're here."

The Mohawk nodded. "Now, there—that's brilliant, that is. They do, they know we're here." Her green eyes fixed his. "With their blessing. However would you think we got here so quickly?"

The Toddler blinked; he knew.

"They showed us the way."

McGarr. Not playing by the rules. After Lo-Annh was lifted, he'd cut her a deal.

Which was when the Toddler lunged for the Mohawk one. If he could just get her head in his hands, maybe he could keep the others at bay long enough to make the lift. Even if they'd already taken the precaution of disabling his cars, they hadn't dropped here out of a bubble; they had to have a vehicle of some kind outside.

And did! One hand clamping down on the back of her bristly head, the other clutching her under the chin.

Somebody swung a club and struck his shoulder.

"Do that again, and I'll snap her neck."

"He's bluffing. He can't snap her neck."

"No, he's not," said the Biddy's daughter. "Me ma told me on the phone: He's a trained killer. With kicks and chops."

"Back off now! Back off!" the Toddler roared, raising himself out of the swirling water and stepping out of the pool. "Everybody into that corner—quick! Quick!"

He had already formulated his plan; he knew what he must do. "Go!" he screamed at the top of his lungs, as loudly as the DIs had screamed at him at Pendleton.

And they jumped, quickly.

"You won't get far," said the daughter.

"Won't I? Why not?" He lifted the Mohawk one off her feet, and she began choking, her hands clawing at his. "You know something I don't?" At the door he flexed his biceps and snapped his hands forward and back. Once. Then threw the dead Mohawk girl into the pool.

Slamming the door, he locked it, then watched through

the glass as the gaggle of Knacker cunts wailed and jumped into the water to try to save her. One vomited; another ran at the door with a slane and smashed at the glass, breaking it.

But they'd not get out. The door was heavy, insulated to keep in the heat, and sheathed in Formica. The window was only a foot square.

"Bastard!" she roared. "You miserable fookin' bastard!"

Aye, and more, thought the Toddler. He could ring up the guards and say he'd been attacked in his bath and had killed the bitch in self-defense.

Or, on the other hand, he could just kill them and say he'd been attacked in his bath. He'd decide which while dressing. Naked, wet, and no longer threatened, the Toddler was now getting a chill. Turning toward his dressing room, he saw—too late—a figure in front of him with something raised over his head.

McGarr swung the chair made out of some heavy wood— teak or oak—that broke as it slammed down on the Toddler's head and shoulders. Yet he only fell to his hands and knees.

McGarr's foot came up, catching him under the chin and toppling the man into the door.

"Open up! Open up! Let us have him! He fookin' murdered Rita just now. Let us fookin' have him!"

Bresnahan reached for the key.

"Careful," said McGarr. "He's still moving." The Toddler's face was streaming with blood.

Giving him a wide berth, Bresnahan reached over and slipped the key into the lock and turned it. From the inside the girls began throwing themselves at the door, struggling to push it open with the Toddler's weight against it.

Feeling the pressure, still conscious enough to realize what would happen to him if they got it open, the Toddler spun around and threw his hands onto the panel. But he began slipping, sliding in his own blood, which was thick now on the tiles of the drying room.

McGarr signaled to Bresnahan, and she moved around the margin of the room, staying well away from the man and the door.

"McGarr!" the Toddler roared. "Help me! Name what you want—anything! Everything! You can't just let me die!"

In the doorway McGarr said, "Hannigan would. I'll tell him what you said, your last words. He'll be relieved."

There was a thump as the girls collectively threw themselves against the door, which opened maybe a foot, something like a bench being shoved into the gap.

The Toddler kicked at it with his foot. "Then at least fuckin' shoot me!"

Why, when there was a more elegant Toddler-like solution to his problem already in play?

"You're a bastard, you know that? A bastard!"

High praise from one who knew whereof he spoke, thought McGarr.

The Toddler slipped and fell to his knees.

The door opened yet more, and a hand with a pipe in it reached around and smashed at his hands.

Turning suddenly, he let go of the door and tried to stand and rush from the room. But again he slipped in his blood and went down.

And they were on him—hacking, swinging, punching, stomping. His face, his neck, the groin, the wound.

Oney Maugham was the last out of the doorway, shears in hand. "Wait!" she shouted. "Don't kill him. Don't! It's too good, too easy."

In the lift on the way down to the ground floor, McGarr said to Bresnahan, "Come back tomorrow, straighten things up," so there'd be no evidence of who might have murdered him, he meant. Not even the dead girl, whose corpse would be taken back to her own people and not left there for the police, if McGarr knew anything about Travelers.

"Tomorrow, if Hughie's any better, I'll drive back down to Midleton, have a talk with the head man."

"McDonagh," Bresnahan put in.

"And the father and mother."

"Maggie and Ned."

"Who knows, with the right legal help, this place might be theirs."

21
CAW! CAW!

 A week and a day later a telephone caller to the Murder Squad asked to be connected to "Peter McGarr, please. It's Eithne Carruthers of River-house, Glencree. I think he'll remember me."

Ruth Bresnahan took the call. "I'm afraid the chief super-intendent is unavailable."

"What about Detective Ward?"

"The same, but I know who you are."

"You do?" The woman seemed pleased.

Bresnahan introduced herself, adding that she had been on staff when the woman had phoned twelve years earlier.

"Then you know all . . . that about Archie?"

"Yes. What can I do for you?"

"It'll be apparent when you get here."

An hour later the woman pointed toward a copse near the

base of the mountain in back of her estate. "You see, it's happened again." A small cloud of crows was circling the tallest tree. "I only hope and pray it's nobody I know."

Bresnahan's wish was the opposite. And was granted some hours later, when she reached the top of the "Cliquot" tree with the help of two Tech Squad climbing specialists.

For there was (or had been) Desmond Bacon, the Toddler, shackled into the "nest" at the top of the giant sequoia that was bobbing, swaying, surging in the stiff breeze. Already the crows had dined massively on his corpse, having removed his eyes and most of his face, the flesh of his arms and thighs.

In a phrase, he was "half picked over," said one of the Techies. "The castration probably occurred before he succumbed. But as you can see from his wrists and ankles, it didn't kill him by itself. He struggled for some long time to produce that damage."

Which could not have been long enough, thought Bresnahan. She only wished McGarr and Ward could have been present to view the corpse. But she had thought to carry up a camera with her, and there would also be the Tech Squad photos.

"What's this—the family thing?" Bresnahan asked some days later when Ward was about to be released from hospital into the care of his son and . . . well, his son's mother.

Who had the audacity to reply, "Well, I hope you can imagine that Lugh is concerned about his father. And it being summer holidays, he'll have the opportunity of being with him more than usual, while Hughie's recuperating."

And you? What opportunity will you have? thought Bresnahan. She had never seen the woman—Leah Sigal or Lee Stone or whatever she called herself—looking so vibrant, there was no other word for her.

With her lustrous hair, which had been made rather darker in recent days, her sparkling china blue eyes, and, well, the shapely rest of her that had been primped, pampered, and provided with the most stylish costumes that Dublin possessed (and she doubtless could afford!), the "L. Ward" aspirant (Bresnahan was certain) looked as though she had knocked a decade off her fully thirty-nine years. Ruth had checked; not for nothing was she a detective.

"Then the shop—my shop—doesn't require a great deal of my time, and his wound *is* draining." The round from Biddy Nevins's large-caliber weapon had come very close to Ward's heart. "He'll need a nurse."

Precisely, thought Bresnahan. And not you who—from all she could learn—had not so much as gone out with another man between having Ward's baby and telling him about their son fourteen years later. It was as though she had been waiting for him and him alone all that time.

Talk about *true* love! And now look at her—preserved, as by suspended animation, and right back in his life. Big time. "May I have a word with yehr mahn?" Bresnahan asked in her broadest impression of the Dublin accent, which was natural to the other woman in spite of her Ph.D. and jewelry and antique expertise.

Bresnahan couldn't help herself. Basically a country girl from Kerry in spite of her now-urbane exterior, she could feel herself beginning to hate the other woman. And to hate herself for so doing, knowing the approach was exactly wrong. Ward would continue his relationship with his son regardless, and she could not be seen to get into a mood or throw a fit every time he did. "Alone, please. Door closed."

Leah Sigal's smile did not change one bit, further angering Bresnahan. "Of course. Certainly. Take all the time you need. We'll wait downstairs in the lobby. Come along, Lugh."

But as she closed the door, her china blue eyes met Ward's. Briefly, pointedly. The situation was not good, Bresnahan gauged.

And she was left alone with the man she had *virtually* been married to for a decade. In the common law sense. Whom she still very much loved and wished to *possess* in the strict sense. Could the opportunity have passed? It felt like that.

She eased herself onto the bed that Ward would need help getting out of. Not only was there the gruesome drain, but he was still weak, and—to be utterly truthful—medicine, nursing, wounds were not Ruth's thing. "What gives here?"

Ward said nothing; he did not know himself. He had nearly died; it had changed him. He was suddenly, totally, irrevocably old, or at least more mature. The aspects of his former life that had interested him, from a new car or a new suit to a holiday in Majorca or winning in the ring, were as nothing now.

What did attract him, however, was putting his own stamp on life—personally, professionally, privately, which he thought of as how he spent the free hours of his days. He would no longer squander that time doing things that were expected of him. By other people. He would do only what he wished.

"Has she said anything to you, made any representations?"

Nor would he lie, so he said nothing.

"Oh, then, she has."

Again nothing.

Were there now tears in Bresnahan's smoky gray eyes? There were. "Look, if you want to get married that badly," she blurted out, "we'll get married. Have babbies. I'll quit; we'll get a house here in town. After all, it's silly to have that big place down in the country without babbies."

She meant the large and picturesque farm down in Sneem, in Kerry, that she had inherited from her father. "We'll have a family, do the *right* thing, so." It was as if she were trying to talk herself into it. "What say?"

She couldn't look at him, and he didn't say.

After a while she just got up and left the room.

Slightly over a month later, when Chief Superintendent Paul Hannigan of the Drug Squad returned from his summer holidays in Portugal, he found that—miraculously—the cloud that had been hanging over him was gone.

"The Toddler bit it," said Sergeant Tom Lyons, one of Hannigan's subordinates, and an impertinent, dangerous chap in every regard, Hannigan had long thought.

Lyons twirled a newspaper down on Hannigan's desk. "He's dead. They found him up in the Cliquot Tree, just like Mickalou Maugham was a few years back."

Hannigan stared down at the paper, afraid to touch it, afraid Lyons might say more. Hannigan had purposely kept himself out of touch in order to postpone what he was certain would be the inevitable inquiry into the business on—

"The Raglan Road?" Lyons dropped another newspaper on his desk. "All dead. Tag Barry, Cheri Cooke, Biddy Nevins. And you'll never guess who shot her, the Biddy."

If Hannigan held his breath any longer, he'd burst.

"Ward."

He let it out in a puffy blast. "No. Go 'way. You're coddin' me."

"After—get this—she shot him with a forty-four. Upper chest. Right through the lung."

"And he plugged her?'

"Head shot. Dead before she hit the floor. But McGarr helped—pumped at least three or four shots into her himself, thinking she was the Toddler."

"Now I've heard everything." Hannigan felt as if he could jump out of his skin. The wee, wonderful bollocks McGarr had put his foot, his arse, his entire career in the effing jam, he had.

Which would make any allegation against Hannigan re the Toddler ludicrous, coming from a man who had shot and killed the Toddler's victim and target. "Ward, now. Tell me about Ward. Is he—"

"Serious? Critical? Was. But he's on the mend. Athlete, very fit. The wound, the circumstances, the loss of blood would have killed any other person. But they say he'll never box again. The shoulder and all."

Hannigan looked away. Well, he thought, you can't have everything. "A shame. A desperate shame, so it is. Jaysis. What about the Tod . . . ler," he added, not wishing to sound too familiar. Or flip. "Who did him? The Knackers?"

Lyons shrugged.

"McGarr investigating?"

Again.

They both knew there wouldn't be much of a search, if any. "And why? Him bein' a scourge, a downright pestilence." Hannigan liked the last word, which made him feel, you know, high-minded and intelligent. He remembered something else. "What's the saying? Strike one Tinker, and you strike—"

"—the whole clan," they completed together.

"Sure, we used to say that, down the country, don't you know? And look how long they waited to get back for Maugham. Didn't they get the bastard finally?"

When we couldn't, thought Lyons, because of you.

"Excellent! *Excellent!*" Hannigan could scarcely contain himself or wait to leave. In spite of the mountain of work that had piled up on his desk in a month, he just had to get out of there and *celebrate!*

"Come 'ere, Tom. Can I share somethin' with yeh?" Share was a word that Hannigan's son, who'd had a bit of a go with the drugs, used these days himself. In recovery, Hannigan hoped. "I've got a touch of Montezuma's revenge." It seemed to fit; weren't all the Latin people greasers of one sort or another?

"And I'm to see me sawbones at"—he pulled out his pocket secretary and flashed it open and shut—"wouldn't you know I'm fookin' late as it is?" Hannigan stood. "Couldn't you paw through this . . ." He almost said "shit" and laughed, but the man would take it wrong. "Just chuck out anything not important."

Not waiting for Lyons's reply, Hannigan steered the prow of his paunch around the desk and out of the cubicle, singing to himself, Freedom! Ah, *freedom!*

At the Horse & Hound, which was his fourth stop—the drive across Dublin being a minefield of enticing pubs when on a toot—Hannigan got yet another pleasant surprise.

The owner took him aside. "See that bottle?" He pointed to a liter bottle of Hogan's Own in a glass case. "It's yours."

Hannigan's head went back. "Ye're jokin' me."

"No. Remember the last time you were in here, right before you went away. You were with the other chief superintendent, the one whose assistant got shot."

"And also shot one of me suspects. Killed the bloody bitch outright." Hannigan began laughing and laughing, letting all his joy at his luck out. He thought he'd explode.

But the barman was humorless, so he was, and didn't even smile. "Indeed. Well, to continue, you two no sooner left than in walked this little Oriental woman. At first I thought she was a child trying to sell me something, and I nearly threw her out. But didn't she place the bottle on the bar and hand me this slip of paper?"

Hannigan took it from the man. It said:

Paul Hannigan is a hard man to buy back, so I'd like you to present this bottle to him from me. So, when he comes in again, let him have a touch or two of this, before telling him what's up and giving him the rest to take home. I include ten quid for your trouble and the loss of custom.

PETER MCGARR

"And didn't she—the little woman—splash out the ten quid and leave? I could hardly believe it. Extraordinary. I didn't know what to say."

Hannigan shook his head; he sighed; he smiled. "I do. I say, 'twas a great day for the both of us." Hogan's Own. It was McGarr's brand all right, and one of the best whiskeys that Dublin had ever produced—aged in old sherry cask to give it flavor and hue. Aged for a decade at least.

"I'll have me one, I will. Instanter, as we used to say in Synge Street. A large glass with ice, please."

When the glass arrived, Hannigan added, "I hope you put the forty quid in your pocket. You know, no register, no government, no tax to pay."

Again the man said nothing. And wouldn't to the police, him being a tight-arsed publican in every way.

Ah, well, there were those who could look out for themselves and those who couldn't get out of their own way, Hannigan quipped silently. Like McGarr and Ward. He began chuckling again. Jaysis, he wished he'd been a bluebottle fly on the wall to watch it. He raised the glass.

Sure, he'd miss the monthly stipend from the Toddler. But sooner or later he'd make an arrangement with whoever filled the little bastard's spats. And he'd again have the few hundred-odd quid tax-free to make life enjoyable. "Will you have one yehrself?" he asked, knowing that too was impossible, given the man.

Who only glanced at him.

"Then I make a toast to meself, I do. To Peter effing McGarr, God bless him, and to me mither's uncle Bill, God bless him wherever he is. And we suspect the worst!" Hannigan drank off a goodly swallow from the large glass, thinking how good it tasted like that.

Which was free. He'd have a snootful, he would. Get fookin' locked and laugh his arse off at them two—McGarr and Ward—and all the other gobshites who toddled around like priests with scarcely enough in their pockets for a decent session.

Until Hannigan turned to make use of the toilet, and the room began spinning. Christ, have I had that much? He managed only two steps before he found himself suddenly on the floor looking up, and two people—no, four—no a crowd of faces staring down. He couldn't talk; he couldn't move; he couldn't even blink. Or, now, breathe.

"And there Hannigan had called it Montezuma's revenge," Sergeant Tom Lyons said to McGarr over the phone the next day.

"After the bloody Aztec king who conducted all the human sacrifices?"

"Aye, but didn't Hannigan have the wrong country altogether?"

"Though the right type of man."

Lyons waited.

"Montezuma being an earlier class of Toddler."

EPILOGUE

As the days of Ward's recovery passed and he grew stronger, he became accustomed not merely to the rhythm of living in the comfortable digs at the back of Leah Sigal's antiques and jewelry shop. He found himself enjoying and needing the daily contact with his son. And, disturbingly, Leah herself.

First, there was the ritual of dinner that the mother of his only child, who was an excellent cook, served in the solarium, a glass-enclosed mini-greenhouse that looked out upon the narrow valley of the River Poddle with a fine view of central Dublin. But more, it was how much Lugh, their son, seemed to appreciate these events in his life, having been deprived of their mutual company for his first fourteen years.

Lugh was always on time for dinner, no matter how distant he'd gone for sports or some other activity after school. Often he'd even have his lessons done so that the three of them could watch the telly together or play a board game (at his suggestion) or just sit in the big fan chairs by the windows and look out over the city and talk.

Lugh always turned the conversation to his father, wanting to hear stories from Ward's youth or about his family or his experiences in sport or with the squad. All the things he had not heard as a child, Ward quickly realized with no little guilt and sympathy for the boy.

Added to that was the way Leah mediated between her "two men," as Ward overheard her confiding to a friend on the telephone, making sure all was well between them and their every need was met. With that same slight smile Ward had noticed weeks earlier and the sparkle in her blue eyes. There always seemed to be a fire in the hearth and something baking in the oven.

When Ward finally became mobile and decided that he should at least dress in street clothes for part of the day, he called Bresnahan to ask her to bring some of his togs over. But before she could even answer the telephone message he left, Leah had gone out and bought him "a few things," including a lounging jacket that was about the most expensive and tasteful thing Ward had ever donned.

In all, he felt as comfortable as he ever had in his life, and he found himself falling into long, deep, delicious, and dreamless recuperative sleeps that he woke from as though reborn.

And none so satisfying as when lying on the couch in the sitting room watching the television late at night after Lugh had gone to bed. He'd only close his eyes for a moment during some advert, and—presto—it was morning.

On one such night he awoke somewhat earlier to discover that he was not alone. For Leah was sleeping beside him and tucked so perfectly into his body that she felt like the warmest, softest pillow. She was wearing some pretty silk kimono that Ward had never seen before.

And either she had raised his left arm and placed it over her, or he had reached for her in his sleep. Because the arm was wrapped over her waist and in the palm of that hand was nested her right breast.

Yet she was sleeping deeply, and Ward dared not move lest he wake her. Because then what? In that position? And because it all felt so . . . right: how their bodies melded together, who she was, how she felt, and the aroma of some fragrant shampoo in her glossy hair that was touching his nose and lips. And also because he was not sure he wanted to leave her, though he knew he should.

It was as if they were glowing or radiant or—Ward didn't understand it—producing palpable energy there in the darkness, the only light coming through the transom to the hall. It was as if they were on fire, some slow but steady and substantial burn.

Of course, he thought of Bresnahan, as he often still did. But his thoughts of her, when he felt Leah easing in beside him and he did not stop her, were not positive. Seldom had Bresnahan and he watched television like that, on a couch, since she was rather larger than he, and it was difficult to see past her, if he was on the inside. On the outside Ward didn't feel completely masculine—with her hugging him—and in all fairness to Ruth, they only infrequently snuggled because after all, they slept together every night. Or had, before he'd been shot.

Because for the near month that Ward had been recuperating at Leah's (or, rather, his son's house), his "colleague" had only phoned him, albeit daily, having quipped the first day that she was no "home wrecker" and that "the best scenario undoubtedly is for you to fulfill your familial obligations. But if you love me, you'll get out of there soon." Recently, however, her calls had become brusque and dispassionate.

And lacking for a week, when—always an early riser—Ward awoke just before dawn to find a cover drawn over them and Leah—could it be?—naked under his hand. And the feel of her! At once full and womanly and ripe, there was no other word for her. She was at once turgid yet soft, warm yet cool, and—when his hand descended—hot. Turning to him, she kissed him so passionately that Ward felt actually dizzy, and without his realizing how it happened, they were suddenly . . . engaged. Totally. But for a moment only.

Because out in the hall, their son, having to leave early for school and a sports outing that would take him away for several days, was calling for her.

Pulling away from him and leaving the couch in the darkened room, she stared down at him for a moment, before reaching for the kimono. To let him look at her. Knowing that in spite of her thirty-nine years she was still more than simply desirable. She was voluptuous. Some long seconds passed before she fitted the kimono over her shoulders, all the while her eyes locked into his. Knowing, feeling, silently rejoicing, that she now had him in her emotional thrall.

And yet more triumphant when over breakfast, Lugh asked her for a lift into school, "since you're going that way." Out to UCD to teach a course in decorative art, as she always did on Wednesday.

"I'm canceling."

"Are you ill?"

"No, I just think I'll stay home." And her china blue eyes met Ward's with a force and a purpose that were undeniable.

"Hughie," she went on, "why don't you go into the sitting room and switch on the telly? There's that show I told you about."

Instead Ward went directly to Leah's shade-darkened bed-room, which was scented with the aroma of her expensive perfume that—could it be?—he loved.

When she found him, she again disrobed slowly where he could see her. "Do you want me?" she asked.

Ward did so much he could barely say yes.

"How much?"

Ward debated only a moment, since what was about to happen was inevitable and beyond his ability to choose otherwise. Why else had he come to her bed, which felt so right, like . . . home? Finally, he knew from his perhaps too extensive tawdry history, things like this were best done when one was at least committed to the experience, he tried to tell himself. "A lot."

"Enough to fill me up?"

Ward did not answer. He reached for her hip and drew her toward him.